erdrive.com

AE

D1101463

FUN & GAMES

FUN & GAMES

ABERDEENSHIRE LIBRARIES WITHDRAWN FROM LIBRARY

DUANE SWIERCZYNSKI

ISIS
LARGE PRINT
Oxford

Copyright © Duane Swierczynski, 2011

First published in Great Britain 2011
by
Hodder & Stoughton

Published in Large Print 2012 by ISIS Publishing Ltd.,
7 Centremead, Osney Mead, Oxford OX2 0ES
by arrangement with
Hodder & Stoughton
An Hachette UK Company

All rights reserved

LP

The moral right of the author has been asserted

British Library Cataloguing in Publication Data
Swierczynski, Duane.
    Fun and games.
    1. Attempted murder - - Fiction.
    2. Hollywood (Los Angeles, Calif.) - - Fiction.
    3. Suspense fiction.
    4. Large type books.
    I. Title
    813.6–dc23

ISBN 978–0–7531–9048–7 (hb)
ISBN 978–0–7531–9049–4 (pb)

Printed and bound in Great Britain by
T. J. International Ltd., Padstow, Cornwall

For David Thompson

Che sempre l'omo in cui pensier rampolla sovra
pensier, da sé dilunga il segno perché la foga
l'un de l'altro insolla.

— Dante
Purgatorio, canto 5, lines 16–18

You're the type of guy that gets suspicious
I'm the type of guy that says,
'The puddin is delicious.'

— LL Cool J, 'I'm That Kind of Guy'

The Piercing screech of tires on asphalt.
The screams —
His.
Your own.
And then —

CHAPTER
ONE

It's all fun and games until someone loses an eye.

— Popular saying

Los Angeles — Now

She discovered Decker Canyon Road by accident, not long after she moved to L.A. A random turn off the PCH near Malibu shot her up the side of the mountain; followed by twelve miles of stomach-flipping twists and hairpin turns all the way to Westlake Village. And she *loved* it, hands gripping the wheel of the sports car she'd bought with her first real movie check — because that's what you were supposed to do, right? Blow some of that money on an overpriced, over-muscled convertible coupe that popped a spoiler when you topped 75. She never cared she was going thirty miles faster than any sane driver would attempt on this road. She loved the ocean air smashing into her face, the feel of the tires beneath as they struggled to cling to the asphalt, the hum of the machine surrounding her body, the knowledge that one twitch to the left or right at the wrong moment meant her brand-new car, along with her brand-new life, would end up at the bottom of a ravine, and maybe years later people would ask: *Whatever happened to that cute actress who was in those funny romantic comedies a few years ago?* Back then, she loved to drive Decker Canyon Road because it blasted all of the clutter out of her mind. Life was reduced to a simple exhilarating yes or no, zero or one, live or die.

But now she was speeding up Decker Canyon Road because she didn't want to die.

And the headlights were gaining on her.

The prick had been toying with her ever since she made the turn onto Route 23 from the PCH.

He'd gun the engine and then flash his high beams and fly right up her ass. She'd be forced to take it above 60, praying to God she'd have enough room to spin through the next finger turn. Then without warning he'd back off, almost disappearing . . . but not quite.

The road had no shoulder.

No guardrails.

It was like he knew it and was trying to spook her into a bad turn.

Her cell was in the dash console, but it was all but useless. The few seconds it took to dial 911 could be a potentially fatal distraction. And what was she going to tell the operator? Send someone up to Route 23, seventeenth hairpin turn from the middle? Even the highway patrol didn't patrol up here, preferring to hand out speeding tickets on Kanan Road or Malibu Canyon Road.

No, better to keep her eyes on the road and her hands upon the wheel, just like Jim Morrison once advised.

Then again, Jim had ended up dead in a bathtub.

The headlights stayed with her. Every few seconds she thought she'd lost them, or they'd given up, or — God, please *please please* — driven over a bump of asphalt where a guardrail should be and tumbled down into the ravine. But the instant she thought they might be gone . . . they returned. Whoever was behind the wheel didn't seem to give a shit that they were on Decker Canyon Road, that one slip of the wheel was like asking God for the *check, please.*

She was almost two miles along the road now; ten to go.

Her Boxster was long gone; traded in after the accident in Studio City three years ago. Now she drove a car that suited her age — a leased Lexus. A car for grown-ups. And it was a fine machine. But now, as she took those insanely tight turns in the near dark, she wished she had the Boxster again.

Decker Canyon Road was notorious for two things: the rusted-out chassis of cars that dotted the hills, and its uncanny ability to induce car sickness, even with safe, slow drivers just trying to make their way up to Westlake Village in one piece.

She felt sick to her stomach now, but she didn't know if it was the road doing it to her, or the events of the past few days. The past few hours, especially. She hadn't eaten much, hadn't slept much. Her stomach felt like it had been scraped from the inside.

She'd been up for a job that seemed like a sure thing: producers, director, writer, star all in place, a guaranteed fast-track green light. It was a supporting role but in a higher-profile movie than she'd done in years. A role that would make people notice her again — *Wow, she's in that? I was wondering where she'd been*. And then it all had fallen apart in less than an hour.

She'd spent the majority of the past week in her Venice apartment, brooding, not able to bring herself to take much interest in feeding or watering herself or even turning on the satellite cable — God forbid one of her pieces of shit appear, or worse, a piece of shit she'd been passed over for.

So tonight she'd gone for a long late-night drive — the best kind in L.A. Enough wallowing. She wanted the ocean air to blast away the malaise. Blasting away the better part of the past three years would be nice, too . . .

And then the headlights were back. Rocketing toward her, practically up her ass.

Number of accidental vehicle crash deaths in the United States per year: 43,200.

She stomped on the accelerator and spun the wheel, tires screaming as she made — barely — the next finger turn.

The bastard stayed right behind her.

The worst part was not being able to see much beyond the span of her headlights and having to make lightning-fast decisions, one after the other. There was no room to pull over, to let him pass. If passing was even on his mind.

She wondered why she presumed it was a *him*.

And then she remembered why. Of course.

At some point she knew Decker Canyon Road crossed Mulholland, and there was even a stop sign. She'd happily pull over then and give him the double-barrel salute as he drove by.

How much farther was it? She couldn't remember. It had been years since she'd been on this road.

The road continued to snake and twist and turn and climb, the tires of her Lexus gripping asphalt as best they could, the headlights bobbing and weaving behind her, like she was being pursued by a forty-foot electric wasp.

Finally the road leveled out — a feature she remembered now. From here, the road would ease up for a quarter mile as it ran through a valley, followed by another series of insane uphill curves leading to the next valley. A few seconds after, everything seemed to level out —

— then she gunned it —

60, 70, 80

— the electric wasp eyes falling behind her —

90

Ha, ha, fuck you!

The Lexus made it to the next set of curves within seconds, it seemed, and all she had to do now was slide and skid her way along them and put even more distance behind her. She applied some brake, but not too much — she didn't want to lose momentum.

Halfway through the curves, though, the electric eyes returned.

Goddamnit!

Right on her, curve for curve, skid for skid. It was like the car behind her was mocking her. *Anything you can do, I can do better.*

When she finally saw the red glow of the Mulholland stop sign out in the distance, she decided to fuck it. Hit the turn signal. Slowed down. Used the bit of skirting that now appeared on the side of the road. *Go ahead, pass me. I'm stopping. I'm stopping and probably screaming for a while, but I'm done with this. Maybe I'll take a look at your license plate. Maybe I'll call the highway patrol after all, you reckless asshole.*

She pulled the Lexus to a skidding stop, her first since the PCH, which felt like years ago. Then she turned left and pulled off to the side.

The car followed her, pulled up next to her.

Oh, shit.

She reached for her cell and power-locked the doors at the same time. The other car appeared to be a goddamned Chevy Malibu, of all things. Some kind of bright color — it was hard to see in the dark. The driver popped out, looked over the roof, made a roll-your-window-down gesture.

Phone in her hand, she paused for a moment, then relented. Pressed the power window lock. The glass slid down two inches.

"Hey, are you okay?" the guy asked. She couldn't see his face, but his voice sounded young. "Something wrong with your car?"

"I'm fine," she said quietly.

Now he moved around the front of his car, inching his way toward her.

8

"Just seemed like you were having trouble there. Want me to call somebody?"

"On the phone with the cops right now," she lied. She had her finger on the 9 but had stopped. Go on, press it, she told herself. Followed by two ones. You can do it. That way, when this guy pulls out a shotgun and blasts you to death, your last moments will be digitally recorded.

"What the hell were you doing, racing up my ass that whole time?"

"Racing up what? What are you talking about? I didn't see anybody on the road until just now, when you slowed down. I almost slammed into you!"

The guy sounded sincere enough. Then again, L.A. was crawling with men who were paid to sound sincere.

"Well, we'll let the police sort it out."

"Oh, okay," the guy said, stopping in his tracks. "I'll wait in my car until they show up, if you don't mind. It's a little creepy, being out here in the middle of nowhere."

She couldn't help herself — she flashed him a withering *Duh, you think?* look.

But that was a mistake, because now he was looking at her — *really* looking at her. Recognition washed over his face. His eyes lit up, the corners of his mouth lifting into a knowing smile.

"You're *Lane Madden:* No way!"

Great. Now she couldn't be just an anonymous pissed-off woman on Decker Canyon Road. Now she had to be *on*.

"Look, I'm fine, really," she said. "Go on ahead. I guess I was imagining things."

"Uh, don't take this the wrong way, but should you even be driving?"

Lane's brain screamed: *asshole*.

"I'm fine."

"You know, I don't mind waiting, if you want to call this in, or check in, or whatever you have to do."

"Really, I'm okay."

The guy seemed to know he'd pushed the ribbing a little too far. He smiled shyly.

"You know, I promised myself when I moved here, I wouldn't be one of those assholes asking for autographs everywhere he goes. And I'm not. Just wanted to tell you how much I'm a fan of your movies."

"Thanks."

"And you're even prettier in person."

"I really appreciate that."

After a few awkward moments the guy got the hint, walked back to the driver's side of his Malibu, and gave her a sheepish wave before ducking back inside his own car and pulling away into the dark night.

Lane sped through Westlake Village, caught the 101. It was an hour or so before dawn. The freeway was as calm as it ever gets. She took a series of deep, mind-clearing breaths. Maybe when she had enough oxygen in her brain she'd be able to laugh about all of this. Because it was sort of funny, now that it was over.

Sort of.

The Malibu guy hadn't been riding her ass; he'd simply been out cruising down Decker Canyon Road for the same reason Lane used to cruise it — the sheer thrill. It only seemed like he was trailing her. Hell, he was probably following her lead. Lane Madden had clearly seen too many action movies. God knows she'd been in too many of them.

They caught her in the Cahuenga Pass near Barham — a two-car team. Malibu had done this dozens of times before. His job title: professional victim. You find your target in the rearview, then start to make a series of subtle calculations that only truly exceptional wheel men can make. A small turn of the wheel, a tap on the brakes, then presto, Hollywood fender bender. Happens all the time.

That was the fun part. The boring part was the aftermath. Bleeding. Waiting in your own car for the highway patrol to arrive. Then more waiting for the EMTs to take you to the nearest hospital. Malibu was stone sober, of course, and his driving record was spotless, since it was erased every time he did one of these jobs. His volunteer work with kids with leukemia (fake) would pop up, as well as his Habitat for Humanity projects (also fake). No one would give him a second glance. Maybe they'd mention his name — an alias, and he had plenty of them — in a newspaper story or two. But mostly they would focus on the actress.

Malibu wanted to take her out on Decker Canyon Road, but it turned out she knew these roads just as well as he did. Sure, he could pull some fancy surefire moves that would nudge her sweet little ass off into the canyon. But that was beyond what had been discussed, so he'd called Mann on the hands-free. The word came back quick: *no*. This had to look as mundane as possible. Something that would make headlines briefly, but nothing that would be followed up.

No, better if she looked like another coked-up actress who was out too late and didn't know how to handle her Lexus.

So he trailed her to the 101. Now it was show time.

Malibu liked working with members of the acting community. They were fun. You knew exactly what they were going to do, exactly how they were going to react. Like they were following a script. They had the idea that they were above it all —

"I really appreciate that."

— that made it all the more gratifying.

Lane was approaching the exit to Highland Avenue — the Hollywood Bowl. It was still painfully early. The sky over L.A. was a pale gray lid. Maybe from here she'd go down to Hollywood Boulevard, then take Sunset all the way back down to the PCH, and then Venice. Make herself a big strong cup of coffee — one of those Cuban espressos she used to drink all the time. Put on some Neko Case, wait for her manager to wake up. Plan her next moves. When life finally stops kicking you in the teeth, you don't whine and count the gaps. You see the fucking dentist and move on.

She signaled to change lanes, and saw the Chevy Malibu in front of her again. Damnit, the same one from Decker Canyon Road. As the moment of realization hit her — *he's braking he's braking he's braking* — the vehicle came to a violent rubber-burning halt.

Lane's body was hurled forward just as the hood was ripped from its moorings and went flying up into the windshield. Glass sprayed. The air bag exploded.

Mann watched the accident from approximately fifty yards away. Now it was time to pull over to the shoulder and be one of those friendly citizens who offers to hold your hand until the police arrive. Only *this* friendly citizen would be uncapping a syringe containing a speedball and jamming the needle into the victim's arm. There would be no hello, no speech, no nothing. Just death.

The speedball contained enough heroin and coke to take down a Belushi-size human being; it would probably stop her heart in under a minute. And if it didn't, there was always something more exotic that could be quickly loaded into a syringe. But better if it looked like a pure speedball. That way, Lane Madden would die and go to Hell still wondering what had happened. The Devil could fill her in.

Lane was numb for a few moments. Her body was telling her she was hurt, hurt bad, but she couldn't find exactly where. The signals in her brain were crossed. She looked around, trying to solve it visually. If she could put together the details, she'd know what happened.

She had broken glass in her lap. The air bag had smashed her in the face. She half pushed it aside. Her right ankle was throbbing. Her foot had somehow wedged itself under the brake pedal.

A few feet ahead she could see the car she'd hit, or the car that had hit her — she wasn't sure what exactly had happened. The driver's head was slumped over his wheel. She prayed she hadn't killed him.

Then someone opened her driver's-side door, pushed the air bag out of the way.

She looked down and saw the needle in a gloved hand.

Even though she was still wrapped in a cocoon of shock, she knew that the needle was the one detail that didn't belong.

The stranger grabbed her left wrist, twisted it, jammed the needle into the crook of her arm, depressed the plunger. Lane's heart began to race. Oh God, what was in that fucking needle? Her vision went blurry. She clawed at the passenger seat, felt the smashed beads of glass.

Lane grabbed a fistful —

— and smashed it into her attacker's eyes.

There was a horrible scream of rage and suddenly the needle was wobbling loose, hanging off Lane's arm. She plucked it out it, threw it to the side, then tried to crawl out of the car. Meanwhile her attacker flailed around, blind, looking for her. Cursing, raging at her.

As Lane's palms dug into the asphalt of the 101, she realized that her right ankle wasn't working properly. The damned chunky metal weight strapped to it didn't make it any easier. Her heart was racing way too fast, her skin slick with sweat. The world looked like it had been wrapped in gauze. Lane crawled away on her hands and one good knee, all the way to the fence at the edge of the 101.

And then she hurled herself over it.

CHAPTER
TWO

California is a beautiful fraud.

— Marc Reisner

Wheels were supposed to be up at 5.30a.m., but by 5.55 it became clear that wasn't gonna happen.

The captain told everyone it was just a little trouble with a valve. Once that was fixed and the paperwork was filed, they'd be taking off and headed to LAX. Fifteen minutes, tops. Half hour later, the captain more or less said he'd been full of shit, but really, honest, folks, *now* it was fixed, and they'd be taking off by 6.45. Thirty minutes later, the captain admitted he was pretty much yanking off/finger-fucking everyone in the airplane, and the likely departure time would be 8a.m. — something about a sensor needing replacing. Nothing serious.

No, of course not.

So after two hours of being baked alive in a narrow tube, Charlie Hardie took the advice of the flight crew and stepped off to stretch his legs. After an eternity of standing around, his belly rumbling, he decided to make a run to a bakery over at the mall between Terminals B and C. Hardie had taken exactly one bite of his dry bagel when the announcement came over the loudspeakers: *Flight fourteen seventeen ready for*

16

takeoff. All passengers must report immediately to Terminal B, Gate . . .

By the time Hardie returned to his seat, carry-on in hand, someone had already commandeered his space in the overhead bin. Hardie glanced forward and back to see if there were any gaps in the luggage where he could slide his bag. Nope. Everything was jammed in tight. Irritated passengers tried to squeeze by him in the aisle, but Hardie wasn't moving until he found a place for his carry-on. He refused to check it. He'd carefully planned his seat assignments so that he'd be one of the first on the plane, guaranteeing him overhead bin space. It didn't matter what happened to the rest of his stuff; Hardie just couldn't lose sight of this carry-on.

"Everything okay?" a gentle voice asked.

A flight attendant — young, smiling, wearing too much makeup, trying to ease the bottleneck in the middle of the plane. Trying to avoid some kind of incident.

Hardie lifted the duffel.

"Just trying to find a place for this."

"Well, I can check it for you."

"No, you can't."

The attendant stared back at him, catching the raw stubbornness in his eyes. She looked uneasy for a moment but quickly recovered:

"Why don't you slide it under the seat in front of you?"

Hardie had tried that once — during his first flight. Some snot-ass flight attendant had given him crap about height and width and keeping the aisle clear.

"You sure that's allowed?" he asked.

She touched his wrist and leaned in close. "I won't tell anyone if you won't."

The flight was quiet, monotonous, boring. Landing, too — a soft touchdown in the early-morning gloom. Hardie was thankful that the hard part was over. Within a few hours he would be back to work in a stranger's home, where he could sink down into a nice fuzzy alcoholic oblivion, just the way he liked it.

Hardie stumbled into his house-sitting career two years ago. He was between budget residence hotels and a friend of a friend had been called off to a job in Scotland, so he asked Hardie if he'd look after his place an hour north of San Diego. Four bedrooms, swimming pool, bunch of lemon trees outside. Hardie got $500 a week as well as a place to stay. He almost felt guilty taking the money, because it was a mindless job. The place didn't burn down; nobody tried to break in. Hardie watched old movies on DVD and TNT. Drank a lot of bourbon. Munched on crackers. Cleaned up after himself, didn't pee on the bathroom floor.

The friend of the friend was pleased, and recommended Hardie to other friends — about half of them on the West Coast, half on the East. Word traveled fast; reliable house sitters were hard to come by. What made Hardie appealing was his law enforcement background. Pretty soon Hardie had enough gigs that it made sense for him to stop living in residence hotels and start living out of one suitcase and a carry-on bag. Rendering him essentially homeless, but living in the fanciest abodes in the country. The kinds of places people worked all their lives to afford.

All Hardie had to do was make sure nobody broke in. He also was expected to make sure the houses didn't catch on fire.

The former was easy. Burglars tended to avoid occupied residences. Hardie knew the standard entry points, so he spent a few minutes upon arrival making sure they were fortified, and then . . . yeah. That was it. All of the "wor?" that was required. He made it clear to his booking agent, Virgil, that he didn't do plants, didn't do pets. He made sure people didn't steal shit.

Fires were another story. Especially in Southern California during the season. Hardie's most recent West Coast gig was in Calabasas, where he watched the home of a TV writer who was over in Germany doing a comedy series. Hardie followed the news reports between sips of Knob Creek, and then without much warning the winds shifted — meaning a wall of fire was racing in his direction.

There was nothing Hardie could do to save the house. So instead, he loaded up every possible thing that would be considered valuable to a writer — manuscripts, notes, hard drives — into his rental. He was still filling every available nook and cranny when the flames reached the backyard. Ash rained on his hood, the top of his head. Hardie made it down the hill and over to the highway, watching the fire begin devouring the house in his rearview mirror. Watching the smoke and choppers reminded Hardie of that old punk song "Stukas over Disneyland." The fact that

19

Hardie was pretty deep into a bourbon drunk at the time made his great escape all the more amazing.

Because that's what Hardie did after the "work?" was done and the house was fortified — drank, watched old movies. When Hardie stopped understanding the plot, he knew he'd reached his limit. He'd put down the bottle and close his eyes. He didn't worry about not being able to hear home invaders, or sirens, or any of that. The stubborn lizard cop part of his brain refused to shut off. Which, Hardie thought, was why he drank so much.

See, it was all one neat little circle.

After the Calabasas fire, and weeks of hawking black gunk out of his lungs, Hardie decided he'd had enough of SoCal for a while. He did some jobs in New York City, San Francisco, Santa Fe, Boston, even DC for one wretchedly humid week. The writer from Calabasas was grateful Hardie had managed to save so much of his material, so it wasn't as if he suffered poor marks on his house-sitter report card. In fact, Hardie had more job offers than he could handle. His living expenses — booze, used DVDs, a little bit of food — were minimal. He sent the rest of his earnings to a PO Box in a suburb of Philadelphia.

When this new California offer came up, Hardie decided it was okay to go back. The house was nestled right on the Hollywood Hills, and the ground was just as dry, probably drier, than it had been the previous year. Which had been an especially bad year for wildfires.

But it was also coming up on the three-year anniversary of the day Hardie's life ended, and he wanted to be as far away from Philadelphia as possible. He didn't want to be anywhere near the Eastern seaboard, in fact.

Hardie made his way out of the cramped tube, trying to stretch his sore body while walking. Nobody would let him. Bodies rushed past him from behind, nearly collided into him from the front. He felt like a human pinball. Down a flight of stairs he came to the luggage carousel and waited for the bags to start being vomited up from below.

Nearby, a little boy, about eight years old, squeezed his mother's hand. He glanced over his shoulder at the automatic doors every time they *whooshed* open. Down the carousel was a girl — dark hair, pretty eyes, vintage purse tucked under her arm. She tapped her high-heeled shoe to a slow, slow song.

The carousel kept churning. Airport carousels always reminded Hardie of a suit of armor, dirty and scuffed, as if a knight had fallen into a trash compactor.

The bags were belched up one at a time. None of them looked like Hardie's. There was a loud cry to his left. The little boy was running toward the doors. A man in his late thirties stopped in his tracks, took a knee, then held his arms out as the boy tackled him. He lifted the boy up off the ground and spun him in a half circle. Hardie looked back at the carousel. The girl with the purse, the one who'd been tapping her shoe, was gone. He guessed her bag had come up.

Finally all of the bags were up and claimed, leaving Hardie to stare at the empty metal carousel, turning and turning and turning.

Figured.

The suitcase contained nothing of real value — a couple of gray T-shirts, jeans, socks, deodorant and toothpaste, some DVD standbys. And Hardie still had his carry-on bag, thank God.

But the loss was still annoying. He would have no change of clothes until the airline located his suitcase — *if* they located it, ha ha ha — and had it delivered. Hardie went to the airline desk near the carousel and filled out a form with boxes too small for even his small, tight printing. He wrote down the address of the house he'd agreed to watch, wondering how the promised courier service would ever find it.

The owner, a musician named Andrew Lowenbruck, had told Virgil that the place was notoriously well hidden, even to people familiar with the tangle of intestines that made up the roadways of the original Hollywood Hills. Some deliverymen insisted that Alta Brea Drive didn't even exist.

Hardie figured he might see his bag somewhere on old episodes of *The Twilight Zone*. Maybe tucked into the background behind Burgess Meredith, or in the overhead bin over William Shatner's head.

Still, Hardie dutifully filled out the missing-bag form, then hopped a dirty, off-white shuttle bus to the rental-car area. Hardie hated renting cars, because it was one more thing to look after. But you couldn't be in the Hollywood Hills without a car. What was he supposed to do? Take a bus to Franklin and Beachwood, then hike on up to the house?

Lowenbruck was supposed to have met him at the place this morning. But he'd sent an apologetic e-mail last night to the service explaining that he had to be in Moscow earlier than expected. Lowenbruck was working on the sound track for a movie by an eccentric Russian director who wouldn't let the unfinished reels leave his native country, so he had to fly out to watch an early cut to start gathering ideas. His original flight was canceled; the replacement left eight hours earlier. Virgil told him that Lowenbruck was known for his "pulse-pounding" action scores — the modern-day Bernard Herrmann, they called him. Hardie didn't know what was wrong with the original.

So . . . Hardie wouldn't be meeting him. But that wasn't unusual. He rarely met the owners of the houses he watched — it was mostly handled by Virgil at the service, who in turn handled things by e-mail and FedEx key exchange.

Which was probably for the better. If they had a look at Hardie, some owners might change their minds.

Instead, Hardie got to know his clients by the stuff they left behind. The photos on their walls, the DVDs on their shelves, the food in their fridges. Stuff doesn't lie.

As it turned out, Alta Brea Drive wasn't too hard to find. Just shoot up Beachwood, the main drag, until you hit a dead end at the fairy tale-looking houses. Hang a sharp left on Belden, which only looks like somebody's driveway — swear to God, it's a real road, don't worry, keep driving. Then, follow the intestinal tract straight up into the Hills until it looks like you are going to drive over the edge of a road and tumble down a ravine to your death. Then, at the last possible moment is another turn, and you find yourself in front of Andrew Lowenbruck's house.

Hardie was thankful it was daylight. How the hell did people do this in the dark?

These roads weren't meant for two-way traffic, let alone a row of parked cars along the sides. But that's what people did up here, apparently — good luck sorting it all out. Still, Hardie made it up the mountain without an accident, and that's all that mattered.

Hardie had been up in the Hollywood Hills before, watching other houses. But never in this specific area — the original Holly-woodland development known as Beachwood Canyon. The whole setup looked way too fragile to Hardie. Back in Philly, he'd had grown up in a $7,000 two-story row house, which was wedged in with hundreds of other row houses on flat tracts of land that stretched river to river.

Out here was the opposite — all hills and heights and precariously perched multimillion-dollar homes. Every time Hardie looked at the Hollywood Hills, he half-expected to hear a loud wooden snap and then *whooosh*. All of the houses would slide down from their mountain perches and end up in a giant pit of broken lumber and glass at the bottom of the canyon.

Which was just one of the many reasons Hardie drank a little bit more when he sat one of these houses.

Hardie pulled up in front and turned off his rental — a Honda Whatever that felt and drove like a plastic box. Forget Alta Brea Drive; Hardie wasn't entirely convinced this *car* was real. But it was part of the airline — rental-car package he'd found online. He didn't plan on driving it much, anyway. All he needed was a way to get to a grocery store to buy food and booze, and then eventually a way back to the airport.

There were two other homes on this twisting bit of road, one on either side of Lowenbruck's place, all three of them clinging to the side of the mountain. Across Alta Brea was a rocky cliff covered in foliage. A crew of two workmen in buff jumpsuits were busy hacking away at the brush with chain saws. On top of the cliff was another of what Californians called a "house." The only part you could see from street level was a turret, standing tall, looking like it was part of a full-fledged castle. That was the thing about these hills. No matter where you built your castle, there was always somebody with a bigger castle, higher up than yours.

From street level, Lowenbruck's place looked like nothing more than a wide, flat bungalow. Spanish-tile roof, freshly painted stucco exterior. On the left was a single-car garage. In the middle was a sturdy front door cut from solid oak, and on the right, windows that would offer you a wide-screen view if tall shrubs weren't in the way.

But Hardie knew this was just the top level. Virgil told him the place had three floors; the other two were built down along the side of the mountain. In his instructions, Lowenbruck called it his "upside-down house."

The house was famous in a minor way. In 1949 a film noir called *Surrounded* had been set here, as well as parts of a 1972 neonoir called *The Glass Jungle*. This was no accident. The director of *Glass Jungle* was a big fan of *Surrounded* and had spent a lot of time on permissions for the location. Later still, in 2005, they remade *Surrounded* — this time calling it *Dead by Dawn* — but left out the house altogether. Hardie hadn't seen any of the films, but Lowenbruck told Virgil there were copies at the house — the sitter should check them out, just for fun. Hardie would check out the first one, but not the others. He had a rule these days: he didn't watch any movies made after he was born.

Seems the movies were another reason Lowenbruck wanted a house-sitter. Every few days some noir geek would just show up and start snapping photos of the house. Some would even try to sweet-talk their way in, as if the place were just a vacant movie prop and not a real place where actual people lived.

Late last night, when he had to catch his sudden plane to Moscow, Lowenbruck e-mailed Virgil to say he'd leave keys in his mailbox.

Hardie looked.

Yep.

No keys in the mailbox.

CHAPTER
THREE

Nobody came, nobody cares.
It's still not about anything.
— Bill Cosby, Hickey & Boggs

Leaving the keys to your $3.7-million-dollar home in your mailbox is never a good idea. But Lowenbruck had insisted — there was no time to FedEx them to Hardie, and he didn't know any neighbors to leave them with. Couldn't Hardie just let himself in? They'd be in the mailbox, what, a matter of eight hours?

Or never.

Hardie pulled his cell phone out of his jeans pocket, pressed the auto-dial number of Virgil's office. He waited. Nothing happened. Upon closer examination, Hardie realized that there were no bars on the screen. Probably the damned hills, blocking everything.

Hardie decided he wanted a beer. Like, yeah, right now. It was super-early in the morning, but maybe that's what he should do. Get back in the Honda Whatever, drive back down to level ground, and buy some beer. Perhaps by the time he got back, the keys would have magically reappeared in the mailbox. If not, drink another beer. Repeat until reality conformed.

Yeah. Sure.

Hardie realized that unless he wanted to guard this damned place from outside, he'd have to figure out some way of breaking in.

He examined the front, looking for entry points, hoping for an obvious weakness. The oak door was solid, locked. The wide-screen windows were locked as well — and wired. Hardie spied the security transmitters mounted in the corners of the frames. Lowenbruck had given Virgil the keypad code, but that was useless with Hardie locked outside now, wasn't it?

Moving toward the right side of the property, past some eucalyptus bushes, Hardie craned his neck until he saw a wooden sundeck hanging off the back of the house. It was supported by narrow metal poles and fitted with a wrought-iron railing. If he could make it onto the deck, he could probably jimmy open the back doors. The only problem: there was no easy way up to the deck. From the edge, there was a fifty-foot drop to the ground. Not unless Hardie wanted to climb onto the roof, and then jump down onto the deck.

The latter, of course, seemed to be the only option.

Hardie sighed. Was he really going to do this? Who knows what kind of trouble he might get into up there. One slip and he could end up with a broken leg down in the ravine, bobcats circling him.

Hardie slid the phone into his pocket, climbed behind the wheel, pulled the Honda Whatever up closer to the garage door, then parked. He stepped onto the hood of the car and scrambled up the slanted tile roof. The tiles were warm from the sun. Hardie had a vision of the damned things breaking loose, sliding down the

28

roof, and shattering on the pavement, one after the other after the other. Hardie was a large man; he didn't know if the makers of Spanish tile took his size and weight into consideration.

But he made it to the peak of the roof without incident. There he paused. The lush bowl of the hills was laid out beneath him, and off in the distance were the hazy glass-and-metal skyscrapers of downtown L.A. Hardie instantly understood the appeal of living here. Even though the sides of the mountain were littered with homes, there was the illusion that yours was the only one that mattered, that the rest of these properties had been assembled here for *your* benefit. No one else had a view like yours, not the homes above nor the ones below. You had a front-row seat to the big show. You could enjoy it anytime you liked . . . when you weren't slaving away on a sound track, that is. Hardie wondered how much Lowenbruck enjoyed his view. He doubted the man ever climbed up onto his own roof to catch this particular vista.

Okay, enough. Sooner or later somebody was going to look up and see Hardie standing here, looking like an idiot.

Hardie spied the deck and began to make his way over to it, arms out for balance. Still, he couldn't help but glance down at the houses below. The different-colored roofs, the pools, the terracotta patios.

And through a clearing in the trees, on the back deck of the house closest to Lowenbruck's, a nude woman sunbathing.

It almost looked like a mirage. The branches and trees made a perfect frame around her body, blocking out everything but her astounding and abundant nakedness. She was full-chested, with pink nipples that looked too delicate to be out in the bright California sun. Her body was muscled, perfectly shaved, and oiled — as far as Hardie could tell — from her nose down. Her skin practically glistened. Hardie wondered why Lowenbruck hadn't left the keys with *her*.

The woman's eyes were hidden behind sunglasses. She held a cell phone to her ear. And while her mouth moved, the words didn't travel the distance uphill.

Hardie froze in place, pitched precariously on the downward slope of the roof. He stared for a few moments before he realized that, fuck, she could probably see him, too.

Probably telling a friend on the phone: *You're never going to believe this, but some idiot is standing up on the roof of my neighbor's place, staring at my tits.*

Hardie continued his descent, placed a hand on the hot tile for balance, then jumped down onto the back deck. Something squished underfoot. Hardie was almost afraid to look . . . then did. Some kind of animal had been up here recently and had left a large deposit on Lowenbruck's sundeck. Not a bird; this beast appeared to enjoy a heartier diet than seeds and grass.

Shit.

Fortunately, Hardie had packed another pair of shoes.

Unfortunately, they were in his missing suitcase.

30

Hardie tiptoed over and tried the sliding glass doors. Miraculously, they were unlocked. Either Lowenbruck forgot or he wasn't in the habit of locking it.

The moment the contacts separated, however, the alarm was triggered — a shrill repeating *bee-BEEP bee-BEEP*. Thirty seconds and counting. Hardie knew there was a keypad by the front door. He needed to reach it fast or he'd have company soon, and that would no doubt push back his drinking by a few hours more.

bee-BEEP

bee-BEEP

bee-BEEP

Just as he was about to step inside he remembered the unidentified animal crap on his shoes. Hardie worked off one shoe hurriedly with the back of the other, reached down, yanked off its companion, then darted through the open doors looking for anything, anything at all, resembling a security keypad.

bee-BEEP

bee-BEEP

bee-BEEP

There were too many things hanging on the walls near the front door, too much clutter. Fuck. Fuck. *Fuck . . .*

Hardie found it and jabbed the code in with two seconds to spare.

The key situation would have to be figured out sooner rather than later — Hardie didn't want to leave the premises unlocked for any period of time, nor did he want to climb the tiled roof again to make a grocery run. Maybe he could have some booze delivered? No. Because that would require a working cell phone, and Virgil had told him that Lowenbruck didn't have a landline.

Anyway, first things first: house check.

The sliding doors from the back deck opened up into a media room — and immediately Hardie knew he'd lucked out. Wall-mounted plasma TV, stereo components whose brand name Hardie only recognized from other houses he'd watched. Overstuffed black leather couch, which Hardie immediately decided would be his home base for most of the next month. The wall shelves contained row upon row of DVDs, many of them classics — which was fantastic. Old movies gave him something to fill the long days. He remembered the special Hell of a Myrtle Beach condo that lacked not just cable or satellite TV but a TV as well. Longest two weeks of his life.

The rest of the top floor seemed to be little more than a life-support system for the media room. The locked front door led to the vestibule and beyond that a winding staircase with wrought-iron rail, leading down to the lower floors.

The stairwell was lined with cardboard standees of 1980s white tough-guy actors, arranged *Sgt. Pepper*-style. Clint. McQueen. Bruce. Sly. Arnie. Van Damme. Segal. And, strangely, Gene Hackman. This was seventies Hackman. Crazy-man Hackman. *Night Moves* and *Conversation* and *French Connection* Hackman. The collage of 2-D tough guys looked like it

32

had been stuck up there for a while. The edges of the cardboard were frayed, cracked, and torn in places, and the material itself was yellowing. The surfaces featured a film of dust, and various body parts — an elbow, a foot — had come unstuck from the wall. Either Lowenbruck really loved his action heroes, or some previous owner had, and Lowenbruck thought it easier to leave the whole thing up.

The next room was a smallish dining area, though clearly nobody ever ate in here. The table was covered in scripts, DVDs, CDs, old newspapers, staff paper, pencils. A peek inside a cupboard door revealed more battered scripts, yellowing newspapers, and about forty copies of a sound track called *Two-Way Split* on CD.

The galley kitchen was clean but spare. Seemed like not much cooking happened in here. No booze in the cabinets, no food in the fridge, except for a box of baking soda and a glass jar of martini olives shoved in the back.

Half bathroom off to one side. Handy. Probably thirty paces between the leather couches and the porcelain throne here. That would make life easy.

On the other side of the kitchen, a door led to a tiny two-person deck with a hard-plastic Adirondack chair and a Weber Baby grill, overlooking another part of the hills. Hardie looked through the window and thought he could make out part of the Griffith Observatory. No other nude sunbathers in sight, however. Which was a little disappointing. Would have been nice to have the ladies in stereo.

Okay.

So, three entrances so far:

Front door;

Back patio doors (if you felt like walking on the roof);

Side patio door (if you were to somehow climb up the side of the house and vault over the railing).

All locks in working order as far as Hardie could tell.

Hardie retraced his steps, passed the gang of action heroes, gave Hackman a respectful nod —

Gene

— then continued down the wide stairs as they spun him around to face . . . a closed set of double doors. Which seemed weird, until Hardie opened them up and walked into a large music studio, soundproofing everywhere.

Ah, so this was the padded treasure in the heart of the Lowenbruck castle: the recording studio. The space was tricked out with enough gear to make the upstairs media room look like a kids' Fisher-Price set. Huge, wide-screen plasma TV, a mixing console the size of a back porch, multiple keyboards, amplifiers, heaps of spaghetti cable.

Virgil had told him:

"Lowenbruck's insanely anal about his studio. Don't even go in there if you can avoid it. Just make sure nothing happens to it."

"I won't."

"I've got explicit instructions here. Like, don't even turn a knob."

"What am I, in high school?"

"Just telling you what's here on the form."

34

"Okay, Virge. It won't be easy, but somehow I'll resist the urge to record my *Pet Sounds* tribute."

Nothing else down here — was there room for anything else? — except two other padded doors. One was open a few inches, and obviously led to a bathroom. Hardie could see a white-tile floor and the edge of a silver mirror. He supposed that when Lowenbruck was in full-on work mode, this was all he needed. His keyboards and a place to take a leak or splash water on his face from time to time. The other door probably led downstairs to the third-floor bedroom.

Hardie was about to head down when the bathroom door flew open all the way and someone screamed and rushed at him and hit him on the head with something really, really hard.

CHAPTER
FOUR

I don't make things difficult.
That's the way they get, all by themselves.
— Mel Gibson, *Lethal Weapon*

The first blow dazed Hardie, made his vision go fuzzy, sent him stumbling one step to the side. The second blow struck him on the upper arm. The entire limb went numb. Some muscle memory kicked in just in time for the third blow. Hardie was able to block the hard, shiny object with a forearm.

With his other hand he snatched out and grabbed a wrist, then twisted it hard. His attacker — a young girl, he could see now — cried out. Hardie yanked her out of the bathroom doorway and spun her into the room proper. Her back hit a mixing board, and her head banged into a monitor that was hanging from the ceiling.

Hardie held up his hands. Tried to, anyway. His left arm was still numb. At least the right one still worked.

"Hey?"

His voice sounded strange to him. Hardie couldn't remember the last time he'd spoken out loud.

The girl was wearing only panties and a T-shirt, and her ankle was bandaged. Her legs were lean and muscled. Her whole body trembled.

"Get the fuck away from me or I'll cut you, I swear to God I'll jam this straight up your ass?"

Hardie looked at the *this* in her hands. He couldn't place it. Long, silver, metal. A tube of some kind. About two feet long, with the circumference of a nickel. Uncapped on the end. Then he looked behind her, into the music studio, and saw others just like it.

A microphone stand.

She had been beating the shit out of him with a mic stand.

Hardie said, in a slow and steady and reasonable voice:

"Give me that."

"I said, stay the fuck away! You people are making a big mistake."

"You *people*? Only one of me here, honey."

There was something vaguely familiar about the girl's face, like he *should* know her from somewhere. Had Lowenbruck sent Virgil anything about her, maybe attached a photo to an e-mail? No, Hardie would have remembered that. Nobody was supposed to be here in the house. No girlfriends, no relatives, no friends — nobody. Hardie wouldn't have taken the job otherwise. That was the whole point. Avoiding people.

Hardie steadied himself, took a step closer. The girl responded by swinging at the air with the mic stand, then inching her way back into the studio.

"Come on, now. Enough's enough."

"Stay the fuck *away* from me!"

"I'm not going to hurt you."

The girl's hands fell to her sides. Her head hung low. Her entire body went limp, and she started breathing strangely. It took Hardie a second or two to realize she was launching into a full-on crying jag. He took a step toward her, said:

"Look, why don't we start with —"

Without warning she lunged. Another hard, mean swing. Hardie was ready this time. He snatched the pole in his hand and refused to let go. She tugged. He held firm. She tugged again. He held on tighter. Uh-uh. Bitch was not getting her mic stand back. Bitch was definitely not hitting him with the mic stand again.

Then she did something Hardie did not anticipate. She lunged forward, pushing the mic stand toward Hardie. His grip was not prepared for this. The mic stand slid through his fist and went into his chest.

Both Hardie and the girl looked down at the pole for a moment before Hardie took a confused step backward. What had just happened?

"Ugh," he said.

"Oh God," she said.

Hardie forced himself to look down. Yep. He'd been impaled. Under his gray T-shirt he could feel blood trickling down across his right nipple, along his belly, past the waistband of his jeans. None of this seemed real. He took a breath, wondering if one of his lungs was going to collapse. Maybe pass out. Any second now.

But nothing yet. Somehow, he was still standing.

"Oh God," the girl repeated, and immediately yanked the mic stand out.

"No, don't do —"

Too late. The metal slid out of his flesh with a soft, wet *shucking* sound — like the meat of an oyster being pried from its shell. Hardie took an involuntary step backward, as if he could remove himself from the damage. The girl, too, edged backward, looked alternatively angry, shocked, and confused.

"I told you . . . I told you I'd hurt you!"

And make no mistake. The wound in his chest really fucking hurt, pain ramping up with every breath, it seemed. But somehow he was still standing, fully conscious. Maybe it wasn't so bad. Maybe it had missed everything vital — the heart, the aorta, the lungs, the liver. Then again, maybe she'd nailed his heart right smack-dab in the fucking center and he was going to bleed out in a matter of seconds.

Hardie looked into the bathroom doorway for a towel, something to press against his chest. Maybe wrap around the wound. He took a step forward. Which freaked out the girl.

"Stay the fuck away from me!?"

"I'm not going anywhere near you. Believe me."

The girl tried to focus on him. Every muscle in her body was tensed, but her eyelids were strangely droopy. The combination of anxiety and lethargy suggested the girl had been playing mix and match in a medicine cabinet. Maybe Lowenbruck kept a bunch of pharmaceuticals handy and this girl knew it.

Whatever. Hardie took a few cautious steps into the bathroom, snatched the edges of a white terry-cloth towel and whipped it from the rack. He quickly folded it in half, held it under the entrance wound. Usually, the advice was simple: direct pressure, stop the bleeding. But what the fuck were you supposed to do when somebody impaled you?

Hardie looked at the girl.

"Why did you do that?"

"You're one of *Them* . . . admit it!"

"I don't know who you mean by *Them*, but I can assure you, I'm not."

"Then, what the fuck are you doing in here?"

"I'm the house sitter."

"House what?"

Her long dark hair hung down in her face, and her skin was dirty in places. Lots of scratches, too, along with a stray bruise or two. She'd bandaged up both of her hands — a sloppy, rushed job. Still, she was a pretty girl. Wide, full mouth, high cheekbones, and eyes that would be striking if she could manage to keep them open all the way — and somebody hosed her off in the backyard for a few minutes.

"House sitter. I watch houses."

"Why would a fucking house sitter go sneaking around the house, checking every room? Don't fucking deny it — I heard you!"

Hardie had had enough standing. He carefully eased himself down to a sitting position. If he was going to pass out, he'd rather do it closer to the floor.

40

"Look, honey, I just got here. Question is, what are you doing here? Because I'm pretty sure my booking agent didn't mention anything about a crackhead with a mic stand, hiding in the bathroom."

She rolled her eyes. "Crackhead. Don't you know who I am?" "Sweetie, I have no idea."

The faintest trace of a smile appeared for a moment, then vanished. Then she started trembling.

Hardie had no idea who she was, but a story started to form in his mind. Beneath all of the patches of dirt and scratches and attitude, she appeared to be a perfectly young and healthy girl — not your average skinny L.A. junkie with buggy eyes and cheekbones that could cut tin cans. This girl had been well fed and cared for until relatively recently. Like, maybe even just a few hours ago. Maybe her parents owned a place farther down Alta Brea, or somewhere else in Beachwood Canyon. Maybe she'd stayed up past her bedtime partying hard, an asshole friend suggesting a quick coke-and-H nightcap. *Mellow out and party all night long!*

Yeah, maybe that was it. She shoots up, she freaks. Knows she can't go home to Mom and Dad. Not in that condition. Sees the Lowenbruck house. Finds the keys in the mailbox. Still freaking, worried about *Them* — parents? cops? dealers? — coming for her. Grabs a mic stand — yeah, that still didn't make sense to him either, but he supposed a weapon was a weapon — then hit the bathroom.

Enter Charlie Hardie, Human Pincushion.

He hoped she had parents. He'd love to send them his emergency-room bill.

With every second that passed, Hardie came to believe that maybe the pole *had* missed all of the important bits. His sister-in-law-nurse back in Philly had told him a bunch of crazy ER stories — thugs rolling in with twenty, thirty stab wounds, yet still smoking cigarettes and annoyed to have to wait around so long even though they don't have proper ID, let alone health insurance.

But Hardie had also heard plenty of the opposite, too. Stupid bar fights where one sloppy stab with a greasy butter knife ends up with one man DOA and another facing a manslaughter beef.

And when it came to medical luck, Hardie was reasonably confident that he'd used it all up three years ago.

Oh God.

She'd stabbed a man.

He was probably one of Them, but still . . . she didn't mean to puncture his chest. She just wanted to knock him out — though her favorite stunt coordinator, Enrico Cifelli, had once told her how ridiculous that was.

Sure, you saw it in the movies all the time. But Enrico told her that blows to the top of the head almost never render the person unconscious. What it might do, however, is cause the diaphragm muscles to freak out, making it difficult for that person to breathe. Left untreated, it would kill him.

Of course, try to keep all of that in mind when you think you're being hunted. This was not a movie set; she hadn't gone through endless repetition, practicing a single move so that it could be filmed. When you're being hunted, you kind of just *wing it.*

And now she'd stabbed a man.

Hardie struggled up off the floor, fully expecting to pass out at any second. Before that happened, the dirty psycho chick had to go. To the hospital, to the LAPD, whatever. He supposed he should involve the LAPD because — well, she'd impaled him.

And broken into the house. Those still counted as crimes, even in L.A.

"Are you okay?" she asked, hand out, as if to help him up. She took great care not to actually touch him, though. She gestured as if Hardie had an invisible force field around his body.

Hardie shot her a look.

"Hey," she said. "I said I was sorry."

Hardie said, "Pretty sure I missed that."

"Well, I'm saying it now."

"Whatever. Does your cell phone work?"

"Why?"

"Well, I'd like to call nine one one, if that wouldn't be too much trouble. Maybe we can call someone for you, too. Like your mom or dad, maybe?"

The girl's jaw dropped. "My *mom?*"

"You look pretty banged up. Maybe you should go to the hospital, too. Maybe they can give us adjoining rooms, just in case you feel like ramming something sharp through my body again."

"You just want me to go outside."

"Unless there's an emergency room in the basement, yeah."

This was getting them nowhere. What was he doing, anyway? Why did he give a shit about this girl, or even this house? Hello, Earth to Charlie: You have been impaled by a steel tube. You belong in a hospital.

She was looking at him. "You say you're the house sitter."

"Yeah."

"What's your name?"

"Charlie. And yours?"

"Last name." This was a command, not a question.

"Hardie."

"I'm supposed to just, what? . . . *Believe you?*"

Hardie thought about taking a better look at his wound but then changed his mind when his chest started throbbing. He took a semideep breath, wondering if he'd feel his lung collapse suddenly. It made him angry. She did this to him, and now she was giving him shit?

"You want to go upstairs and trade driver's licenses? Because that's all I've got. I seem to have left my birth certificate and Social Security card at home. Sorry."

"That's just what you'd want, isn't it? Me to follow you upstairs."

"Isn't that what I just said?"

The girl's eyes darted around wildly as she processed his words. Then her brain seemed to slip back into gear.

"Okay, let's say you're not one of Them."

"Let's do more than say it. Let's believe it, because I'm fucking *not*."

"If you're not one of Them, how did you get into the house? I have the keys."

"Ah, from the mailbox, right?"

So Andrew Lowenbruck *had* left the keys after all. Sorry, good sir, that I ever doubted you. Seems like this skinny, spoiled party girl went helping herself. Hardie smiled, but that just seemed to piss her off.

"I asked you," she repeated, making sure he understood every syllable, even though her voice was trembling. "How. Did. You. Get. *In?*"

"Yeah. I heard. And thanks to you, I had to walk across the roof and use the sliding doors on the deck."

"Shit — did anybody see you?"

"See me what?"

"When you walked into the house, did anybody see you? Was anybody watching?"

Hardie thought about his walk across the tile roof and almost said, *Well, yeah, there was this woman with amazing tits who caught me breaking into the house,* but that didn't seem like a good way to put this girl at ease.

Before Hardie had a chance to answer, the girl pushed herself back a few inches, creeping away from him, shaking her head back and forth, pure panic on her face.

"No . . . oh God, what if they saw you? Shit, if they saw you . . ."

Back to *them* again.

"Nobody's outside. It's just you and me, honey."

Well, and the sunbathing babe.

This was getting old fast. Hardie was wondering what he was going to say to Lowenbruck about all of this. Because after he got this girl calmed and into his rental car, he would have to call the police — and then Virgil. But there wasn't any way around that. Lowenbruck would need a report for his insurance. Especially if she broke anything. God knows what she did to this place since helping herself to the keys. Goldilocks only ate porridge and smashed chairs and fell asleep in beds. And Goldilocks wasn't a teenaged junkie.

Wait.

The girl had obviously helped herself to the keys, but how did she manage to deactivate the alarm? It had been set when Hardie had opened the sliding doors.

The story in his head changed.

Maybe this wasn't a college girl. Maybe this was one of Lowenbruck's barely legal exes. She didn't have keys, but she knew the security code because he never bothered to change it. She runs into trouble, goes to the first place that comes to mind.

Either way, Hardie had to get her out of here and the police thing over with. He was exhausted. Being stabbed in the chest didn't help his mood either. He hoped it was a few stitches and a couple of Vikes kind of situation . . . not a go-to-a-hospital-for-major-surgery-because,-oh,-your-lung-is-collapsing kind of situation. He still didn't want to look down at the wound.

46

Hardie took a step forward, held out his hand. "C'mon."

The girl seemed outraged by the suggestion.

"Don't you come anywhere near me."

"We both need a trip to the hospital. We can sort this all out in the waiting room."

"You don't understand. I'm not leaving this house. I don't care what you say or what you do, but I'm not leaving."

No, Hardie didn't understand, but add it to the long, long list of things he didn't understand.

And then the world around them fell silent.

CHAPTER
FIVE

Arnold Schwarzenegger: *Where did you learn*
how to do that?
Rae Dawn Chong: *I read the instructions.*
— *Commando*

He found the transformer, traced the power lines to the underside of the house. Slashing the wires was foolish; you wanted to be able to resume power quickly if need be, or cover your tracks. So he used a putty knife to strip away the layer of gray utility clay bunched around the cable, carefully placing the chunks in his jacket pocket. Soon the copper cables, insulated in layers of lead and rubber, were revealed, and he carefully disconnected them from the digital meter.

A few feet away, the HVAC unit, resting on a pad of concrete, shut down and spun out to a total stop.

"Power's out. Hooking up the governor now."

"Good."

He screwed the loose wires into a small hard-plastic box that could be controlled by remote. Power was gone, but it could be back on line if needed.

Next up: security system, satellite dish, gas lines, water. All the things you took for granted until you pushed a button, flipped a switch, or turned a knob and nothing happened. And the security system? That was a joke because it depended on a battery, as well as a landline to notify the company. Disable both and they'd have no idea. Nope, nothing wrong here.

Hardie looked around the recording studio. It was hard to tell at first what was wrong — just that something suddenly felt *wrong*. He stood up, glanced down briefly, then up again. Maybe it was him. Maybe his brain was shutting down, his soul preparing to depart his body and simply shutting off all of his senses before it left.

No . . . the girl seemed to hear it, too. Her head snapped to the left, then the right. She touched her lips.

"What was that?" she asked.

"I don't know," Hardie said. "Stay here."

"Where the fuck are you going?"

Hardie ignored her, then started climbing the stairs, keenly aware of his heart pumping the blood that enabled his limbs to move. In his mind's eye, he saw his heart working okay, just hanging in there . . . until a fat artery suddenly popped out of his heart, twisting and leaking like a severed garden hose, whipping around his chest and spraying his lungs with dark blood.

Knock that off, Hardie told himself. You're going to think yourself into the grave.

As he wound his way back to the first floor, the cardboard action heroes seemed to raise a collective eyebrow.

Buddy, you have no idea what you're getting into.

"Shut up," Hardie muttered.

This house-sitter guy could still be one of Them.

Easy.

He didn't act like it. But that would be just like them, wouldn't it? All jokes and smiles and friendliness, all meant to put you at ease, help you relax, then, *wham!* You were done.

Just like her Good Samaritan on the 101. Walking up to her car, needle in hand, jabbing it into her arm when she was at her weakest —

Now "Charli?" here was turning his back on her. Probably on his way to the front door to let his buddies inside. The bastards had needles on the highway. What would it be this time?

Sorry, Chuck, she thought to herself. *You may be telling the truth. You may be one of Them. Either way, I'm going to have to stop you.*

Lane pulled herself up, using the edge of the kitchen counter. She had to move quickly. He was already halfway across the dining room.

The alarm had clued her in — snapped her out of a half sleep, actually. She'd set the alarm system for that very reason. While the intruder walked around, Lane got herself together. Listened. Waited. The intruder's steps were methodical. Whoever was inside was clearly searching. She heard the faint creak and hum of the refrigerator door opening. The rattle of a doorknob. The opening of cabinet doors. Slowly. Carefully. Searching. Searching for *her.*

So when he made it to the second floor, the choice was simple. Him or me.

50

Now Lane limped up the staircase behind him. Damn it — he was almost at the front door. She hurled herself up after him, speed-hopping, resting her injured foot for a fraction of a microsecond before using her good foot to vault herself forward. If he opened that door, it was all over.

Hardie stepped into the vestibule, looking around for something out of place. All at once the silence was overwhelming. He was tempted to open the door to see if something had happened outside, like maybe the Rapture or Armageddon, but then a thought occurred to him. Hardie moved into the media room, then saw his reflection in the darkened flat-screen. After a few seconds he figured out what was missing: No digital time readouts on the components.

The girl appeared in the room, bloodied mic stand still in her hand. The fact that it was *his* blood vaguely bothered Hardie.

She leaned forward and whisper-yelled: "What are you doing?"

"The power's out," Hardie said.

"Oh God. So they know I'm in here. They saw you walk in, and they think I'm in here . . ."

"Uh, you *are* in here."

"They didn't know that before you showed the fuck up!"

"Please, for the love of God . . . who is *they?*"

But the girl was already starting to panic, looking around at the windows and doorways, as if expecting a heavily armed unit of commandos to come storming into the house, spraying mace grenades and bullets.

Hardie had to admit, it was all starting to feel seriously strange to him, too. The power *just so happens* to go out just after he got his dumb ass stabbed in the chest? None of the previous explanations his lizard brain had come up with seemed to fit now. If it was just the girl, that would be one thing. People on drugs cooked up some truly weird shit in their fevered brains. But this was no simple cocaine-fueled delusion. Hardie was living in it, too.

He went to the front door, and, as predicted, the digital security panel was still lit. These systems always run by backup battery. That way, if home invaders cut the power, you can still call for help.

The girl appeared behind him and took him by the wrist. Hardie flinched at her touch.

"Come back downstairs with me," she said. *"Please. I don't want them seeing us through the windows."*

"Hold on. The security's still working. There's got to be a panic button or something on here."

"No! Don't you dare touch that!"

"Why not?"

"They could be anybody. What if they just put on a bunch of fake security team uniforms and come knocking? How would you be able to tell the difference between what's real and what they want you to see?"

"Just curious — do you realize how little sense you're making right now? Or is this the drugs talking?"

BEEP.

Hardie's eyes flicked to the right.

52

The security display panel?

Dead.

"Security's out, power's out, everything."

"Okay. O'Neal — the wasp nest on the door?"

"Mounted, loaded, and ready."

"Okay, let's get bags ready, A.D."

"On it. How is your eye, by the way?"

"Focus on the task at hand."

"Sorry — just asking."

"Ask me when the production is over. Now go."

By the time Hardie put it fully together — that, yeah, someone on the outside was fucking with them — the girl had already taken up a position in front of the heavy oak door, mic stand in hand. Her whole body trembled. She was wild-eyed. She pressed her free hand against the door, as if trying to sense what was on the other side through the power of touch.

Hardie took a step forward. "You need to let me through."

She whisper-yelled at him: "No, I will *not* fucking let you through. Don't you understand? That's what they want! You open this door, and we're both dead."

"If you don't let me through so I can get to a hospital, then I might be dead, and *you* might be going to jail. Is that any better?"

This was wonderful. Already this gig had earned its place in the House Sitter Hall of Fame.

Hardie took a step forward. The girl raised her weapon — the bloodied mic stand — and pointed it at him.

"Want me to go now?"

"No. Wait to see if he comes out on his own. He might think the whole area is out and step outside to check."

"How about I get into position, anyway, and wait for your signal?"

"Go ahead."

Hardie didn't know if he should swat the mic stand to the side, try to snatch it out of her hands, or give up.

"Are you really threatening to stab me with that thing?"

"I won't let you open this door."

"Look. I believe you. There is some kind of *They* out there. *They* are most definitely fucking with us. But I don't want to sit here and wait for them to make a move. I used to be with the police. I think I can handle myself."

Even Hardie knew that last line sounded full of shit. Yes, he sort of used to be something like a cop. But that had been three long years ago. A lot of drinking and poor eating and general sloth had atrophied his muscles. He was slower, larger. His liver wasn't talking to him anymore, and his heart gave him little friendly reminders every so often that he might want to get his ass up and move around a little. The mornings he felt good simply meant that he'd passed out before he could have any more to drink.

So . . . *I can handle myself?*

Sure, Unkillable Chuck. Whatever you say.

The fact remained — he wanted to look outside and see what the hell was going on. Maybe it wasn't just this house but the whole block. Maybe World War III had kicked off, and he'd be able to see downtown L.A. go up in a flash of blinding light.

But the girl was still stubbornly blocking his way.

"You can't handle these people. Believe me."

"Still nothing."

"Playing it safe, I guess. Okay, go head. Take it."

"On it."

Hardie heard a car engine rev, though at first he thought it was the power kicking back on. Then came the screech of tires, which quickly receded into the distance. Wait a second now . . .

He went for the door handle. The girl held up the edge of the mic stand so that it pointed at his throat.

"Don't. I'm warning you."

Hardie said, "Let me look."

"Use a window."

Hardie didn't want to get into another wrestling match with this psycho chick. She might end up stabbing that damned mic stand in another part of his body. His luck, his goddamned eye. So, fine, he'd open the front door later. Hardie sidestepped away from the girl and made his way to the wide-screen windows in

55

the living room. He pulled aside the dusty curtains, then looked outside, and then immediately muttered, "Fuck *me*."

Hardie had pulled up what . . . thirty minutes ago? His Honda Whatever was gone.

CHAPTER
SIX

A far-fetched story must be plausibly told,
so your nonsense isn't showing.

— Alfred Hitchcock

The Lane Madden production was supposed to be the easy one.

After Mann received the green light, O'Neal observed the actress for a few days. He reported back, which only confirmed that Mann's original idea was best: a "Sleeping Beaut?" — late-night OD after a party. The narrative in Mann's head went something like:

After a career slump and well-publicized descent into booze and drugs, and eventually a court-ordered alcohol-monitoring anklet, a B-list starlet is given a second chance with a part in a new indie prestige film. Feeling good, she decides to celebrate. She can't handle it; she relapses hard. She ODs in her Venice Beach apartment.

If all went well, Mann thought, the actress wouldn't even wake up for her own death. She might feel a slight pinch somewhere in her dreams, and then she'd feel wonderful, and then she'd feel nothing at all.

Mann had a three-man support team (O'Neal, A.D., Malibu) all set to move when SURPRISE — the actress got her ass up and went for a late-night drive up the PCH. They reported it to Mann, who told Malibu to follow her, see if any opportunities presented themselves. Malibu pushed for a Decker Canyon Road crash, but the thought made Mann uneasy. Too many wildcard factors — including the idea that the actress might survive a plunge into the canyon, or live long enough to place a 911 call describing the car that had run her off the road. When it seemed that Lane was headed down the 101 toward Hollywood, Mann put a new plan into play — an old reliable. Drug overdose followed by a crash. Easy, simple.

Only not so simple. A.D. and O'Neal had tracked her up into the Hollywood Hills while Mann staggered off to have an eye patched and Malibu stayed at the scene to give a report to the police.

The court-ordered ankle bracelet made it easy to trace Madden's movements through the Hollywood Hills. They'd hacked into it the day before and had been following her movements on their phones ever since. Toward the end of the chase, however, she got smart and used something — probably a rock — to break the bracelet and tossed it into a clump of eucalyptus bushes down at the bottom of a steep hill. All seemed lost until they picked up some blood splatters near Alta Brea Drive.

There was only one house on this flat steep slope. A quick phone call revealed the owner's name, and that settled it. The actress was obviously there, slipping inside like some fucked-up Goldilocks who knew the bears were about to devour her ass.

They weren't bears, though.

They were highly trained professionals, part of something they loosely (and semijokingly) referred to as the Guild.

The Guild was a small brotherhood that specialized in invisible acts. They considered themselves the unseen architects of modern history. No footprints, no forensic evidence, no hint of the hand behind the act. Mann and her kind didn't provide something as crude as a "hit"; rather, she strived for an *airtight death narrative*. You could look, but you would not find anything. You could question, but there would be no answers — other than the obvious.

Few people knew they existed.

Those who did called them by their nickname:

"The Accident People."

O'Neal and A.D. were ordered to watch the house until Mann could make it up to Alta Brea. Once Mann arrived, O'Neal and A.D. reported that no one had entered or exited in the past hour. With one good eye — and oh, the cut eye almost made it personal, it truly did — Mann noticed a small white house down the hill below Alta Brea Drive. A quick call to Factboy confirmed that the occupant, an actress, was away on a horror-movie shoot in Atlanta. The house would be a perfect staging area. Mann broke in, secured it, then set up a surveillance post.

So now Mann watched from below and started to craft a new narrative:

Drugged-out B-list starlet crashes her car on the 101, staggers away in a haze, thinks she can just leave her mess behind for someone else to clean up. Wanders into some poor bastard's home (celebrities were known to do that, too) only to die in a guest bathroom . . . or no, wait, she wanders the hills for a while, which explains the scrapes from tree branches, and the grass stains on the bottoms of her feet.

Once they had her again and made sure she was dead, they'd dump her in the canyon. Even better: march her body out to the edge of a mini-canyon, then *whoops*, good-bye, Lane Madden.

Cars and drugs were popular methods of celebrity death, but accidental falls were surprisingly popular, too. Maybe Lane would enjoy a lucky trifecta? People wouldn't focus so much on the wrecked car or the speedball as on her stupid plunge off the edge of a cliff in Hollywoodland. That was it. Right there. Lane Madden's final narrative.

But they had to get her out of the house first.

And they had to do that *just right*.

Celebrity deaths were always scrutinized. By reporters, by cops, by fans. Even your average American idiot, having put in years of forensic study watching *CSI*, knew that the evidence told the story.

So if you needed everyone to believe your narrative, you had to get the details perfect.

Mann could not kick down the doors, guns in hand, screaming, looking for their target. That was *not* being invisible. They had to use their brains and pinpoint her location by other means. Mann was smart, and was regarded in extremely small circles as the best. Lane Madden was a vain little bitch, probably still out of her mind from the injection. This shouldn't be too difficult . . .

They needed to operate within the parameters of the narrative. Narrative was *everything*.

But first, they needed to get rid of the intruder.

He had shown up unexpectedly. Parked right in front of the garage, then went to the mailbox and flipped the top like he owned the place. Which was not the case. The owner was a man named Andrew Lowenbruck, who was currently landing at Sheremetyevo International Airport in Moscow. Who was this guy? Did the actress figure out a way to call for help? Had she left him a note in the mailbox somehow?

This intruder was fucking with Mann's narrative. She needed him identified, then eliminated from the scene.

"Okay, go ahead," she told O'Neal. "Take it."

Number of vehicles stolen in Los Angeles every year: 75,000.

Hot-wiring cars? For punks and crackheads. O'Neal preferred to go high tech: hacking the onboard navigation system, popping the locks, and firing up the engine courtesy of a hunk of metal flying twelve thousand miles above the surface of the earth. It took maybe fifteen, sixteen seconds from the first keystroke. He was getting better at it all the time. New skills, new ways to pay the bills.

Then again, O'Neal shouldn't go breaking his arm to pat himself on the back. Rental cars were notoriously easy picking. Nobody thought twice about override commands and remote starts — if anybody was looking. Which they weren't.

The only disappointing thing was that the vehicle was . . . well, a Honda. Perfectly okay car, don't get him wrong, if you were a suburban dad who worked in a cube and equated kinky with jacking off to photos of a New Jersey Housewife. The instant he slid himself behind the wheel, O'Neal felt that much lamer. Good thing he'd be driving it for only a couple of minutes — off the road and into a safe haven. In this case, a storage facility on Vine, right under the 101.

O'Neal made an efficient search of the interior, reporting details to Mann over a hands-free unit as he worked.

"Okay, nearly full tank, one twelve on the odometer. Small black duffel bag in the passenger seat."

Then O'Neal popped the glove box and found the rental papers — the driver had simply stuffed them in there, like every other human being on the planet.

"Vehicle rented to a Charles Hardie, eighty-seven Colony Drive, Philadelphia, Pennsylvania one nine one five two."

"Good," Mann said, then thumbed the vitals into the phone, sent it off to the researcher. Within minutes, a short but complete summary of Charles Hardie's life would be winging its way back.

Soon the man who called himself "Factboy" had the basics nailed down. Factboy knew better than to bore Mann with the minutiae of Charles Hardie's life — high school attended, last book checked out of the library, blood type. What mattered now was what Hardie did for a living. Why he was here, at this address on Alta Brea Drive, right now, in the middle of their business.

"He's a former consultant with the Philadelphia Police Department," Factboy said. "Now he's a freelance home security specialist, working with an agency out of Dallas."

"Home security?" Mann asked. "We didn't trip any alarms."

"No, he's not a guard. Hardie's just a house sitter. The owner of the house, one Andrew Lowenbruck, is away for a month. Hardie's here to watch the place."

"And he shows up now, of all times?"

"Seems legit to me. Lowenbruck left just last night according to the agency's records. Hardie caught a red-eye, made it here this morning."

"So he wasn't called in because of the target," Mann said.

"There's no indication. No phone calls have been made from the residence, or from the target's phone."

Factboy waited for the smallest indication that Mann was impressed by how much he'd cobbled together in such a short span of time, but Factboy knew better. Mann wasn't impressed by miracles; they were expected.

Factboy had a large array of digital tools at his disposal, but lately his weapon of choice was the National Security Letter, something the FBI invented over thirty years ago but really came into its own after the Patriot Act. NSLs were lethal little mothers. If presented with one, you had to open up your files, no questions asked. Didn't matter if you were a used-car dealer or a US Customs official — all your base belong to them.

And the NSL came with a nifty feature: a built-in gag order, lasting until your death. Say one word about the NSL, and you can be thrown into prison. Before 9/11, the FBI used NSLs sparingly. But in the hazy, crazy days that followed, the FBI handed them out like candy corn on Halloween — something like a quarter of a million in three years alone.

Factboy had quickly learned how to fake them. He could even send one digitally. No voice, face, no human contact whatsoever.

This was just like his relationship with Mann — which, like "Factboy," was a code name. They had never met. They probably never would. But hey, as long as the checks cleared.

"You said he was a consultant," Mann said. "What kind?"

"I'm still working on that."

"Work harder."

Mann disconnected. Factboy stood up, slid the phone into the pocket of his cargo shorts, stepped on the metal handle to flush the toilet, then opened the stall. The men's room was crowded. He walked over to the one open sink, splashed some lukewarm water on his hands and face, then went outside to rejoin his family.

They were on vacation.

Factboy had a real name, but he made it a point never to reveal it. His real identity wasn't even known to Mann, who accounted for roughly seventy percent of his income. Factboy presented himself as a ghost in the system, a man (or maybe a woman!) living off the grid somewhere in a country where extradition laws do not apply, with servers spread throughout the globe with a nominal headquarters in Sweden. Trying to catch Factboy would be like trying to grab a fistful of smoke — physically impossible. But if you needed information quickly, Factboy could find it for you quickly, cleanly, untraceably.

In reality, Factboy was a suburban dad, thirty-four, with two laptops, a smartphone, and really, *really* good encryption software.

And right now, he was on vacation with his wife and two kids at the Grand Canyon, ready to have a nervous breakdown.

This was unusual for Factboy, who spent most of his waking hours in his attic office "programming." A total lie. He was busy retrieving information, then selling it to people who would pay him a lot of money for that information. This took anywhere from ten seconds to a couple of minutes, depending on the type of information. Nothing — *nothing* — took more than a few minutes. The rest of the time Factboy watched 1980s-era horror movies, prowled message boards, and jacked off. Which was pretty much his life twenty years ago, too, come to think of it, down to the same movies. A wife and kids hadn't changed things all that much.

The problem was, Factboy had to be available to Mann more or less all the time. While the info retrieval might take ten seconds, the request might come in at 3:13 a.m., and Factboy was expected to respond within seconds.

Factboy excused himself to go to the bathroom quite often.

So much so that Factboy's wife thought he had irritable bowel syndrome. Instead, he was usually sitting on top of the toilet, thumbs flying over the tiny keypad on his phone, fielding a request, hoping he wasn't too late.

Then he'd flush.

Lately, though, the wife had started in on him about spending more time with his family. Usually this was something that politicians or executives said after being caught with a dead ladyboy in their secret apartments, but the wife meant it for real. More time. *Quality* time. She thought they should travel. They should go see the Grand Canyon, she said.

Factboy and his family lived in a modest three-bedroom in Flagstaff, AZ — just an hour away from the Canyon. They'd never seen it.

Sensing that refusal might lead to separation, possibly divorce, and a smart enough lawyer might start taking a close look at Factboy's revenue streams, jeopardizing pretty much everything, Factboy caved.

They went to the Grand Canyon. Stayed at the El Tovar, the oldest resort hotel, which looked like a huge pile of smoky timber perched within yards of a big gaping hole in the earth.

Within minutes of arriving at the South Rim, Factboy started having panic attacks. He wasn't particularly afraid of heights, though the mile plunge to the bottom of the canyon was kind of terrifying. Instead, he found that he was completely freaked out by the lack of a fence. Not even a halfhearted little mesh-wire number. Not so much as a guardrail. Nothing. And there were kids everywhere — Factboy's kids included — dancing, posing, goofing around, completely *oblivious of the fact that certain death was just one fucking ooopsie away.* Factboy couldn't bring himself to look. He couldn't bring himself to not look.

And then he received his urgent request from Mann.

One look at the screen and he told his wife —

"I've got to use the facilities."

The "facilities?": marriage code for number two.

"Now?"

"Yes. Now."

"Everything in place?" Mann asked.

"Yep," A.D. said. "All he has to do is step outside."

CHAPTER
SEVEN

Who's they? I want you to tell me who they is.

— John Aquino, *Blow Out*

Hardie couldn't believe what his eyes were transmitting to his brain.

"Where the fuck is my *car?*"

"Get away from the window," the girl scream-whispered behind him. "Please, I'm begging you. You looked, you're upset, now move the fuck away before something *really bad* happens."

"It was *just there.*"

"Are you really this dense? Or haven't you heard a word I've said?"

But Hardie was too focused on the stretch of asphalt in front of the garage. The sight absolutely boggled his mind. It didn't make sense. When he finally glanced down at the psycho chick crouched next to him, mic stand in her hand, he decided he'd had enough. He darted for the door. He thought he was moving pretty fast, but she was a lot faster, even limping. The girl easily closed the distance, slid herself into the space between him and the wall, and again pointed the edge of the mic stand at the hollow of his throat.

"No," she said.

Hardie tried to push her out of the way. "Move."

"*They* took your car, don't you realize that?"

"Well, I'll just force *Them* to give it back. Move."

"You can't go outside. You go outside, you're dead."

"I can still catch them."

Hardie was half-serious about that. The roads up here were twisty. Winding. They — *whoever* — just stole it a few seconds ago. He heard them do it. Maybe he had a chance — slim, he knew, but it was still a chance — at catching them on foot. But then what? Leave this girl here, by herself, in the house he was supposed to be guarding?

She hissed at him:

"Get down! It's bad enough they saw you?"

Hardie sometimes marveled at how quickly things could spin out of control. He'd been in L.A. only, what? . . . ninety minutes total? . . . and he'd already lost all his possessions except for the wallet in his back pocket, the useless set of car keys in his front pocket, the cell phone with no service, and the clothes on his back. He'd jumped off a roof and landed in unidentified animal crap. Hardie half expected this crazy bird to force him to strip, then make him jump off the back deck into the wilds, just to show him — *that's how Hollywood does ya.*

Then Hardie remembered that his carry-on bag had still been in the passenger seat of the Honda Whatever, and a tiny knot of grief formed in his stomach.

Hardie believed there were two kinds of things in the world. Things that could be replaced, and things that could not. He'd spent the past three years giving away

69

or tossing everything in his life that could be replaced. This turned out to be most things in his life. Clothes, CDs, kitchen utensils, old books. All of it junk. You could soak it in lighter fluid and it wouldn't matter. Because somewhere, out there, was another copy. But his duffel bag, the one he never checked at airlines, the one that never left his side, was full of things that could not be replaced.

And now it was gone.

Hardie pulled the cell out of his pocket. Fuck this. At the very least, his rental car was stolen. He needed to report it.

The girl touched his arm. "They won't let you call."

Hardie eyeballed her. "What do you mean?"

"I tried to use my phone, too. They've stopped the signals."

Hardie checked the screen. No bars. Just like earlier, when he tried to call Virgil. At the time, he thought it was just because he was up in the Hollywood Hills, where service was shitty. Maybe he'd get lucky.

Hardie said, "It's the mountain. Nobody's jamming anything."

"Look, I've been to countless parties up here. Calls are dropped all the time, but a service blackout like this? For, like, hours? No. It's *Them*."

Well, it *was* Them.

Mann's team was equipped with a suitcase-size digital portable jammer — normally reserved for police and military use — as well as handheld jammers given

70

to each operative. These devices were easy to obtain and extremely useful for operating under a blanket of silence. Mann insisted that all of her employees have them on at all times during every production.

To cover the immediate Alta Brea area, Mann had O'Neal power up the larger, more powerful jammer in the van — the same kind police use during hostage situations and drug raids so that the bad guys won't be able to connect to the outside world.

With the handhelds, Mann opted for simplicity. Every time you talk on your cell, you use two frequencies — talk through one, listen through another. The simplest way to block your cell is to jam one of those frequencies. This makes your phone believe there is no service at all, and it tells you so. You can curse at the phone and shake it, but it will do no good. Cell phones are stupid that way.

To stay in touch with her operatives, Mann issued multiband intrateam tactical radio units with encryption designed to look like ordinary phones, including hands-free Bluetooth devices so they could look like pretty much every other asshole in L.A.

No bars — no service.

No car.

Get ahold of yourself there, Chuck.

Breathe.

Let's think this through.

All of this talk about *Them* and *ooh, watch out, THEY might see you?*.

Bullshit.

What Hardie had interrupted was probably a home invasion. Two addicts who knew that Lowenbruck had left on a long trip; maybe even one of them glommed his security code from some party. Hell, maybe the security company even sold them the code — it wouldn't be the first time.

So we have this girl and probably some crackhead boyfriend. Lots of expensive AV gear on the top floor, even more expensive recording equipment on floor two. They hear Charlie on the roof, then on the deck, and then he's in — and they're freaking out, scrambling, not thinking straight. Chick goes downstairs; boyfriend slips out the front. Takes the opportunity and steals the Honda Whatever. Now this chick would be all about getting away while she could.

"I'm telling you, get away from the window?"

Hardie reached out, grabbed her wrist, and squeezed.

She cried out. The metal mic stand fell out of her hand, clattered on the hardwood floor.

"Please stop sticking that thing in my face."

As he continued squeezing, the girl's eyes widened, her mouth opening in a silent scream. Then she looked down at Hardie's chest, and her expression changed completely. From pain to revulsion.

"Oh God, your chest . . . ," she said.

Hardie was halfway through the motion of looking down at his chest when he realized he was being an idiot.

But by then it was too late, because she had already shoved the palm of her free hand up into his jaw.

Lane always thought it was funny that she became known for the action movies. It had all started with that stupid remake *Dead by Dawn*. A woman-on-the-run story, and that summer, she'd been the face du jour. *EW* and *Vanity Fair* and everybody else had made a big deal about her first shoot-'em-up, having previously dismissed her as the sweet-but-dippy friend of the hero's girlfriend in a trilogy of vapid preteen comedies. But after *Dead*, the only scripts she saw were actioners, and she found herself in what seemed like an endless succession of grueling mixed-martial-arts sessions. It felt like she spent more time being thrown around onto vinyl mats than on a stage actually *acting*. She used to run lines in her sleep; now boyfriends complained about being kicked and rabbit-punched in their sleep. Enrico used to work her *hard*.

The move she pulled on this asshole now came from a heist thriller called *Your Kiss Might Kill Me*, where she'd had to (believably) overpower a former Navy SEAL/bank guard who had at least two hundred pounds on her.

Funny how it came back to her so easily.

Hardie's head snapped back, his teeth smashing together so hard it sent jagged bolts of pain through his skull. She'd gotten him *good*. He staggered back on his heels, instantly aware of the mic stand she'd dropped on the floor. If she stooped down, picked it up, and rammed it through his guts, well, then he'd die a ridiculously stupid death.

Fortunately she opted for kicking the living shit out of him instead, throwing a rapid succession of punches, chops, and kicks at his face, torso, balls. She clearly had training, but the coke and whatever else buzzing around in her bloodstream made her hits sloppy and unfocused.

Hardie absorbed the blows, waited for his moment, and then lunged, wrapped his thick arms around her, and squeezed. The girl struggled and opened her mouth to scream — which was the moment Hardie flipped her to the floor, blasting the air out of her lungs. While she was still stunned, he straddled her, pinning her arms under his thighs.

"You finished?" Hardie asked.

"G-Get off me?"

"Shhhh. I'm two hundred forty pounds. You're not going anywhere."

The girl struggled a bit more, as if she could summon the adrenaline to prove him wrong. But then she stopped and looked up at Hardie defiantly.

"So, what now?" she said.

"What now? Well, for starters, how about you tell me where your boyfriend took my rental car? It's not that I give a damn about the car. But I've got a bag inside that means a lot to me, and if I don't get it back, I'm going to track him down and beat the living fuck out of him."

She narrowed her eyes. "Beat who?"

"Your boyfriend."

She huffed.

"Boyfriend?"

"Boyfriend, husband, accomplice, whatever . . . whoever took my fucking car."

"Don't you get it? *They* took your car . . . *your own people* . . . so whatever this is, what are you waiting for? Just do it already. Do it!"

Hardie could feel her body start to shiver. Her lips trembled, too, and her eyes slid to the corners.

"Hey."

Hardie gently touched her chin and moved it slightly. Her eyes found his again. He'd seen plenty of overdoses back in the job. She wasn't quite there, but whatever she'd shot herself up with, she'd flirted with the edge.

"Let's cut the bullshit, okay? I'm not *Them*, there is no *Them*."

Now she focused on him again. Narrowed her eyes.

"You really don't know who I am, do you?"

"I have no idea. You kind of look like this actress, what the hell's her name . . .?"

"Lane Madden."

That was it. Now Hardie understood why she'd looked familiar. Over the past decades he'd studied faces, coaxing unwilling witnesses through countless descriptions, running his eyes over an endless stream of black-and-white photos in mugshot binders. He'd come to the conclusion that God was a shameless self-plagiarist, because he had no problem using the same molds over and over again. A lot of people resembled a lot of other people.

"That's her. I guess you've been told that before."

"All of my life."

"So what's your name?"

"Lane Madden."

Hardie started to laugh, but the sound died in his throat, because now that he looked at her and saw the stone sincerity in her eyes, he knew she was telling the truth. Holy shit. He'd been stabbed and beaten by Lane Madden. In any other circumstance, it'd be an amusing little story to share with the world. *Hey, guess who rear-ended me on Beverly Boulevard! Winona Ryder!* Now, though . . . not so much.

Lane — *Lane Madden?* — looked up at him.

"Can you please get off me?"

Hardie was already shifting his weight off her body, embarrassed. Confused, but embarrassed. He'd been straddling a celebrity, not subduing a drugged-out teenager. Every cell in his body wanted to apologize. He felt her tense up beneath his thighs. Hardie tried to lighten things up.

"You're not going to try to stab me or punch me in the jaw again, are you?"

"I'm going to assume for the moment," Lane Madden said, "that you're *not* one of Them. But let me say for the record, that if you *are* one of Them, and this is you playing dumb just so you can kill me later, then you're a big fucking asshole."

"I promise I'm not going to kill you."

Hardie lifted one knee off the floor and eased himself off her body. Lane rolled over, coughed, then worked herself up into a sitting position, resting her back against a wall. They were near the media room — the oversize plasma screen, the DVDs, and leather couches.

76

Hardie had this theory, two years running, that he was living in a kind of purgatory. This was further proof. All he wanted to do was watch a movie, crash on the couch, get his booze on.

Now he was sitting on the floor of a house in the Hollywood Hills with a coked-up actress who thought people were trying to kill her.

Hardie rubbed his head.

"Did I walk into a movie set or something? Because that's what it feels like all of a sudden."

"I wish. Believe me. Just promise me you won't open that door, okay?"

"There are no hidden cameras anywhere, right? This isn't some reality show, is it? Because if it is, I'd really like to leave the set now."

"No. It's not. This is all totally real."

"So, I'm guessing you know Lowenbruck?" Hardie asked.

Lane took a moment to think about it. "Who?"

"The composer. Guy who owns this house. You know him, right?"

She looked around now, as if she just tuned in to the fact that, oh yeah, she was squatting in someone else's home.

"No. I found the keys in the mailbox, just like I said."

"How did you turn off the security system?"

"I didn't. I wasn't on when I got here."

Nice one, Lowenbruck. Why not just prop the front door open a few inches, tape a note to it saying, NOBODY HERE. BURGLARS, HELP YOURSELVES.

"Then why did you set it?" Hardie asked.

"So I'd know if anyone was coming. God, I feel like I'm dreaming. None of this is happening. I keep hoping I'm going to wake up in front of the TV."

Hardie nodded. He knew,exactly what she meant.

Hardie followed Lane back through the house to the bathroom. It was a compromise; Hardie wanted to stay on the top floor, and Lane wanted to be in a room without any windows. Once inside, she closed the door, then pointed Hardie to the toilet. Very gracious of her. He saw her bloodied pants balled-up inside the sink, as well as a single shoe. Lane leaned against the sink, let her head tilt back. She exhaled heavily, then shuddered.

Now that he knew who she was, Hardie saw her in a different way. She had a *presence* about her. This was no complete stranger telling him a crazy story. It was someone he *sort of, kind of* knew, which made it difficult to completely dismiss what she was saying.

Hardie realized how ridiculous that was. He'd seen this woman act in silly comedies; he didn't really know her.

But she was famous. Why would she lie?

(Because, duh, famous people were crazy!)

Lane Madden leaned in close and, through trembling lips, told him everything that had happened to her. The creepy race along Decker Canyon Road. The weird guy in the Chevy Malibu. The engineered accident on the 101. The forced speedball. The fistful of safety glass. The narrow escape to the edge of the 101.

"Now do you believe me? Does that sound like a series of coincidences?"

78

Hardie had to admit that, yeah, it sounded odd, even for L.A.

"What happened next?" he asked.

"I pulled myself over the fence and limped up toward Lake Hollywood. I used to come jogging up here, and I knew there were houses everywhere. I thought maybe I could yell for help or something."

"So why didn't you?"

"Because I thought about the kind of people who were after me. They weren't some carjackers or something. They were organized. They had a plan all worked out. What if I knocked on the door of some family — and the assholes who were after me hurt them, too? I couldn't put innocent people at risk. So I kept running. I thought I could outrun them."

"Limping all the way?"

"I did my best. You kind of forget about pain when people are trying to kill you."

Hardie didn't know L.A. geography all that well. Was it possible to limp from the 101 all the way up here? Seemed kind of implausible. Wasn't there, like, a mountain in the way?

"So did they follow you?"

"God, yeah. Just when I thought I'd lost them, I'd see another one of them rounding the corner. It was spooky."

She touched his leg, poking at him with her fingertips.

"That's when I realized how they were tracking me — and this is what really freaked me out, because it shows you how freakin' connected they all are."

"How did they track you?"

"My ankle bracelet."

Hardie stared at her for a moment, waiting for the rest of the story. When he realized that was the extent of her explanation, he squinted, tilted his head and said:

"Huh?"

"The ankle bracelet. You know . . . the kind the court gives you when you've fucked up one too many times?"

Blank look from Hardie. Lane smiled slightly and leaned back.

"You really don't know about this? Like, this is the first you're hearing of it? I thought pretty much the entire world knew I was wearing that damned thing. All of those jokes on those late-night shows, the pictures on the websites . . . God, they fucking love it, thinking they're so clever, asking me to flash a little leg."

"Were you under house arrest or something?"

"No . . . more as in, if I take so much as a sip of beer, some guy in a monitoring station somewhere will know it, and they'll call the L.A. County prosecutor."

Hardie nodded. "So you think they were able to track you with it."

Lane tapped an index finger on her own temple. "I don't *think* they did. I *know* they did. Because I smashed the fucking thing off with a rock, threw it away, and ran even faster. Haven't seen them since. I came here to pull myself together."

"So you just broke in."

"Well . . . yeah."

"What made you pick this house? Weren't you worried about the people inside? You know, putting innocent lives at risk, and all of that?"

Lane took a breath.

"Look, I was coming around the bend down there — you know, turning up from Durand? And I saw the owner of this house step outside. He had luggage and his keys. He locked his door, put the keys in the mailbox, then drove away. I figured his house was empty. No one could get hurt. So I ran across the street and got the keys and let myself in and took a mic stand from the studio and hid in the downstairs bathroom and now we're all caught up."

"What time was this?"

"I don't know — a couple of hours ago?"

That couldn't be right. According to Virgil, the client — Andrew Lowenbruck — caught his flight late last night, not just a few hours ago. That was the whole reason for leaving the keys in the mailbox . . . right?

"So let me get this right — a couple of hours ago you saw the owner of this house leave?"

"Yes."

"So you do know Andrew Lowenbruck?"

"Who?"

Hardie smiled. "The owner of this house."

"No, no idea. Why do you keep asking me that question? Everybody in Hollywood doesn't, like, know each other."

It was an old cop trick. Asking the same question over and over again. You'd be surprised how many people answer it differently the second, third, fourth time around.

Hardie watched Lane carefully. He was no mastermind interrogator — as a matter of fact, he'd never interrogated anybody before. That wasn't his job. He'd observed Nate do it countless times. Nate claimed that Hardie's observations were invaluable, and that he was good to have in the room. Hardie knew that was crap. Nate Parish was the genius detective with a mind like a lynx. He wondered what Nate would make of the actress and her story.

Actually, Hardie wondered what Nate would make of the whole situation. No doubt he'd have it figured out in 10.7 seconds. He was like goddamned Sherlock Holmes, plucking a few details out of the air and piecing them together into a logical, hard reality.

Not Hardie.

Not with his slow, lizard-like brain.

Lane reached out and touched his hand. "Hey, I'm not boring you or anything?"

"No. Just thinking. Keep going."

"So I waited in here. I was hoping they'd give up, and later I'd have a chance to go for help. But apparently they're still out there. And now they know I'm in here."

"You think so?"

"I don't know . . . no. I think if they knew for sure, they'd come kicking in the doors. But then they probably saw your car, and—"

"Ms. Madden —"

"You can call me Lane, you know."

"Okay, Lane. I've saved the million-dollar question for last. Why do you think these people want to kill you?"

She hesitated. "I have no idea. All I know is, they're serious."

"You have no idea at all?"

"Isn't that what I said? I was out late last night driving, just to clear my head — and I hadn't been drinking, thank you very much, you can ask my manager, Haley. And then, *boom*, they came out of nowhere."

Hardie considered this.

"Let me see your arm."

"Why?"

"Just let me see where they injected you."

She obediently made a tight little fist and extended her arm, showing him the crook of her elbow. Hardie looked. There was a needle mark, as well as some bruising around it. She'd been injected hard, and some veins had collapsed around the site. Still, she could have done it herself. Like shooting up before/during/after a Hollywood party.

"Mind if I touch you?"

Lane smirked. "You've already put me in a bear-hug death grip and sat on me. Now you're asking if I mind if you touch me?"

"Just thinking of the lawsuit. Don't want you and your lawyers tacking on extra items."

Lane raised a right hand.

"I give you permission to touch me, Mr. Hardie."

"Call me Charlie."

Hardie gently took her by the wrist and rotated her arm inward. So strange to touch her. So strange to touch another female human being, actually. When was the last time he'd done that? He examined her arm quickly. No finger-shaped bruises. No other marks at all, except for random scrapes and cuts.

"Huh."

"What?"

"Just wondering why a speedball."

"Because they probably wanted my death to look like an accident. Like I was some dumb two-bit cokehead actress who went out cruising late and ended up rear-ending some poor father of three or something."

"Why go through all that trouble?"

Lane looked at him. "I told you, I don't know. Why did that deranged idiot shoot John Lennon?"

Hardie tried to keep an open mind, swear to God he did. But even the slow, lazy lizard part of his brain was screaming BULLSHIT at every turn.

The kind of killers Hardie encountered back in Philly were idiot scumbag husbands who beat their wives with baseball bats and tried to dump their bodies in storage lockers registered to their real names. Gangbangers looking to make a name for themselves, undercutting one another with cheaper and cheaper hits to the point where you could take out a witness in a major drug case for about the price of a fucking iPod. Drug-gang hitmen, Russian-mob enforcers. The killers he knew didn't work in coordinated packs, and they certainly didn't try to make their work look like an accident. That was the whole point. A death was not supposed to be an Act of God — it was meant as an Act of Vladmir, To Teach You Not to Steal From His Stash.

"Let me take a look outside and see if I can't put your mind at ease, huh? And then we can get to a hospital."

"No. No fucking way. That's what they want. God knows what they'll do to you the moment you set foot outside. Don't you understand? These people operate on a completely different level."

Hardie muttered:

"They."

Factboy gathered more intel on Charles D. Hardie. Slowly, it painted an interesting, if kind of sad and deadbeatish, kind of picture.

Hardie had been filing tax returns as a "house sitter" for the past twenty-three months.

He didn't make much.

The address on the rental agency turned out to be for a house that had been on the market for twenty-seven months.

The house was crap.

Debit-card statements revealed that he lived in hotels or the places he watched.

He didn't spend much. Movie rentals.

(Who the hell went to an actual store and rented movies anymore?)

All bills went to a PO Box in Philadelphia.

The person who paid for that box lived at 255 Dana Street, Abington, Pennsylvania.

So far, no connection between Madden and Hardie, outside of a few DVD rentals on Hardie's debit card. Nothing from the past three years. But previously he'd rented some romantic comedies where Madden was featured in a supporting role: *How to Date a Zombie, The Hook-Up, Never the Bride.*

(Factboy's wife had made him sit through that last one. He wanted to use a fork on his eyeballs, just to escape the theater.)

Anyway, it was safe to assume that Hardie recognized her. Also safe to assume Madden had shared the events of the past few hours with him.

Factboy told all of this to Mann, who disconnected without a word of thanks or good job or anything. Good thing he wasn't in this business for the ego-boosting. Factboy pretend-flushed, then rejoined his family, who were hot and cranky, and tired of waiting around for him.

Mann needed this production concluded immediately. Another, much bigger and more complex job on the other side of the mountain was pending. This silly little bitch was taking far too much time and money.

Somewhere in all of this, there would have to be a visit to an ophthalmologist. The mobile doc who'd patched it stressed he wasn't an expert but thought it could be a severe corneal abrasion — definitely something that needed proper attention, not a quick fix. The wound burned and itched like crazy; it was all Mann could do not to scratch or rub around the edges.

Another reason to move things along.

The bright, warm sun helped distract Mann from the pain. She rubbed more sunscreen on her breasts, dried her hands with a white terry-cloth towel she'd found in the house.

Then a voice spoke into her ear. O'Neal.

"Heads up, y'all. We've got another guest."

The driver of the Dodge Sprinter kept the engine idling as he engaged the parking brake. For a precarious moment, the van seemed like it would roll back down Alta Brea and crash into something that cost millions of dollars. But the brake held. The driver, in shorts and a company polo shirt, stood up and stepped into the back, wiping his face with a sleeve. He looked like he'd been up all night.

O'Neal spoke quietly: "Uh, anybody expecting a package?"

Mann, down below, said, "Keep watching."

After a few seconds the driver emerged with a piece of luggage. He hopped out of the back, checked his computerized clipboard, typed in a few things, then popped out the long handle and started rolling the bag up to the house. The wheels bumped on the uneven paving blocks.

"Courier's got a bag," O'Neal said, "and he's headed to the house. Repeat; headed right to the house."

"Hang on a minute," Mann said.

"We don't have a minute. I need to know what you want."

Mann said nothing.

Which pissed O'Neal off. Not that it mattered, killing the delivery guy. But it was one more detail, one more annoying errand extending this job into super-bugfuck-crazy overtime. If that was the case, then Mann should let him know right away. If not, O'Neal should have the opportunity to coax him away from the place. Jokes aside, this was literally a matter of life and death.

The delivery guy pushed the handle back down into the bag and steadied it against his leg.

"Okay, he's there," O'Neal said. "About to knock."

Mann's voice, in his ear:

"Good. Let him."

CHAPTER
EIGHT

I'm kind of a big deal.
　　　　　　　　　— Will Ferrell, Anchorman

The knocks were rapid-fire gunshots that echoed loudly in the big, empty top floor. Hardie hated to admit it, but his entire body did an involuntary jolt. So did Lane's. Their heads both whipped around at the same time. Hardie stood up from the toilet seat. He felt blood trickle down his chest.

"Okay," Hardie said. "You stay here."

Lane grabbed him by the wrist with both hands and pulled him toward her.

"No! This is where you leave, and then somebody kills you, and then they come in after me. Don't you ever watch movies?"

Hardie rolled his eyes.

"Could be a neighbor, coming to see if the power's out."

"Could be the people, oh, I don't know — trying to kill me! Look, neighbors don't talk to one another up here. They certainly don't go knocking on one another's doors."

"I'm not going to open the door. I'm just going to take a look through the peep-hole."

"You're unbelievable."

"What?"

"You put your eye up to that and they'll shoot you through it. Blow the brains out of the back of your stupid fucking head?"

No, Hardie wanted to tell her. That is not how they do it. They don't knock, they don't get all clever with peepholes. They just pull up to your front door and shout your name and open fire and take away everything you've ever cared about . . .

"Wait here," Hardie said.

Hardie didn't have a real weapon, and the kitchen was utterly disappointing. He opened a drawer and saw nothing more lethal than a bunch of plastic utensils from takeout joints, still sealed in plastic. Freeze or I'll spork you to death, motherfucker. He'd feel better with something vaguely deadly in his hands. He checked another drawer, then another. Best Hardie could find was a little plastic corkscrew, ninety-nine cents at finer liquor emporiums everywhere. But not exactly deadly. The thing would probably shatter in his hands if he tried to use it.

There were three more knocks — just as loud as the first three.

Lane limped into the kitchen, steadied herself against a counter.

"Promise me you won't open the door."

Hardie slid the cover of the corkscrew into a hole on the base. He tucked it between his fingers. Maybe it wouldn't be so bad. If things got ugly up close, at least he'd have a shiv.

"Promise me?" Lane repeated.

90

Hardie told her to please be quiet, and to go hide somewhere and leave him alone for a minute. Let him do his job. Which was protecting this house.

First Hardie checked the front windows, angling his head around so he could see the entranceway to the house. Was there someone — one of THEM! — crouched down, waiting to pounce? Or maybe a guy with a knife in the shrubs along the concrete pathway? Or maybe someone suspended above the doorway, Tom Cruise/*Mission Impossible* — style?

No.

Instead, Hardie could see a courier van, big-ass Dodge Sprinter, parked in front of the house. A delivery dude in polo shirt and shorts, clipboard in his hand. And Hardie's missing bag, leaning up against the delivery guy's leg.

Delivery Dude looked around, knocked again. He looked impatient and sweaty. Dude had the look of a hangover about him, and Hardie was pretty damn near an expert on them.

Lane appeared by his side. Scared the fuck out of him.

"Who is it?"

"Delivery guy," Hardie said. "He's got my bag."

"What bag?"

Hardie craned his neck for a better look. Certainly seemed like his bag. The right color and design. The white airline tag stuck to the handle, fluttering in the breeze. And there was the telltale sign: a Spider-Man without a head. His boy had slapped a sticker on there years ago. The head came off; Spidey's body was left behind, now fused to the fabric of the bag and drained of almost all color thanks to months of constant travel. Hardie left it there because it helped him ID his bag when it came off the carousel.

His bag. Brought by the airline, as promised.

Not *Them*, Delivery Dude.

Hardie walked back to the vestibule and squinted through the peephole mounted in the middle of the door for a better lock. He was either a delivery guy or a hired killer. Us or *Them*. As if to answer, the guy called out —

"Delivery?"

— and knocked again, as if it were the last time.

Could he be one of *Them?* Lane said it would be easy for them to dress up in uniforms and pretend to be cops, or whoever they wanted. No big deal to scrounge up a big ugly truck, a clipboard, and a goofy-looking polo shirt. But then, where did his bag come from? What, was the airline in collusion with these killers?

No.

The very idea was ridiculous, and Lane Madden here — well, clearly she had some issues with reality. She wouldn't be the first actress to have that kind of problem. Hardie felt lighter; this could all be over in a minute. Not only did Delivery Dude have his bag full of underwear and T-shirts, but he probably had a way of communicating with his dispatcher. LAPD could be up here in a matter of minutes, and then Lane Madden would become their problem. See you in the tabloids, honey.

(Delivery Dude could also have a Glock tucked into the waistband of his cargo shorts and be waiting for you to open the door to give him a clear target! Remember what happened last time someone called out for you, and you looked outside?)

"What are you doing?" Lane asked.

"Saving you from *Them*."

"Goddamnit, no!"

Hardie put his hand on the door handle, took a breath, then pressed the latch with his thumb and pulled open the door.

The device mounted on the door frame was called a wasp's nest.

Nothing fancy, really. You simply mounted it at face level, set the trigger mechanism, and then you were good to go. All the target had to do was open the door, and, *boom* — load in the face.

The load, though . . . now, that's what made the wasp's nest fancy.

The spray was a weaponized poison that rendered you unconscious within a second, then killed you about a minute later by temporarily shutting down the part of your brain that regulates your heart. After it finished its job, the poison broke down into little untraceable pieces of nothing. A coroner could order all the tox screens he wanted but wouldn't find jack shit.

And the targets almost never saw it coming.

Something clicked and hissed —
PSSSSSSSSH

— and Hardie felt cold drops spray his face. Even before his brain could form the thought, his body knew something was Real Fucking Wrong. His hand fumbled with the door handle and he felt crazy-weak all of a sudden, overcome with chills and drowsiness, and he didn't know what was happening, screaming NO NO NO at his mind as if he could talk it out of shutting down and

CHAPTER
NINE

*They will stop at nothing . . . They are ubiquitous
and all-powerful.*

— Geoffrey O'Brien, *Hardboiled America*

Once, in his early twenties, Hardie had an operation
to fix a deviated septum. A young nurse with soft
skin and pretty eyes held his hand as they wheeled
him to the cold, bright operating room. For a
moment, Hardie didn't care that his face was about
to be mauled with sharp knives. At that moment he
was under a warm blanket and holding a young girl's
hand and then she let go and somebody asked him
to count backward from ten but he couldn't even
remember saying nine and then he was blinking and
waking up and the pretty girl's hand was still holding
his and she smiled and said, see that wasn't so bad?

That's what it felt like now — he had a dim memory
of being with a pretty girl.

But now that he was awake, he saw there was no
pretty girl.

He was wrapped up in black plastic.

Actually, a body bag.

★　★　★

And with that realization came another: Hardie couldn't get air into his lungs.

There was no air in here at all, like he was a kid hiding under a thick blanket, and the boogeyman was outside, and as much as he wanted a lungful of clean, fresh air he didn't dare lower the blanket.

Frantic, Hardie's fingers searched for a seam, a zipper, something, anything. But his fingers didn't appear to be working right. Finally his fingertips found the opposite end of the zipper, the one without the little thing you pull on. He pushed it with his index finger, trying to get it to move. *Come on.* His finger trembled. He pushed harder. He needed air. If he didn't get air soon, he would pass out again. And this time he probably wouldn't wake up. Hardie pushed again. The zipper moved a quarter of an inch. It was enough.

He jabbed his finger through the opening and ripped downward, which killed his chest, but it didn't matter, because his chest would really fucking be out of luck if he didn't get any air into his lungs.

Number of accidental suffocations per year: 3,300.

Hardie sucked in oxygen greedily, then pulled the plastic womb down over his head, then shoulders, then body. Hardie realized where he was. By the front door. He'd passed out here and somebody had put him in a plastic body bag. That same somebody had just left him here, like garbage waiting to go out. Hardie didn't know whether to be pissed or insulted.

Hardie didn't know what time it was — power was still out. He couldn't even hazard a guess as to how much time had passed. Sun was still up.

He listened; the house was eerily silent.

And then he saw he wasn't the only thing on the floor.

Next to him, in another black plastic bag, was something suspiciously body-shaped. And next to that bag was another black bag, too small for a body but big enough for, say, a human head.

Hardie opened the zipper on the bigger bag first, fully expecting to see the face of a famous actress. In which case he would owe her a serious apology. Because she was right. Hardie should never have opened the door. He should have stayed hidden in the bathroom.

Instead, it was a guy inside, and it was a fuzzy second or two before Hardie realized, oh shit, the delivery dude. Somehow they'd dosed them both and wrapped them up in body bags faster than you could say *duck, you suckas*. Which meant that the small black plastic bag probably contained his luggage. Maybe his shoes.

The house was utterly still. Was somebody in the house on another floor? Or were they outside, getting ready to walk back inside at any moment?

They.

Hardie climbed to his feet, his joints popping, head swimming. He half expected to look down and see his body still there, proving he was dead and this was an out-of-body experience. Next he'd see a bright light up on the ceiling and hear some short, pudgy lady telling him not to go into it. But no. There was no body on the floor; Hardie was still using it.

A few steps forward, toward the front door.

Just go, he told himself. Don't think. Go. Walk away from the house. Remember, they stole your car. So you have to walk. Or run. Running would be good. I mean, what else are you going to do — stay?

Stay and do what?

You can barely breathe. You've been beaten and impaled and sprayed with some knockout shit and left for dead. The smart thing to do is not be the hero. Remember what that got you last time? It damn near got your stupid ass killed, that's what. It got everybody else's asses killed. You're never going to forgive yourself for that, and you know what? You shouldn't.

So what are you going to do? March back inside, charge through the house, your chest bleeding and your head still swimming, to try and play the hero? They've probably already got her. She's probably in a plastic bag, just like you were a few seconds ago. They're just cleaning up, because they're anal killer types who don't want to leave any forensic evidence. When they finish, they'll come back up for you. So now's a good time to leave. You want to be a hero? Leave the house and run until you find a cop. Report everything. Let the professionals handle it.

Get out. Get out now, you idiot. While you still can.

What are you waiting for?

Hardie took a few steps toward the front door, then froze. Probably a bad move to open that up. Last time he opened it, he had ended up in a body bag. Only insane people repeat an action and expect a different result. Insane people, and Hardie's mother-in-law.

But somebody had to walk into the house. Somebody had to zip up Hardie and Delivery Dude into body bags. Somebody was making little creepy fucking noises downstairs. What did they do, go across the roof and in through the back deck doors?

Which actually wasn't a bad idea.

Climbing up onto a roof with a chest wound, a barely functioning left hand, and a head full of junk — all while trying not to make a sound? Not recommended.

Hardie made it up, anyway, using a metal hose fixture as a foothold. He put his upper arms on the slanted tile roof, then swung his left knee up and caught the edge. Heaved himself up once; didn't make it. Heaved again, then rolled over onto the roof. Hardie took a deep breath, then cautiously made it to his feet and started up the slanting roof.

The delivery van was still out front, but someone had moved it off to the side. It sat behind a white van now. Nobody in either vehicle, far as Hardie could tell. Up here he had a better view of the castle up on the hill. He could make out a name, too: SMILEY, someone had carved into the stone face. There was scaffolding covering the structure; the owner must have work in progress. Nobody in the windows; no signs of life whatsoever.

Hardie turned to face the opposite direction and . . . hallelujah, the topless chick with the phone was still there. She had a phone. Her mouth was moving. That meant she had service.

Thank you, God.

Please ignore the bad shit I've said about you over the years.

Mann, awaiting confirmation, glanced up at the house. This was taking way too long. Her eye burned and itched like fuck. It had been a long night without a break. Time for all of this to be over.

And then she saw him.

Charles Hardie, standing on the roof, looking down at her.

Hardie knew this moment wouldn't last forever. Any second now the faceless fuckers who'd put him in a body bag could show up, or the woman could go back inside, or an earthquake could start rumbling, or a wildfire could break out . . . so he had to move now. He could either go back down into the house and do something really stupid and heroic . . .

Or he could be smart for a chance and call for help.

Be *smart*, you idiot.

Quietly as he could, he eased himself down the slope of the roof and jumped down to the driveway. He took great care to bend his knees as he landed to cushion the blow. He fell over, anyway. Picked himself up, then scrambled out onto Alta Brea and followed it back down to Durand until he was level with the third floor of the Lowenbruck home. Hardie glanced over at it, wondering if Lane Madden was dead or alive. He couldn't do anything about that except get to this woman and have her call 911 and wait for the cavalry to arrive.

Right?

Hardie reminded himself:

You've been stabbed. You're in no condition for a close-quarters brawl with god knows how many people.

You are not equipped to save people. You are not in the hero business. Remember, this is what got you in trouble three years ago. You're no good.

You had thought you might be a hero once, but you were wrong. People stronger and smarter and more ruthless taught you that. You are nothing. You're one of those people in movies who gets killed in the first act. A nameless hood. Someone the screenwriter didn't even bother to name.

Don't pretend to be what you're not.

Hardie hurriedly stumbled down the path toward the nice naked lady with the phone and braced himself for a scream.

He really, *really* hoped she wouldn't scream.

Because if she screamed, then he'd have to somehow convince her to go inside and make the phone call, because those faceless cocksuckers could pop their heads out of a window and start shooting at the both of them. A million bad film-noir scenes flashed through his head — guys slapping their meaty palms over the mouths of screaming dames, their leading-man eyes reassuring them that *Hey, I'm the good guy, everything will be okay.* Of course, this was not the way it happened in the real world. Hardie fully expected the woman to attempt to bite off his thumb and then knee him in the balls, then go ahead and scream, anyway.

Hardie took a few more quick steps, trying to project the most nonthreatening and peaceable version of himself. Hands out — look, see, no weapons.

The woman remained perfectly still, as if she'd fallen asleep and was completely unaware of the bleeding, trembling man barreling toward her. Not like this kind of thing happens every day in L.A. Or does it?

She continued her conversation. Hardie caught the tail end of it:

". . . you know me. I like constant updates. Hang on a second."

Finally Hardie caught her attention, because she turned her head slowly to face him. It was impossible to read her reaction behind her sunglasses. She said calmly:

"Let me get back to you."

The woman wiggled a little until she'd propped herself up on her elbows. Her breasts hung full and wide from her tight, athletic frame.

"Uh, miss . . . please don't panic. I need you to call the police. It's an emergency."

"Hi, Charlie," the woman said.

CHAPTER
TEN

No, no, I sock 'em in the jaw and yell
pop goes the weasel.

— Samuel L. Jackson, *The Long Kiss Goodnight*

Hardie stopped moving. Dropped his hands. Felt a rush of blood to his head.

"Gotta say, I'm a little surprised to see you up and moving around," the woman said. "But I guess that was a miscalculation, splitting the dose between two grown men. Usually we load those things with enough for just one. Have to make a note for next time, I suppose."

"Who the fuck are you?" Hardie asked.

"Interesting you didn't run for it. In fact, you came down here to borrow a phone and call for help. You probably consider yourself the hero type. So if I tell you to just walk away and pretend like none of this happened, you couldn't, am I right? You just couldn't. It would run counter to your very DNA."

Hardie stared at her.

"Well, don't be rude," the woman said. "Aren't you going to say something?"

Hardie could think of nothing to say to that, other than:

"You have very nice tits."

The woman smiled.

"You like them?"

"Anybody would like them."

"You probably don't think they're real." She let a fake sigh escape her lips and threw her head back wearily. "Nobody thinks they're real."

Hardie shook his head, something approximating a confused smile on his face.

"I honestly don't think I'm the best judge of what's real and not real. What happened to your eye?"

"Let's not talk about my body parts, okay? Let's talk about our situation. Usually, my inclination is to throw money at the problem. It's easy, clean, and has been proven to truly motivate people. But I don't think I can bribe you. Sure, you might go along with it, buy yourself some time. Or maybe you think, worst-case scenario, you can always track me down and seek your revenge later. Because that's what tough guys do. Still, even if I believed you'd take the bribe and keep your mouth shut, it's a loose end, and I'm not in the business of loose ends."

Hardie said, "What about the dead delivery dude in a plastic bag? Was he another loose end?"

The woman smiled. "That's a sad story, actually. He used to be a comic-book artist, but he had trouble making ends meet. He joined the delivery service a few months ago. About a half hour from now, he'll be found in North Hollywood, bullet through his brain, victim of a carjacking."

"That is really sad."

The woman lowered her head slightly. "Would it help if I told you the woman up in that house — the one you think you're protecting — deserves to die?"

"What girl?"

The woman smiled.

"*What girl*. Good one, Charlie. But believe me, she's pretty fucking far from innocent and deserves everything she's got coming. If you knew what she did, you might even help us. Hold her down while we finish her off."

Hardie had one of his usual take-stock-of-your-current-situation moments and realized he was standing on a downward slope of the Hollywood Hills, surrounded by multimillion-dollar upside-down homes, talking to a topless vigilante / killer. Okay. Just wanted to make sure he had it right.

"What about the dead delivery guy in the plastic bag? Did he deserve it?"

The woman sighed, shook her head. "No, he didn't. Just like you, he's an innocent victim, caught up in a tragic yet hopeless situation."

A barking laugh exploded out of Hardie.

"What's so funny?"

"Nothing."

The woman wrinkled her nose, then reached to her side and started to root through her bag. Here it comes, Hardie thought. Maybe a little snub-nosed revolver. Maybe a Taser. Maybe a crossbow with flaming arrow, for all he knew. He took a step back . . .

The woman sat up and held out a fat plastic tube. "Here. Would you do the honors?"

The tube was sunblock. Ordinary brand-name, SPF 25.

"You want me to rub this on you?" Hardie asked.

"If you don't mind."

Hardie looked at the tube in her hands, then back up at the woman, trying hard not to make eye contact with her breasts. Anywhere but her breasts. Even when you're negotiating with a killer, you had to have some standards.

"Where?"

"Where do you think? You've been staring at them long enough. The girls could use another coat. Come on, don't be shy. Kneel down next to me."

Hardie's brain screamed: *She has a weapon! She has a weapon!* Still, Hardie found himself kneeling down. The only other option was to run, and if she did have a weapon, then what good would running do? This way, at the very least, he was closer to her phone. And if he could somehow grab her phone . . .

"What's the matter?" she asked. "You have the strangest look on your face."

"I think I'm having what they call an existential moment."

"You don't need to make this complicated. Just open the top and squeeze into your hands, and let nature take its course."

"You know what? I think I'll pass for now."

Hardie held the tube out for her.

The woman smiled. The edges of the bandage that covered her right eye — under the sunglasses — crinkled a little.

106

"Still the faithful husband. Which is really impressive considering how long since you've seen them."

Hardie said nothing.

"Oh, don't be coy about it. You're still wearing the ring, and I know all about your wife, Kendra, and your son, Charlie Jr., who live at 255 Dana Street in Abington, Pennsylvania."

A cold little ball formed in Hardie's stomach. The address. God, she knew the address. How the hell did she know the address? How long had he been here — couldn't be more than an hour and a half? And yet she knew the fucking address?

"Here's the thing — and honestly, I'm done toying with you. Either we end this now or somebody will pay your wife and son a visit in the very immediate future. You can end this in a matter of seconds, or this can go on and on."

This stranger knew the address, even though only two people in the world were supposed to know that address. What else did she know?

The woman pulled a syringe out of a small bag sitting next to her. They were so close, Hardie could just reach out and touch her. The sun was hot on his back.

She said, "Do you understand?"

Hardie nodded.

"You're not going to make this difficult, are you?"

Hardie shook his head no.

"Show me your forearm."

"What's in that?"

"Does it really matter? I promise you, it's painless. Think about your family."

"I hate needles."

"Don't be a baby."

She took the protective plastic cap off the syringe. Hardie made a fist with his left hand, pumped it a few times, then smashed it into her right eye. The lens of her sunglasses shattered. The force of the blow sent some of the plastic shards directly into her eye.

The good one.

She didn't scream, to her credit. Instead, she sucked in a fortifying gulp of air and gritted her teeth and jabbed at Hardie with the syringe. But he anticipated the move and grabbed her wrist, freezing it mid-jab. Then Hardie punched her in the face again, knocking her earpiece loose. Hardie saw it bobbling there, half in, half out. He snatched it and tossed it down the hill. *Now* she screamed, a blast of sheer, angry red-hot rage, then turned and went scrambling, nearly naked, down the side of the hill. While she was distracted, Hardie grabbed her phone.

Hardie stood up. Maybe it was the knockout drugs, maybe it was the lack of oxygen to his brain, but he felt like the world had come to a screeching halt.

Kendra and Charlie.

Fuck.

Despite everything — the separation, the exile, the lack of communication, the precautions. They were in as much danger as they would have been if they had gone on living together, in their old row house — the one with all the bullet holes caulked over and repainted. All of the past three years had been for fucking nothing. The crazy topless killer bitch knew the address!

Not *the* address, thank God. Hardie didn't even know it, and Deacon Clark had made the arrangements with the help of some buddies in WITSEC. They weren't in witness protection; they'd "gone ghost," which is what Deke and the rest of the FBI called it these days.

However, 255 Dana Street *was* Deacon Clark's address — where Hardie sent all his checks and birthday cards and gifts. And if these creepy bastards could get to Clark, then it was only a matter of time before they would get to Kendra and Charlie. And that couldn't happen.

Hardie staggered back up the hill toward the house.

CHAPTER
ELEVEN

Buddy, you're in the wrong place at the wrong time.
— Willem Dafoe, *To Live and Die in L.A.*

They had the actress cornered.

She had nowhere to run. First floor — clear. Second floor — clear. Third floor — everything clear except the bedroom closet. Only place left she could be hiding. So they braced themselves and prepared for her to go totally bugfuck when they opened the door. O'Neal took one side, A.D. the other. A.D. put his hand on the knob, looked over at O'Neal. O'Neal gave it the old one, two . . . NOW.

A.D. opened the door. O'Neal aimed his Taser at —
Nothing.

O'Neal pushed aside dress shirts, jeans. Kicked a pile of shoes. The closet was one hundred percent devoid of people. Where the fuck was she? She couldn't just *disappear*. Unless they were somehow wrong and she had never entered the house in the first place.

No no no. She was hiding somewhere.

A.D. signaled with his hands: an invisible cell phone to his ear. Meaning: *Should we contact Mann?*

O'Neal shook his head. *Not yet.*

This didn't make sense.

O'Neal and A.D. had had the front covered; Mann had had the back. Nobody had left. They had secured the house carefully, methodically. O'Neal replayed the scene in his mind.

The moment the interloper — Charles Hardie — opened the front door, the wasp's nest did its thing. Both men were down in a matter of seconds. Hardie fell inside. The deliveryman dropped his clipboard, staggered back a few steps like he was on a dance floor, then collapsed. The beauty of the poison spray was that it would finish things off for them. First it stuns, then it kills. All they had to do was bag the bodies, keep them out of sight, then go find the target. O'Neal and A.D. put on their gas masks, grabbed a bunch of plastic body bags, and sprang into action.

Bagged the bodies, the suitcase, the clipboard, anything that belonged to either man. A cleaning team would be sent in later to make sure every stray microbe was removed from the premises, but protocol remained: bag it now.

O'Neal slapped a proximity sensor on the front door. If the girl somehow eluded them and went out the front door, they'd know it instantly.

They split up. Both were equipped with Tasers and jab pens. The former wouldn't leave a mark; the latter wouldn't matter, because one jab stick on a body covered in scrapes and bruises wouldn't be detected. O'Neal scoped out the downstairs, ready to unleash the Taser, then follow through with the pen.

They had checked every inch of the studio. Under the mixing boards, in closets. The bathroom. Tapped the ceilings, the walls. Nothing. It didn't make sense.

Fatigue was setting in big time; there were too few of them, and they'd been on the job for way too many hours. For fuck's sake, this was supposed to be over last night. Mann should have rotated another team in here, started fresh. O'Neal knew Mann was injecting a little bit of the personal into the equation. He'd never say that to her face — wasn't worth it. Still, if he were running things . . .

In the middle of hazy nothing, Mann heard her earpiece purring. God bless whoever's calling me. She scrambled through the grass, blinking away blood, and her fingers found the piece. She put it to her ear.

It was Factboy.

"Hey, I found something you should know," he said.

"Not fucking now," Mann said.

The plan was to go in all stealth.

Hardie reasoned that they didn't know he was coming. The topless lady in the sunglasses would be busy digging around the bushes for at least another few minutes, trying to find her stupid hands-free thing. (Good luck with that, honey.) It wasn't too late. Lane was still alive. Topless had confirmed as much:

You know me. I like constant updates. Keep searching.

And Lane Madden knew who these people were, what they were all about. Hardie didn't have to stop them. He didn't have to solve the case. Which was never his strong suit, anyway. He didn't have to root out corruption at the highest levels of government, or dismantle the nuke, or any of that crazy hero shit. He just needed to find out who these fuckers were, and then dutifully report it to Deacon Clark, who would get the FBI up their asses sideways.

So . . .

Stealth.

Don't let them see you coming.

Inflict maximum damage as quickly as possible.

Get the girl.

Get the fuck out.

Of course, Hardie had no idea how many of them there were inside the house. Could be one guy in there or a dozen. There had to be at least two, right? One to steal his Honda Whatever while the other kept watch on the front of the house?

Whatever. Keep it stealth.

Hardie finished his charge up the hill and came around to the front of the house. Nobody in sight. He crouch-walked to the front door and saw the device the crafty fuckers had stuck to the door frame.

Hardie was no mechanic, but even he could see how it worked. Your victim opens the door, a little leg thingy falls, and then a nozzle sprays the knockout shit. Well, the leg thingy was down; payload spent. Hardie grabbed the box by the edges and pulled. It came loose easily. He tossed it in the bushes. Maybe it would come in handy later — at their trial. *Exhibit A, Your Honor. The little box of death that almost murdered me!*

Hardie put his hand on the doorknob and took a mind-clearing breath. This was it. Remember: stealth.

He twisted the knob and pushed open the door and —

BEEP BEEP BEEP BEEP BEEP BEEP BEEP BEEP BEEP BEEP BEEP

A.D. looked at O'Neal.
 O'Neal signaled.
 Check it out.
 A.D. hit the stairs.

Fuck fuck fuck fuck fuck, Hardie thought, looking for a place to hide, some kind of weapon . . . *anything*.

Up on the first floor in record time, silent the whole way. The actress might be up here, waiting to ambush them. Then A.D. saw the front door, still cracked open. The empty body bag on the floor.
 Goddamnit. The house sitter.
 Charlie Hardie.
 If Hardie had run for the literal hills, that meant someone (probably A.D.) would have to waste even more time chasing him down. A.D.'s first impulse was to go through the front door and see if he was still within view — after all, the alarm had only been triggered a few seconds ago. Then he wised up. The road ran down behind the house. He could just go to the back deck and see if Hardie was headed down toward Belden. If so, then he could back out and run down his stupid ass with the van.

A.D. darted through the media room and was two steps onto the deck before he realized he'd stepped in animal shit. Great. O'Neal would never let him live this down. He scraped his shoes on the wooden planks.

And somebody grabbed him from behind.

Number of accidental falls per year: 14,900.

There wasn't time for Hardie to take a good look at his attacker, but at least this one was fully dressed. Looked young, too, with one of those shaggy haircuts all the teenagers seemed to have these days.

Hardie propelled him forward toward the edge of the deck, using all of his weight to body-check him into the railing. The force of the blow was so intense, the guy immediately vomited — whatever he'd eaten last came spraying out of his mouth and made a four-story drop to the grass below. His arms flailed uselessly at his sides, trying to find something to hold on to. It probably hurt like hell. Hardie didn't care. He couldn't waste any time with this one.

Hardie took a few steps back, then ran up and placekicked him in the balls, sending the guy up and over the railing. He saw the guy's legs kicking out like he was riding an invisible bicycle, and then he disappeared.

There.

Two down.

Who the fuck knows how many to go.

Which is exactly the moment Hardie went stiff, tried to curse, then hit the patio floor.

CHAPTER
TWELVE

Swell.

— Clint Eastwood, *Sudden Impact*

And *that* would be fifty thousand volts, motherfucker.

O'Neal gave him fifteen seconds in the back, enough to drop him. Then another ten seconds to discourage him from getting up again.

He hooked the Taser back onto his belt, then took the pen out of its zip case and popped the top. O'Neal didn't know how this stubborn bastard had survived the wasp's-nest blast — maybe they'd underestimated the payload for two people. But he wasn't going to make it through this.

If O'Neal were ever to be stopped and searched by the LAPD, the pen could be easily explained as an EpiPen, used in case of an allergic reaction (and O'Neal had the requisite card in his wallet to back up this claim). But the pen actually contained a dose of something a mob-backed scientist perfected back in Vegas during the go-go sixties: an injectable heart attack. Works within seconds, utterly untraceable.

Heart attacks were the leading cause of death of men in Hardie's age group, followed by cancer and strokes. Someone had actually come up with a stroke simulator, deliverable by injection, but why go for the third-most common when you could use the best?

O'Neal *loved* the pen.

He'd use it all the time if he could.

He lifted up Hardie's arm for a direct vein jab. Sure, it would work if you stuck it pretty much anywhere. The muscles would absorb the toxin and diffuse it to the bloodstream soon enough. But O'Neal preferred the straight shot right to Aortaville.

He unlatched the safety mechanism with a flick of his thumb, then pressed down on the top to activate it.

Enjoy the afterlife, my friend.

One common misconception about the Taser is that it renders you briefly unconscious.

Au contraire.

You are completely cognizant. Entire body racked with the worst kind of pain imaginable, but cognizant nonetheless. You are even fooled into thinking you can speak, and most people think they're delivering a Tourette's syndrome version of the Gettysburg Address at five thousand words a minute. But in reality, you're not saying a thing. Your body has just ridden the lightning, and your mind is patiently waiting for it to come back.

Most people, that is.

Like most Philly cops, Hardie had had Taser training. And if you have Taser training, you have to ride the lightning at least once. It's a rule. Just so you know firsthand what you're dishing out.

Hardie's first time became a kind of legend in law enforcement circles. Because just a few seconds after the training officer put the contact pads on Hardie's back and gave him a fifty-thousand-volt kiss and started to explain the effects of the shock, Hardie coughed and began to stand up. He shouldn't have. Not so quickly. The training officer blinked and halted his speech, kind of stunned. He quickly hem-hawed and said the unit must be defective or carrying a low charge, and he asked Hardie if he'd be up for another shot in a few minutes. Hardie told the training officer that if he came near him with one of those things again, he'd shove it so far up the man's ass, he could use it as an emergency pacemaker.

Of course, this immediately made the rounds, and cops were calling Hardie "shockproof" and trying to egg him on for another go, even placing bets as to how long it would take Hardie to get up afterward — five seconds? Eight? Maybe even three? Hardie told everyone to go fuck themselves. He didn't think he got up fast. He thought he was down for an eternity, and in massive fucking pain the whole time.

Just like now.

No idea how long he was down.

But the split second the paralysis eased up, Hardie executed something that could only be described as a kind of break-dancing move — something half-remembered from his childhood in the early 1980s. He wasn't going for style; he was trying to get up from the floor as quickly as possible.

But his move had the bonus effect of colliding with O'Neal's hand, the one holding the heart-attack pen, which —

THWOK

— slammed down into his own thigh.

Shit!

Shit Shit Shit . . .

The shit took three or four seconds to absorb, and O'Neal yanked it back out after one, maybe two . . . maybe closer to one . . . but enough of the shot got into his system. Shit shit shit *shit*. He may even have hit a vein, which was seriously bad news. O'Neal dropped the pen and crab-walked backward, toward the sliding doors. Shit fuck shit fuck SHIT. There was only one thing he could do now. Get himself out to the van. Ignore the vise grip in the middle of his chest, the jolts of pain in his arm, the sudden feeling of impending FUCK THIS HURTS AND I AM GOING TO DIE.

Hardie meanwhile had no idea what the hell had just happened. He coughed — which hurt — and rolled over in time to see somebody crawling back into the house through the living room like a toddler on crack. Had his leg even connected with anything?

Doesn't matter.

Get up.

There are probably more of these creepy assholes in the house.

Get up and go find them.

Save the actress.

Save your family.

119

O'Neal didn't know how many times he fell on the short walk from the front door to the van. Didn't really care. He pumped his fists, trying to keep the blood flowing, and slammed them into his chest from time to time. He was a young man, kept himself healthy — fuck, he'd trekked to the North Pole not too long ago, and that was his idea of a relaxing vacation — but the toxin in his chest didn't seem to care about any of that. It wanted him dead. Quick. That's what it had been designed to do.

The only thing that would discourage the toxin was inside the van, already loaded in a syringe.

Things were simple now:

If O'Neal could get to it, he would live.

If not . . .

A.D. coughed. The acid vomit burned his throat. The pain in his legs was unbelievable. His stomach felt like it was twisted up in a knot. But he was alive. That's all that mattered, right? He'd fallen off the top of a house and he was somehow still alive and he wanted to scream FUCK YOU, ASSHOLE at the top of his lungs.

Mann stood up. Opened her eyes experimentally. Some vision. Not all of it gone. Which was good. This was not over.

CHAPTER
THIRTEEN

You're muckin' with a G here, pal!
— Sean Connery, *The Untouchables*

After dead-bolting the front door, Hardie made his way downstairs for a hurried systematic search of the house — room by room, closet by closet, around corners, behind curtains. With each turn, Hardie was totally prepared for someone to pop out of a hiding space and try to stab him with something sharp. Which seemed to be the running theme this morning.

But there was nobody here.

Not even Lane Madden.

Hardie called out her name, experimentally, once he was sure none of the bad guys were still inside. Part of him wondered if she had been a mirage or a hallucination. Maybe all his drinking had finally caught up with him and he was seeing things. Instead of pink elephants, it was famous people.

Hardie knew that was ridiculous. She'd been here; he didn't impale himself in the goddamned chest.

This could only mean that they'd already gotten her. Killed her, bagged her, put her in the van across the street. And the two guys who were inside were just cleaning up after themselves; Hardie had interrupted nothing more than their janitorial work. All those fake heroics. All for nothing. Another person was dead and Hardie had completely failed to stop it.

Worse than that — he'd failed the moment he opened the door. She'd begged him not to do it. Stubbornly, he had. And that had gotten her killed.

Hardie pulled the stolen phone out of his pocket, checked the screen. Yep, still had service up here. So it wasn't the mountains. It wasn't the house. It was them, somehow blocking everything except their own phones.

Well, joke's on you, assholes.

The one person Hardie trusted in this world was named Deacon "Deke" Clark, and he was a special agent with the Philadelphia FBI. Back in his previous life, Hardie and his partner, Nate, had worked on a joint task force, and Deke was the man in charge. If Hardie could reach him this morning and convince him this whole thing was real, Deke would have a bunch of dudes with suits and guns rolling up into Beachwood Canyon and taking out these cocksuckers within thirty minutes.

Maybe they were top-drawer assassins, highly organized, with a bit of a specialty. A little flashy, just like the rest of L.A. But that was all. They could be arrested. They could be stopped.

Hardie pressed 1. The screen changed, then asked for an eight-digit pass code.

"Oh, no."

Frustrated, he typed in random numbers. The phone shut down and powered off completely.

"*Fuck!* You fucking assholes. Oh, you are such fucking assholes! All of you can just suck my cock!"

Utter silence greeted his outburst.

Then, downstairs, something moved.

Hardie made his way down the staircase, ears cranked to maximum. No idea if his mind had just invented the sound or not. Hadn't he just checked the bottom two floors?

No.

There it was again. Someone was definitely moving up from the bottom floor. Maybe one of them had broken through the windows down on the bottom floor and was making his way up to finish Hardie off. Maybe it wouldn't be with a needle this time. Maybe they'd decided this was a special occasion, and it was time to break out the automatic weapons.

Hardie steeled himself. The footsteps were coming closer. When the person cleared the top stair, Hardie pivoted his body and threw the hardest punch he could muster through the open doorway.

Right into Lane Madden's face.

Hidden away in a pocket of the third floor nobody knew existed, Lane Madden had heard the magic word echo through the house:

Fuck!

Could it really be him? Was her would-be protector somehow still alive?

You fucking assholes!

She had been sure Charlie was a goner. He opened the door — against her pleas, mind you — and some kind of mist had exploded, hitting him in the face. Lane didn't hear it. She was too busy hauling ass back down the stairs, running for her life, thank you very much. Down one flight, then the second, not stopping until she reached the bedroom closet and squeezed past Andrew's pants and shirts and ran her fingers along the drywall searching for the sweet spot, the one he'd shown her two months ago because he thought it would impress her.

My own personal panic room, he'd called it.

But Andrew really used the secret space to hide his drugs and master tapes.

Even the real-estate agent who'd sold Andrew the house didn't know about it. Andrew had been moving stuff into his closet when he tripped over a shoe and tumbled forward. His hand caught the sweet spot, and the entire wall — which appeared to be a seamless piece — tilted a few inches to the right. Andrew cleared out the clothes and wiggled the wall until it opened all the way, revealing a second closet — double the size — behind the visible one.

Andrew did some digging and learned the house had been built by some rich dude back during Prohibition — he'd built a few houses up in Beachwood Canyon during its earliest days, apparently. Clearly it was a place to hide booze until he could move it somewhere. Andrew decided that, in the spirit of the house's original owner, he would likewise use it to store organic materials that the government currently did not allow its citizens to use, buy, own, or sell. He kept an *amazing* stash of pot back there.

They'd been bored one night, and Lane had asked if he was carrying anything, and a smile broke out over Andrew's sweet face and he said, *Do you want to see something cool?*

Something cool that had just saved her life.

Just a few minutes ago, Lane had heard them outside the door, tapping it, pushing against it. They don't know, she told herself. They don't know.

They didn't know.

Then they went away.

Lane decided to sit here for as long as it took. She knew the human body could go without food for close to a week, and water for a couple of days. Maybe Andrew would be back in a few days, and they'd be forced to withdraw and move on. It was a ridiculous thought — Charlie the House Sitter had said Andrew was in Russia . . . but still, maybe he wasn't supposed to be gone too long. Maybe he'd know and come back for her and make everything okay.

Then she heard Charlie yell *Fuck!* and she realized that maybe this nightmare was over, maybe she wouldn't have to wait.

Hardie stood over her unconscious body and prayed he hadn't killed her. There would be some horrible irony there, duking it out with three crazy strangers to save a fourth, only to end up accidentally killing her. He might have a tough time explaining that one.

Lane coughed, then moaned.

"Oh, thank God," Hardie said.

He carried her semiconscious body to the middle of the floor. Blood had spurted out of her nose, and one eye was already puffy. She was in shock. You would be, too, if someone punched you in the face.

Hardie followed the shock playlist: elevated her legs (on a stack of music composition books he found in the studio); made sure she was breathing; checked her pulse to make sure it wasn't racing.

"Lane."

"What . . . ?"

"Lane, you're okay. Just relax and breathe, everything's going to be okay."

That was important with shock victims. They were like five-year-olds waking up in the middle of the night after a bad dream. You had to reassure them. Let them know you were in control of the situation, and that you weren't going to let anything bad happen to them. Well, again.

"What . . . happened to me?"

"I seem to have punched you in the face."

"You . . . wh-what?"

"I thought you were one of Them."

Despite the blood and the shock, Lane smiled.

"You said *Them*. I guess you believe me now."

"I guess I do."

Hardie went to the bathroom, wet a rag with cold water, then used it to wipe away some of the blood from her face. Her eye was even more swollen now. Which was not good. He went back to the bathroom, rinsed out the rag, then folded it into quarters, which

126

he put over Lane's eye. Guess it was all about stabbing and eye injuries up here in the Hollywood Hills today.

Her lone eye stared up at him. It was a beautiful eye.

"I thought they got you," she said.

"I've been told I'm stubborn. Guess I didn't want to die yet."

"Are they still here?"

"They're definitely still outside, and I'd imagine they're pretty pissed off. One of them was out back, sunbathing, watching the house. I think it was the same one who shot you up on the highway, because her left eye was bandaged up."

"A blonde? Kind of severe-looking?"

"Yeah. Only she's going to be even more severe-looking, because I punched her in the face, too."

"What is it with you and punching women in the face? Is that your signature move or something?"

"It's quickly becoming a specialty."

"What about the others?"

"I threw one of them, who looked kind of young, off the back deck balcony. Oh, and that was after I made him puke. And then there was a third guy. Older, bigger. I had no idea what I did to him, but he crawled away like I'd hurt him bad."

"Those sound like the guys who were chasing me from the one oh one."

Hardie didn't want to pressure her or anything — she'd been through a lot and was probably still in shock. But he had to know.

"Where the hell were you?"

Lane's one pretty eye looked up at him.
"I found a secret closet."

Those five words sounded funny, even to her.

Sounded like complete and utter horseshit, actually.

But what was she going to do? Say, *Oh yeah, by the way, I knew about the secret closet because this house actually belongs to my secret boyfriend?* Lane couldn't involve Andrew any more than she already had.

She should never have come to his house.

When she started limping in like a crazy woman toward Lake Hollywood Drive, Lane tried to fool herself that this was the only way out. All along she knew she was running toward Andrew's house.

Sweet, sweet Andrew — her secret nonboyfriend. The non-boyfriend that no one else on earth knew about. The nonboyfriend who was the exact opposite of her for-show, management-sanctioned actor boyfriend. Who was a complete and utter douche.

As she ran for her life, she knew Andrew was pretty much the only person in Los Angeles County who would not think she was crazy, who wouldn't judge her, who wouldn't turn her away. Who understood her situation, and what had happened three years ago. Exactly the kind of person you want to have in your corner when hunted by faceless killers.

And . . .

He wasn't home.

Why wasn't he home?

Lane was mildly hurt that he hadn't told her somehow — even in a Twitter DM — that he'd gone off to Russia. Russia, as in halfway around the fucking world. True, the last conversation they'd had was a sloppy drunken late-night phone fight, but that wasn't enough to send someone fleeing to another hemisphere . . . was it? Maybe it was.

So she'd lied to Charlie the House Sitter about knowing this place, figuring the less she drew Andrew into this mess, the better. She lied about not knowing the security codes, lied about not knowing the owner of the house. Over the past six months they'd spent a lot of time in the bedroom on the bottom floor, getting high and talking about stupid things.

It had been very nice to just talk about stupid things.

"Secret closet?" Hardie said, raising an eyebrow.

"I swear to God, it's this weird closet behind the closet. I crawled in there to hide, and I must have tripped the opening mechanism. I crawled back in there and closed it behind me and —"

"Secret closet," Hardie repeated.

"You don't believe me? Go down and take a look for yourself. It's all there. Along with a couple pounds of pot, if you're into that sort of thing."

"Oh, no, I believe you about the secret closet. Totally makes sense. This is L.A., and L.A. is full of weird shit."

"So, why are you looking at me like that?"

"Because I don't exactly believe that you just so happened to find it while you were stumbling around in the closet, looking for a hiding space. You knew about it."

"If I knew about it, then why wasn't I hiding inside it when you came into the house this morning?"

"Because you were angry," Hardie said, "and you thought I was one of them, and you wanted to kick one of their asses. So, no, I don't believe you just happened to find this magical secret closet."

Lane blinked, but her face didn't betray a single emotion. Hardie supposed that's why they paid her the big bucks.

"What, is it a little too deus ex machina for you?" she asked.

"Look, you're talking to a guy who used to work with cops. And if there's one thing cops are good at, it's sniffing out bullshit. You go stomping around in it all day long, you get to be kind of an expert."

Lane ignored him.

"You don't know what that phrase means, do you. *Deus ex machina*. "God from a machine." Where an impossible problem is suddenly resolved by some new character, ability, or object."

"I know what it means. Mr. Roach taught that in freshman-year English."

"Gee. I didn't learn that until drama school."

"And now you're changing the subject, trying to distract me from your previous serving of bullshit."

"You thought I was lying before about people trying to kill me. And look who turned out to be telling the truth."

"There's probably a Latin term for that, too, what you're doing, but I can't think of it. Look, I don't give a shit about your personal life. I'm not going to sell

130

your secrets to the tabloids. And I don't care what your boyfriend Andrew —"

"I don't know the owner of this house! Whoever the fuck he is!"

"— was into, I really don't. But if you do know, you probably know what he keeps in this house. Like, for instance, maybe something useful like a gun."

Lane blinked.

"There are no guns in the house. I checked when I first broke in here. Do you think I'm an idiot? You're lucky I didn't find a gun, because if I had, I probably would have shot you in the head."

Hardie had to concede that one. Though he wouldn't go so far as to call himself lucky. If he had any kind of luck, it was the get-hit-by-a-car-and-discover-you-have-cancer kind of luck. *You're probably going to die from your injuries, but we're also going to give you chemotherapy, just in case you make it through.*

But still, Hardie thought about the magical secret closet and the stash of pot. Maybe Lowenbruck did a little dealing on the side.

And if so, just maybe he kept a piece with his stash.

Hardie helped Lane to her feet, then brought her into the bathroom. Her eye was swelling up pretty good. He hoped she didn't go looking in the mirror, because she might decide to come after him with the mic stand again.

"Lock yourself in here," Hardie said. "Don't open the door for anyone but me. I'll be right back."

"What are you going to do?"

"Check your magical secret closet. Maybe help myself to some grass."

Lane giggled, despite herself. She was probably still reeling from the punch to her face. But even as he spoke the words, Hardie heard the shrill voice in the back of his head. *Yeah, you're a real clown. But that's all you're good for. You can't protect her. You can't protect anybody.*

Downstairs, in the bedroom closet, was the secret room, as promised. And, yes indeedy, there was pot — three tightly packed bricks of it, as well as a box full of loose pot in tiny Ziploc bags. No guns. Not even a knife. What did this guy use to cut into the bricks of pot? His ninety-nine-cent corkscrew?

The pot was essentially useless to him — unless he could use it to barter with Topless. Maybe she could toke up, ease the pain in her eye. Hardie's mother had been a stoner, so to rebel he became a drinker. Why couldn't Lowenbruck have kept a wet bar or something down here? Why couldn't this have been Prohibition, and there'd be a jug of brown lightning hidden away?

For that matter, why couldn't this be just another gig?

Hardie wanted so badly to pop awake on a comfortable leather couch, half-empty bottle of Knob Creek resting against his crotch, and realize he was having a seriously *weird* fucking dream with celebrities in it.

CHAPTER
FOURTEEN

I can still see!

— Rumored original final line of Roger Corman's
X: The Man with the X-Ray Eyes

The two of them — Mann and O'Neal — briefly reconvened in the back of the van on top of the hill. O'Neal was shocked when he saw Mann. She had blood streaked down her cheeks and seemed to be wearing her bikini top upside down. Then again, O'Neal was sure he'd looked better, too. He'd self-administered the adrenaline in enough time to counter the heart-attack special, but he felt like 160 pounds of wet shit. His skin was clammy yet warm. Sweating out of every single pore of his body. Head pounding. If this was what a heart attack felt like, then O'Neal swore to eat a bullet the moment his primary doc told him his cholesterol was looking a little high. He'd fucking mainline oatmeal if it kept his arteries clean.

"What's our plan?" O'Neal asked.

Mann sat down on a crate, ripped open a first-aid kit, started squeezing some antiseptic into a patch of gauze.

"I want to know more about who we're dealing with. Get Factboy on the line and tell him I want everything in ten minutes. If he gives you an excuse, tell him we're severing our business relationship."

O'Neal watched Mann work on her face. More blood trickled down her cheek. The eye wounds looked hideously painful. He waited for Mann to flinch. She didn't. Her fingers moved around her eye, flicking pieces of plastic away from the corners of her eye. Which was not easy with compromised vision and no mirror.

"Can I help?" O'Neal asked.

"Yeah. By calling Factboy."

Factboy sat on the toilet and read about the death and life of Charles Hardie.

He didn't need to file an electronic National Security Letter this time. The story had been all over the local paper three years ago. (He didn't think he should mention that little tidbit to Mann just yet.) Seems Hardie had worked with a detective named Nate Parish — who, in turn, was part of a joint Philly PD-FBI task force dedicated to cleaning up Philadelphia at all costs. (Factboy had visited Philly once. Good fucking luck with that.)

Albanian gangsters had broken into Nate Parish's suburban home and shot the detective and his family — thirty-eight-year-old wife, ten- and six-year-old daughters — to death, execution-style. Also at the scene was Hardie, who had been *almost* shot to death. He'd flatlined and everything, but EMTs were able to revive him. A couple of surgeries later at Pennsylvania Hospital, it became clear that Hardie was going to

134

make it. Within six months he was walking around again.

But the strange thing wasn't that Hardie survived; it was that Hardie had survived *twice*.

The first time was at his own home, which the gunmen had visited before they hit the Parish house. The Albanians sprayed heavy artillery all over Hardie's place, with him inside. One reporter compared the scene to something out of Kabul. Broken windows, chopped-up woodwork, severed plants, exploded chunks of brick.

But Hardie survived the attack, even though he took anywhere from one to three bullets. (See, the Philly PD couldn't really tell because he received more bullets from the same guns during the *second* attack.)

Anyway, badass Charlie Hardie not only survived but was able to rouse his bleeding self, make his way to the garage, start up his car, and race to his friend and partner's house to warn him the Albanians might be coming for him, too.

But it was the worst thing he could have done.

Oh, if only he could take that back . . .

The gunmen arrived not long after Hardie did, giving them a second opportunity to kill him. They even stopped to reload, according to one account, and continued the execution. This time, Hardie didn't get up and chase after them.

But he also didn't die.

A local columnist dubbed him "Unkillable Chuck."

At first everyone said he was a hero. A "Philadelphia-style hero," some columnist said. Hardie had tried his best and lost — just like Rocky. That didn't mean he didn't give it his all. And that was something to be commended.

Soon, though, the tide turned, as it is wont to do. Some city council members questioned Hardie's role with the Philly PD — was he a consultant or a hired thug? What had he done to piss off the Albanians so badly? Rumors of double-dealing and corruption spread through local papers and blogs. Hardie refused to comment; so did the Philly PD.

After that . . . the coverage pretty much died. Hardie spent six months recuperating, then went into exile.

Factboy had to admit, the story hit home. Turns out Hardie had a wife and kid, too, and luckily they weren't home when the gunmen paid a visit. Factboy had a hard time thinking about something like this happening to him — to *his* wife and kids. It's the kind of thing that went through his head in the middle of the night when he couldn't sleep. This chosen profession of his.

Which made what he had to do next more than a little creepy.

But hey, it was his job.

O'Neal gave Mann the highlights as she finished repatching her eyes. He knew better than to try to persuade her to visit a hospital — or even the mobile doc they kept on retainer. She'd want to stay, finish the job. But that didn't mean he couldn't try to talk a little sense into her. Maybe propose a viable alternative.

"What about the team — on the other job?"

She pressed tape to her brow. "What about them?"

"They're not on until tonight, and I know they're in the area. Why not bring them over and have them finish these two off?"

"No."

O'Neal ran his tongue along his teeth, looked down at the floor, tried again.

"It could be a home-invasion scenario. Simple enough. She holes up here, at her boyfriend's place. Only somebody's robbing the place at the same time. Things go south, she mouths off, gets shot . . ."

"Way too coincidental. And the minute you involve guns is the minute everybody and their mothers start picking apart the narrative. With guns, it's almost never an accident, unless you've got a ten-year-old kid, inattentive parents, and an unlocked cabinet."

Right. The narrative. With Mann everything was about the narrative. And she was so anti-gun, you'd think you'd find her out on weekends, arms linked with Oprah Winfrey and George Clooney, singing "Kumbaya?" at a rally.

"This could be over in twenty minutes," O'Neal. "Don't dismiss it."

"We can't use the first team."

"Why not?"

"Because they're already busy."

O'Neal knew there were two jobs this weekend, and he had to admit, he was bummed to be in a backup role for the second. For some reason, Mann had wanted two completely different primary teams. He knew little about the other job, other than that it was "on the other side of the mountain" and set for that night. Making this a kind of twilight doubleheader for Mann.

"What about a fire? We can light it from the bottom. It's L.A., and it is the season. Completely plausible. We can even figure out a way to pin it on her."

"It's sloppy. The actress and Hardie could make it out. And too hard to control. Once a fire breaks out, it could wipe out dozens of homes before the fire department makes it up here. The arson investigators would have a field day."

Yeah, O'Neal thought. But they'd be dead, wouldn't they?

He held his tongue. This was why she was the director and he was the deputy. Not for lacking of trying, though. Maybe someday he'd earn a top spot on the production team. He'd put in the hours, certainly.

Mann finished up by running a wet wipe over her eyes, to remove the dried blood and dirt. She pulled a black dress over her bikini, and applied lipstick as best she could without a mirror. She could pass for an aging Hollywood Hills trophy wife who'd endured a particularly rough crow's-feet plastic surgery session.

"I'm going back down to the other vantage point. I'll check in with A.D. Make sure he's still functional."

A.D. was indeed still functional.

He'd passed through shock and come through it okay, all things considered.

Now he was directly under the bottom floor, keeping watch. If they were going to bolt, they'd most likely try it from the windows closest to the ground. The drop wasn't too crazy; you could survive. Hell, he survived being kicked in the balls and falling from the top floor. A drop off the bottom floor? No problem at all.

"You sure you're okay?" Mann asked, crouching down next to him. "You can still see and hear?"

"Yeah. You know, I'm kind of surprised about it myself . . . but I'm still in this. Don't count me out, boss."

"I won't."

"How's your eye? You can't even tell with those glasses on."

"I need you to focus."

"Okay, I can focus. What do you want me to do?"

"How far do you think you can crawl?"

Mann knew O'Neal was impatient to finish this. So was she. But you don't go this far and make a mistake at the very end. The narrative was everything. Now that she knew a little more about Hardie, she'd figured out the perfect way to eliminate him.

He wouldn't even know it was coming.

CHAPTER
FIFTEEN

It's quiet. Too quiet.

— Movie cliche

The first hour slid by Hardie and Lane on the second floor, taking up a position in the hallway between the bathroom and the stairway to the lower level. Their weapons: a corkscrew and a slightly used mic stand. Hardie wanted to make a run for it right away. The Indians were wounded; this was the time for the cowboys to make their getaway. But Lane refused — no way, no how — and reminded Hardie of what happened the last time he tried to walk out the front door. Hardie had no choice but to concede her point. Didn't mean he had to like it.

They didn't say too much to each other. Lane had either sobered up or had descended into a deeper level of shock. She complained about her eye hurting and stared at the soundproofed walls, breathing slowly, blinking every so often. Clearly, it hurt when she blinked.

Hardie cracked his knuckles, bending each finger and pressing it with his thumb until his joint popped. Then he continued pressing down with his thumb, even when his joints had nothing left to give.

"Will you stop that," Lane said.

"Sorry."

The waiting killed Hardie. He didn't want to spend the day sitting in the hallway. He wanted *Them* to make the next move NOW. Show themselves. Reveal some weakness. At least give him a sense of how many were out there. At least three, with one possibly incapacitated. But there could easily be more. Topless could have called in reinforcements. Hardie would have.

Hardie was reminded of zombie movies. He wasn't into them, but his son loved them. A few lone human beings vs. insurmountable odds. Wave after wave of dead people coming after you, ripping apart drywall, busting through windows, trying to snack on your brains . . .

But these motherfuckers weren't zombies. They were smart. They were determined. They had gear. They had plans. They had ambitions. They had huge breasts. And they had all the time in the world.

He racked his brain for some escape route, some ruse, some way of communicating with the outside world.

"Who will report you missing?" Hardie asked.

"Huh?"

"When you don't show up at home, who will miss you?"

"Sad to say, the only person who will notice will probably be my manager, Haley. I told her we'd talk sometime today about future projects. But I've flaked out before and not returned calls. Sometimes for days. She won't think anything of this at first."

"Yeah, I know the feeling."

"What about you? Who will miss you?"

"Absolutely nobody. Not for at least a month."

"We won't be able to survive here for a month."

"So I guess it's up to you. You're the famous one. Somebody will eventually come looking for you. Maybe they'll retrace your steps."

But Hardie knew that was bullshit the moment he spoke the words. If these guys wanted the death to look like an accident, they would have already scooped the car and all traces of Lane Madden.

Sometime during the second hour Hardie went to splash some water on his face. He was feeling sick to his stomach. Probably because the last thing he ate was that stupid dry bagel in the airport. Hardie turned the cold-water knob. The faucet ran for a few seconds before the pipes rumbled. The faucet spat at his fingers, then went dry. Fuck, come on! Not the water, too.

No food. No power. No way to call for help. No nothing.

It drove him mad.

In the hallway, Lane was throwing up.

Hardie gathered up the remaining towels from the bathroom and helped her clean up her face, then wiped the floor. But the odor of gastric bile was making him sick, too. He had to choke it back, swallow, keep his head clear. Try to, anyway. His head was really starting to pound.

Of course, this was to be expected — they had both been through an absurd number of shocks and traumas this morning. Lane had been in a car crash and hunted up and down the Hollywood Hills in the dark. Hardie had been beaten, impaled, poisoned, suffocated, and Tasered. Adrenaline kicks in during these kinds of situations, but adrenaline doesn't last forever. Human bodies need time to recover. They need water and food and rest and sleep — all things they didn't have or couldn't afford.

So of course, they were feeling like shit, throwing up, and ready to lose their minds.

But . . .

Some ultraparanoid part of Hardie's mind thought it could be something else.

These fuckers didn't use conventional weapons. They went in for poisons. Cars. Electricity. What if they had managed to pump some kind of toxic fumes into the house? And after making them puke like a freshman at a kegger, it would kill them.

Hardie tried to discern if anything smelled strange or left a weird taste in his mouth. Nothing, of course . . . and why would it? Only gas companies helpfully laced their natural gas supply with a delightful rotten-egg odor so you'd know when your pilot light had blown out. If you wanted to kill someone with some powerful, exotic, untraceable poison, you wouldn't go advertising it. You'd just pump it in.

Should he try to go around the house, sealing off all the vents?

Hardie rubbed his eyes. Lane had rested her head against his shoulder and shut her eyes. It would have been a tender moment, quite possibly even a mildly erotic one, had she not been trembling and smelling faintly of vomit.

Hardie thought more about *Them*. Tried to climb inside their minds and guess what they'd be doing next.

Then he remembered what one of them had said.

"Lane."

"Uhhhh."

"Lane, you still with me?"

"Just want to sleep."

"I need you to tell me who we're really up against."

Lane's eyelids slowly lifted.

"I told you. I don't know."

"I told you I met the lady with the one eye, right? Topless Cyclops?"

"Yeah."

"She told me that you deserved this. That I should ask you why."

Lane blinked as if she'd been slapped. She made a show of recovering. Huffing, shaking her head.

"Of course she'd say that."

"Yeah, I understand that. But I still don't think you're telling me everything. And while I'm sure you have your reasons, we might die in here. Because of something you didn't tell me. You tell me that you have no idea why they're trying to kill you, yet you seem to know an awful lot about them."

Lane stared at the wall.

"What, is it that you still think I'm one of them?" Hardie asked. "If that's the case, then —"

"No, it's not that . . . It's . . ."

"What?"

Lane started to rub her eyes to wake up a little and remembered that it really hurt. She tasted the inside of her mouth and found that it was absolutely foul. She stretched and then looked at Hardie.

"Okay, listen, this might sound a little insane. Like I'm telling you about the boogeyman. But an ex-boyfriend was the one who told me about these people. I thought he was full of shit and he was just teasing me. I didn't believe they were real until this morning . . . God, this is going to sound *stupid*."

"Highly doubtful."

She hesitated again.

"In L.A. you hear stories. Rumors about killers who go after famous people and make it look like accidents. You joke about these killers like kids joke around about the boogeyman — but inside, you're scared to death the rumors are true. Some drunk guy at a party will tell you he knows how Marilyn Monroe really died, or how John Belushi's OD wasn't really an OD. And then everybody will get quiet, because everyone else will have heard the same things."

Hardie felt himself easing back into cop mode. Commenting as little as possible, listening to everything. Evaluating.

"Anyway, my ex once told me — *swore to me* — these people were real. Said they had protection at the highest levels, that they were bankrolled by the richest people on earth. They clean up the messes. That's how he put it. After a while he'd start joking around with me. *Don't make me call the Accident People.*"

"So you think he called them for real."

Lane was stunned.

"No! Not my ex. Point is, I believe what he said. He'd be in a position to know."

"So, he's what — an actor?"

Lane nodded, said his name.

It was the BLOND VIKING GOD.

Everybody knew the BLOND VIKING GOD.

The entertainment press gave this particular actor the sobriquet after his first gig — a supporting role in an Oscar-nominated war flick. From there, it was indie thrillers, then a big-budget superhero role, and then finally his own producing arm. Everything he touched turned into golden celluloid. He was as famous as famous could get. A $40 million-dollar man in a downsized Hollywood where nobody — nobody — could command those kinds of numbers. He could open a flick. Open it big. Guaranteed.

His name was uttered at least once every few minutes all across America, usually in the form of a punch line like, "Well I'm no BLOND VIKING GOD, but . . ."

And for a brief while, he used to date a cute actress from a bunch of romantic comedies named Lane Madden.

Lane put her fingers to her temples and lowered her head.

"It's not like I have proof to show you. But he swore to me they were real, because he met them once."

"What happened?"

"He didn't tell me much."

"What happened?"

Lane sighed. "Four years ago — before we even met — he was at this party out in Malibu. Things got out of hand. Too much booze, too much coke. There was a stupid fight. Someone ended up dead. Another actor. Somebody who was kind of over, you know? But the party had a bunch of people who weren't over, who were worth a lot of money to a certain studio. If word got out about what had happened at this party, it could ruin their careers, ruin the studio. So the studio called them in — the Accident People. They rolled into Malibu and cleaned everything up. Made it look like the guy fell while out for a run. Told everyone at the party what to say. The whole thing was scripted, like it was a movie. Nobody questioned it; the police never linked him to the party. Everyone was told that if they even breathed a word about what had happened, it wasn't just their career on the line. It was their life. Because the *Accident People* will be back to you."

"Did Blond Viking God kill the has-been?"

"No! *God*, no. He was just there and watched these people work. Totally freaked him out. Said it was like someone pried off the lid and showed him how Hollywood really works. From then on, he told me, he was always a little more respectful when it came to writers and directors and special-effects people because some of them — when their commercial careers were over — graduated to the ranks of the *Accident People*."

"You make it sound like a promotion."

"Ordinary directors only get to work with stuff that appears on a screen. When you work with the Accident People, you're playing around with real life. You're writing secret history. They take their work seriously. At least that's what my ex told me."

Secret history.

Secret closets, secret kills. Accidents.

The implications of this finally hit Hardie.

This explained their weird behavior, their methods, their tactics. Hardie realized now that barricading themselves in was exactly what *They* wanted. To keep them both contained until they could be "dealt" with according to script. They didn't behave like other killers, because they wanted something besides death. They were trying to make the world conform to their little twisted vision, and they'd keep working at it until they got everything right. The longer they hid inside, the longer they'd have to nail down their big secret plans.

Well fuck that, Hardie thought.

CHAPTER
SIXTEEN

*All the best stories in the world are but one story in
reality — the story of an escape.*

— A. C. Benson

Andrew Lowenbruck kept a tiny charcoal grill on the
side deck. A miniature kettle-shaped thing, big enough
for four hamburgers and maybe a couple of hot dogs
wedged in here and there. It was damn near useless as a
food preparation tool, but to Hardie, it might be their
ticket out of here.

There were only a few ways to light charcoal
briquettes. Some already came soaked in lighter fluid
— which to Hardie's mind was cheating — but most
came without. You either had to use a chimney starter
and bunched-up newspaper, or some matches and
lighter fluid. Hardie didn't remember seeing a chimney
starter outside. And frankly, Lowenbruck didn't seem
too much like a hard-core griller. So there were
probably some lighter fluid and matches around.

Hardie crept upstairs and found both under the
kitchen sink, along with an unopened container of
cleanser with packaging straight from the 1980s. The
lighter fluid was in a small metal box, squeezable. The
matches were wooden and long enough to take an eye
out.

Now all he needed was something flammable. Something that would go up quickly and send a lot of smoke into the air . . .

Hardie carried the fluid and matches into the living room and saw them instantly.

Sly.

Arnie.

Bruce.

Mel.

And yes, even Gene.

The cardboard standees.

"Sorry, boys," Hardie muttered. "You can come find me and beat the shit out of me later."

Hardie shoved the matches into one pocket, lighter fluid into the other, then walked down a few steps until he was eye level with the bottom of the standees. He fished out the lighter fluid, then soaked the bottoms with multiple squeezes from the tiny metal can. It was like trying to piss up a wall. The fumes were harsh and instantly put him in mind of summertime cook-outs. Something Hardie hadn't done for years, didn't think he'd ever have the chance to do again.

He made his way back down the stairs, opened the box of matches, shook one out, flicked the head along the lighting strip on the box. Nothing. He tried again. Nothing. One more time — and the match snapped in half.

"What are you doing?" a voice whispered behind him. Lane.

"Getting us out of here, that's what."

"By doing what — setting the house on fire?"

"Exactly."

"You're kidding me."

Hardie looked up and noticed the stream of fluid led right to Stallone. Made sense. If someone's going to go first, let it be the Philly guy. The guy who embodied that kind of can-do-in-the-face-of-hopeless-odds kind of spirit. Strains of Bill Conti pumped through his head.

"You're going to kill us," she said. "Is that your big plan? Make it easy for them?"

"No. We're going to get some towels wet and seal up the cracks under the door down there. Then we're going to do the same to the other door, and we're going to wait in the bedroom on the bottom level."

"Where we'll die of smoke inhalation! I've worked on action movies, Charlie. I know how this works."

"No, we *won't*. Fire travels up. This is an upside-down house. It'll burn the roof, then start to come down slowly. Meanwhile, a whole lot of black smoke travels up. And the minute we hear a siren, we'll be safe. You said these people work in secret, right? They arrange accidents and nobody's the wiser? They skulk around and take out people on the sly? Well, let's see them try to kill us in front of a bunch of firefighters. What are they going to do — wipe them out, too, along with the EMTs? No. Fuckers lose this round. They wanted to keep this quiet, so I'm going to make it as loud as possible."

Lane stared at him for a moment, then turned to throw up.

"I knew you'd like the plan," Hardie said.

Then he finally got a match to light.

Back in the small house below the Lowenbruck residence, Mann had a new narrative all prepared:

Starlet gets drunk and high, cracks up her car on the 101. She flees the scene, leaving her totaled Lexus behind. She wanders into the hills. She gets lost. Confused. Finally, she collapses. A jogger finds her five days later — four days after she's been reported missing.

So that meant removing her body from the house and planting it out in the hills. Which was not a big deal; there were plenty of spots they already had mapped out without the slightest risk of discovery. The jogger would be one of their own people, with the requisite bulletproof background. Four days of exposure to the elements and wildlife would leave the body in an ideal state. And finally, Hardie could be left in the house for later discovery. Heart attack. Simple enough to arrange.

First, though, they needed the bodies.

And to do that, they'd gas them.

While Mann kept watch, A.D. crawled and ran a robot pig down the gas line and then restored service.

The pig was a piece of detection equipment that gas companies used to test the integrity of their lines — a cylindrical robot that looked like an unlit light saber from the *Star Wars* movies. The pig checked for leaks and corrosion and made sure the pipe was performing to standards.

152

Mann's pig, however, was modified to perform a few additional tasks. For one, it could force a crack in a gas line. It could also accelerate the delivery of the gas into the house, fill it in about a quarter of the normal time. Finally, the pig was equipped with a filter that could strip away the t-butyl mercaptan — the odorant additive that gives natural gas its distinctive smell. Natural has no scent. An entire room could be filled with natural gas and even those with the keenest of senses wouldn't know it. Just like nature intended.

Once A.D. deployed the pig, O'Neal sat in the van and used a tablet computer to guide it to the oven near the top floor. This would be the easiest place to fake a leak. The pig could be used to compromise the connector joint. If forensic examiners ever looked at the pipe, faulty workmanship would be to blame.

But that was the worst-case scenario. What would happen was, the gas would overwhelm them — it would only take an hour or so before the fumes completely filled the house — and they'd recover the bodies. Maybe Hardie, a troubled, depressed cop who watched his best friend die, could even be set up as a suicide. Lane, meanwhile, would be transported elsewhere. No connection whatsoever. The windows could be opened; the air exchanged; the crack in the gas pipe connection mended.

The events of this horrible wretched day — erased.

Which was why Mann was completely stunned by the massive explosion that suddenly rocked the top of the house.

CHAPTER
SEVENTEEN

*If you have any doubts as to how to end a movie,
set everything on fire.*
— Samuel Z. Arkhoff in conversation
with Brian Helgeland

Vomiting, Lane would later realize, probably saved her life.

She didn't know that at the time. Midheave she felt something slam into her from behind. Immediately she started to choke, and when she was finally able to draw in some air, on her hands and knees in the middle of the hallway, Lane was overwhelmed with the odor of something burning.

Holy fuck —

It was Charlie.

Nausea and vomiting was immediately forgotten, as if her brain realized there were bigger things to deal with, hunched its shoulders, and said, *Okay, you win. Go do what you have to do.*

Half crying, Lane kicked the one door shut, then the other, then grabbed the pile of wet towels from the floor and slammed them into Charlie's burning form. What was that line from grade school? Stop, drop, and roll. Well, Charlie was already stopped and dropped. Should she roll him? She should. She touched his sides

154

and was stunned by the heat emanating from his body. She rolled him anyway.

"What the . . .?" Mann said, looking up at the fireball from down below.

O'Neal barked into his phone. "The hell did you do, A.D.?"

Directly underneath the house, A.D. missed the initial blast. He felt it rock his body, though. He rolled over until he was able to gaze up at the smoke and the fire licking the sides of the house. Did *he* do that? No. He couldn't have. The pig wasn't loaded with any kind of explosives. From his vantage point, the holocaust looked otherworldly, like it was happening at some great distance instead of just a few floors away. Kind of cool, actually.

"A.D., answer me! What the hell happened, man?"

"Wasn't me," A.D. said.

All of that dark smoke. So beautiful against the hazy gray skies.

Every year there are a handful of natural-gas explosions in the United States. Few of them are powerful enough to knock down a structure.

The injuries to anyone present inside can range from minor to moderate burns, depending on how many cubic feet of gas has accumulated inside before ignition.

Hardie groaned. He didn't lose consciousness — at least he didn't think so. He was just . . . confused. He couldn't remember falling down the staircase or hitting the floor. And how did striking that wooden match spark a blast? There was no gas in the air, far as he could tell. Unless they pumped in something that was both undetectable *and* extremely flammable . . .

In which case they were kind of fucked.

Hardie could see the fire raging behind the double doors leading to the staircase. The doors were beginning to peel and warp. He could feel the heat radiating from them. They needed to move.

He rolled his head to the side in time to see Lane pausing in the doorway that led to the bottom floor. She seemed unable to make up her mind. Which was fine. He couldn't blame her. Maybe she thought he was already dead, and had to figure out how to save herself. Lane made her way back to Hardie.

"Go," he told her. "Get out of here now — I'll be fine."

"Go where? Outside to the people who are trying to kill me? This is them, trying to flush us out."

"Well, it's working," Hardie said. Smoke was filling the room now, seeping under the door and through the soundproofing ceiling panels. "We can't stay in here."

Lane disappeared behind his head. The next thing he felt was the agony of her touch under his shoulders, trying to heave him up. Hardie screamed and rolled out of the way.

"I can do it, I can do it . . ."

"I was just trying to help!"

"I know, but it's better if I do it."

Pressing his palms to the carpet, Hardie pushed himself off the ground and staggered to his feet. He coughed. Fuck, the smoke worked fast. Lane led the way downstairs. Hardie followed, closing the door behind them. Not that it would do much for long. A serious fire like the one raging above their heads wouldn't take long to eat its way down the house.

"We need to get A.D. out of there," O'Neal said. "Like right fucking now."

O'Neal, now standing outside the van, scoped the scene. What a clusterfuck. Fire and smoke everywhere, eating up whatever fuel was inside the top floor. There wasn't much, from what he remembered. Leather couches, flatscreen TV, DVDs and books and papers and other things that would burn fast. The owner lived like a transient.

In his ear, Mann said:

"Listen."

Off in the distance — sirens. Probably fighting their way up Belden now. Fires were serious business in these dry hills. You had to smash them out before they took hold and turned into something that could eat up millions of dollars' worth of homes within sixty minutes.

"We go in there, we're caught at the scene, it's all over," Mann said. "Better one of us than all three of us."

"Jesus, are you serious?"

"If you were down there, you'd know what to do, wouldn't you?"

O'Neal nodded until he realized that Mann couldn't see him. "Yeah," he said. Another reason they all kept the heart-attack pens zipped up and on their person at all times.

"We need to recover the pig," Mann said. "They find the pig, the narrative unravels. Then they've got a cause. Then they've got something suspicious. We also need to know the conditions inside."

O'Neal usually bit his tongue when working with directors, but he couldn't control himself. He kind of just blurted it out.

"*What* narrative, Mann? Do you really think this is holding together?"

"The narrative is intact," she said. "Keep your head together and your eyes open. If they're still alive in there, they're going to try to make a break for it. They come out of that house, we need to be prepared to deal with them."

Out the windows. That was their only chance. Sure, a dozen people might start taking shots at them but it was better than no chance whatsoever.

"Lane?"

She was already crouched in a corner, back against the wall. Hardie went to her, tried to get her to her feet. "Come on, what are you doing?" he asked.

"Get on the floor. Smoke fills the top of a room first."

"No! We've gotta go out the window, now!"

"Don't you hear that?" she cried. "That's sirens! Your plan will work. They'll get here in time, and when they get here, they'll come in for us."

"That plan was for a slow fire," Hardie said. "You know, with smoke lazily rising up into the sky, and the fire engines arriving before any real damage. Maybe you missed this, but the entire fucking top of the house just blew up. The fire is hungry and spreading fast. If we don't go out the window now, we're going to die."

Smoke from a major fire can fill a room in as little as forty-seven seconds.

This was all for a reason.
That's how Lane knew she was going to survive.

Her dating Andrew, knowing about this secret room, Charlie being here to force her into action . . . all of it. They could have easily killed her on the 101. Or even before that, up on Decker Canyon Road. But somehow, through a chain of ridiculous circumstances, she had survived it all. Everything connected. Even the stupid action movies she'd been doing over the past three years had paid off. How else would she have been able to smash a fistful of glass into that bitch's eye? Or take down a big guy like Hardie?
This was all for a reason.
In other words, Lane was meant to live through this.

Hardie was done arguing. He grabbed one of Lowenbruck's bedside lamps and used it to smash the glass out of a window, tapping every jagged edge of the frame. There. Now all he had to do is convince Ms. Famous Movie Actress to leap out of the thing. And if she refused, well then, Hardie was seriously thinking about throwing her ass out of it. Because if they stayed in this burning house, she would die. Simple as that. And he wasn't going to let her die.

Before he pulled away from the window, however, Hardie happened to glance down.

He instantly wished he hadn't done that.

Mann glanced up to see Charlie Hardie looking down at her through the open window, twenty feet up, calm as can be. And if you're in a burning house, the last thing you should be is calm.

He even *waved*.

Somehow Hardie must have figured out what they were up to, and he started the fire himself. Even if he killed them both in the process. Unbelievable the balls on him.

For once, Mann wished she carried a gun. There were many (many) reasons why they shouldn't, but if Mann had a gun, then she could lift it and squeeze off a shot and explode this guy's heart, just for screwing with them.

"Having fun, Charlie?" she shouted up to him.

Then Hardie disappeared from view, into the haze and smoke and darkness of the bottom floor.

Hardie pressed his back against the wall, stomach sinking to the bottoms of his feet.

160

Lane was right. They were everywhere. They weren't afraid of the sirens. They didn't give a shit. They just wanted the two of them to come outside, where they could finish them off . . . somehow. He didn't see Topless carrying any weapons, but that didn't mean a thing.

Hardie's mind reeled. If they *did* jump down, and if they weren't instantly stabbed or Tasered or sprayed or shot or bludgeoned or electrocuted or irradiated with a mini tactical nuclear weapon . . . could they make a run for it? Down to the house on the next hill seemed to be the best option. But that's where Topless seemed to have set up camp. She was lurking around down there, and no doubt with friends. Uphill seemed to be an even worse idea. Was it possible to run to either side? Hardie tried to remember what the landscape looked like. The geography up here confused him, none of it made any rational sense.

What was the alternative, though? Stay and burn? No. They had to jump now.

"Lane, c'mon."

Nothing.

"Lane?"

Everything is going to be okay.

Everything is going to be okay.

Like a mantra:

Everything is going to be okay.

In Catholic grade school a priest once told Lane — whose name was Lorianne back then — Lorianne Madinsky — that God never gave you more than you

161

could handle. As bad as things might seem, He knows you're strong enough to deal with them.

Lane had stopped being a Catholic back when . . . well, long before she'd stopped being Lorianne Madinsky. But some of the belief structure was still there, hardwired inside her mind, and it served to explain how the universe worked when there were no rational or obvious explanations.

So if she was supposed to endure all of this . . . it had to be because she was strong enough to endure it, that she was somehow meant to endure it, and that *everything would be okay.*

It had to be. Otherwise God would have killed her years ago, right?

So Lane crawled back into the secret closet.

"Lane?"

Where the hell was she?

Hardie dropped to his hands and knees. Visibility was getting bad on the bottom floor. Had she already succumbed to the smoke? No, if it had hit her, it would have hit him, too. Hardie checked under the bed — nothing. He scurried over to the opposite corner, and all at once he realized where she'd gone, damnit.

Hardie charged into the secret closet just as the smoke began pouring into the bottom floor in earnest, gathering up at the low ceiling and working its way down. He could hear the sirens now, too, but he didn't think that would do them much good when they were sucking in noxious fumes in a matter of seconds.

Smoke was going to fill the room in under a minute. They had to get out of here.

Or he could just lie down and die.

Because that's what you did before, isn't it, Charlie? You thought you were so big and bad, pushing yourself up off the ground, sneaking out the back way, then storming your way to the garage and firing up the car and smashing through your own doors and hauling ass all the way out to Nate's place, bleeding all over your upholstery. But that's okay. Because you thought you were some kind of hero. And look how that turned out. Now, go ahead. Lie down and die. Nobody expects anything more from you. This is what you do best. *Lie down and die.*

Hardie told the little voice inside his head to go fuck itself, and he reached out into the darkness of the closet.

"Lane, goddamnit?"

Hardie's fingers brushed against her. She moved away, yelling at him to get out, to save himself, they didn't want him, they wanted her. Hardie ignored her and managed to wrap a hand around her forearm and pulled forward. She yanked her arm backward, screaming at him to leave her alone, it was over, save himself. Her arm slipped out of his hands.

And then everything started to collapse around them.

Interlude With
Mildly Famous Killers

Barstow, CA — Now

The psychopaths came out of the desert, looking for some breakfast.

First diner they found was in Barstow. Not a chain, which was good. Chains sucked. They liked homegrown joints. The girl gestured to a car, eyebrows raised, but the young man shook his head. Eggs first, get a car later. The young man said he could really go for some scrambled eggs with hot sauce, some jalapeño peppers maybe. The girl shook her head, patting her stomach. The young man laughed, replied that he had a cast-iron stomach. She rolled her eyes. He smirked at her, then put a hand on her shoulder.

"You ready for this, Jane?"

Jane nodded.

The young man, who called himself Phil, slid his hand down her chest until it was directly over her tit. He squeezed it gently, as if checking the firmness of supermarket produce.

164

"For good luck," Phil said.

Jane pursed her lips and blew him a silent kiss.

Inside the diner, the air-conditioning was cool on their skin. Neither Phil nor Jane sweated much, but it was god-awful hot outside. The place was almost deserted. They'd missed the breakfast rush, if such a thing existed out here. Phil looked around quickly, saw that the place didn't have quite the setup they needed.

"Let's keep going."

Jane looked around, then nodded in agreement.

A few joints later, Phil found an ideal spot: a gas station mini-mart with notions. While it couldn't quite call itself a diner, or even a lunch counter, it had a little breakfast nook with some pale white disks that claimed to be made from eggs, English muffins, some fruit and cereal. There was a flat-screen TV mounted up in the corner playing cable news. Most important, it was still an out-of-the-way gas station. Enough customers to make this interesting; not enough to worry about being overwhelmed. A doughy-looking married couple in their forties. A bored-looking teenager with an eyebrow piercing. A female trucker with tattoos.

Phil and Jane entered, and Jane made a beeline for the breakfast nook and examined the faux eggs. Phil lingered by the door. He smirked at the counter guy and then reached behind to flip the lock before pulling a gun out of his jacket pocket. Jane, near the breakfast nook, had one to match. Everyone in the mini-mart froze in place, not quite believing what they were seeing.

Phil pointed the muzzle at the counter guy.

"You mind putting on *Truth Hunters?*"

"Wh-what?"

"You've got the TV remote back there, don't you? I'd like you to put on *Truth Hunters*. It's my favorite show."

"It's not . . . I don't think it's on now."

Phil kept speaking as if he didn't hear the man's response.

"I love the reenactments. They make me laugh, because they're creepy and cheesy at the same time. You almost feel the danger, you can almost picture yourself there, at the other end of the gun or the knife or whatever, am I right or what? . . . and then the cheesiness sets in, and you realize you don't have to be scared at all."

He glanced over at Jane, who nodded once.

Now he was back, waving a gun in their faces. "But it's a far cry from the real thing. As you're all about to find out."

Next came the part psychotic killer Philip Kindred loved best — the arranging, the stripping. He ordered the middle-aged wife and the trucker to strip down to their underwear, and then the doughy husband to take off his pants but leave his shirt on. Phil told him that his sister didn't want to see his flabby man-tits, it would just make her upset. The teenage girl with the piercings was forced to pick up a box cutter and bungee-style cords from the small hardware section, and then to put a paper bag over her head. She was fine right up until the paper bag part, and started freaking out, but then Phil shoved his gun into the side of the wife's chest and threatened to blow her breasts off. Jane was already working on the paper bag, cutting out a little eyehole. She handed it to the pierced girl, who was crying when she slipped it over her head. Jane had clearly done a nice job, for when the bag was on, its edges stopped at her shoulders, and you could see one of the teenage girl's eyes peeking out through the hole.

Phil, meanwhile, unpackaged the box cutter, quickly loaded a blade, and then looked up at everyone.

"Okay, who's ready for some fun and games?"

Jane nodded. There was a happy, toothy grin on her tiny face.

CHAPTER
EIGHTEEN

*Perhaps we can dispense with the fun and games
now, yes?*
— Taylor Negron, *The Last Boy Scout*

Hollywood Hills — Now

After the fire burned for another fifteen minutes, and
the engines started to assemble and tap into water
mains, and there was no sign of any living thing inside
or outside the house, Mann resigned herself to the new
narrative.

Now they had a fire story.

Mann took a few fast deep breaths to clear her mind,
to blow the fatigue out of her skull. Timing was
everything now, as was sharp thinking. Arson
investigators were shrewd and tenacious. You might
think that fire was nature's eraser, destroying everything
in its path and wiping the slate clean. An arson
investigator would tell you that you were being an idiot.
Fire told a story like nothing else. It was simple,
elemental, predictable, and utterly traceable. Mann
knew that if you were using fire in your narrative, you'd
better know how to tell a fire story.

That was why she considered it a last resort.
Untraceable poisons were the best — the heart-attack

stuff, for instance, was a godsend. Car crashes could be investigated, but it wasn't too difficult to have a vehicle do what you wanted. Falls were good, too, in a pinch. Bathtub drownings.

Fires, though, were a motherfucker.

She needed facts. Something that would help her firm up the new narrative. It shouldn't be difficult; she knew how the story would end:

Recovering starlet with history of drug abuse gets into a car wreck, freaks out, flees the scene, goes to a boyfriend's house in the Hollywood Hills, is overwhelmed with guilt, shoots up again, and then sets the house on fire in a fit of drug-addled psychosis, thinking she can cover her tracks.

Not Mann's best story line ever, but considering this whole early-morning abortion of a job, it would have to do. But did the facts support it? Would they support the actress lighting the house on fire?

And where did Charlie Hardie fit in?

She had no idea.

Where would the bodies be? What were they trying to do as the fire raged on? How did the fire even start? Was it one of those freak events where a charge from a cell phone ignited the gas in the air? Or did Hardie decide to light one up while he was waiting them out? No. Hardie didn't smoke, according to Factboy, not for three years. Neither did the actress. So, what, then? Did they cause the blast?

Were they dead or alive?

O'Neal, up in the front of the van, was trying to figure that out. He used the dash-mounted scanner and a pair of headphones to listen to the progress of the firefighters just down the street. The fire was worst on the top floor, as expected, but smoke was everywhere. As they cleared each room, he waited for mention of a body. Either body would be welcome. Any sign of progress in this long, tortured morning.

Finally there was excitement on the line. They'd discovered someone. Cries went out for medical assistance.

O'Neal told Mann, "They're pulling out somebody. Still alive."

"Okay," Mann said. "Which one?"

O'Neal held up an index finger, kept listening to the scanner chatter, trying to put the pieces together.

"Tell me it's the actress."

"Hold on. Male, they're saying."

Silence on the line. Finally, O'Neal was back.

"Shit, I think it's A.D. They're talking about getting him to the hospital fast — he's alive but not doing so well. Vitals are crashing."

Mann ignored it. A.D. knew the risks; they had to stay focused.

"Hardie and the actress have to be in there. Give the firefighters time to make their way through the house."

"Did you hear what I said? What's the plan with A.D.?"

"A.D. can take care of himself for now. He won't say a word, and we'll come up with something for him later."

170

Yeah. Like an air bubble in an IV line.

A.D. wasn't the focus right now; he was an unfortunate casualty. Horrible to admit, but you could find A.D.'s pretty much everywhere. Many young, creative minds were eager to break into this rarefied line of work. Confirming the field even *existed* took a great deal of effort and networking and background checks and psych exams — and only then, if you were lucky, would you be able to apply for a support-team job. Still, there were plenty of names on a list somewhere. If A.D. were to die, his corpse would be trampled into pulpy bits by the people eager to take his job.

So forget A.D.; they had to keep their minds on the actress and her new friend, Charlie Hardie.

O'Neal removed the headset, let his shoulders fall, and shook his head. It had been a long day, and it just didn't seem to want to fucking end. And they had the other production later this afternoon. He hated the idea of rolling to another job with all of these loose ends still to clean up.

Mann's cavalier attitude toward the possible death of one of his crewmates didn't help much either. What if it had been him down there? Up until this moment, O'Neal had assumed he'd have been rescued. One Guild member saving another.

Goddamnit all to *fuck*.

But at least their targets were somewhere in that smoldering house, and they were most likely dead. He had been watching the front, and Mann had the back

— from two angles. Neither target had passed their line of vision.

Let's just find their corpses already so we can move on.

There was a cough in the darkness.

"Charlie?"

"Right here."

More coughing, hacking, hand waving in the near dark.

"Where are we?"

"I don't know."

The only people who could answer that question were dead.

In 1925 a bootlegger named Jimmy Smiley from Philadelphia went west to spend some of his ill-acquired fortune. Through the early part of the decade, Philly had been a wide open town. He'd made money hand over fist selling beer and brown lightning to the mooks in the row houses — that is, until the city brought in a Marine general to clean things up. Smiley sensed the glory days were over and lammed it out to the sleepy, sunny farm town that was L.A. Oranges. That sounded good to Smiley.

Back then, Beachwood Canyon was a new development, and Smiley's money was as good as anyone else's. Smiley thought big, and he thought ahead. He found a plot of level ground that looked to be higher than anyone else's in the immediate area and

172

set about re-creating his East Coast manse out in California — only bigger. He made sure the castle had five garages — again, thinking ahead, he knew that Los Angeles was so sprawling that the more cars you had, the more power you'd enjoy. He made sure each of his six children had their own large, sunny bedroom. He made sure his wife had the kitchen of her dreams.

And Smiley made sure his mistress had a place as well.

Back on the Main Line, Smiley had bought the young lady her own apartment near Reading Terminal Station, just a train ride away.

But out in Hollywoodland, Smiley decided to keep her a little closer.

So he purchased a plot of land a little farther down the mountain and had a four-story "upside-down" home built for her. And since it wouldn't do to be seen by his neighbors trotting on down the lane for nightly visits, Smiley had a second construction crew build a secret tunnel connecting the main house up on top of the hill to the mistress's bedroom down below, boring straight through the bedrock of the mountain itself. Smiley hinted to the construction crew that the tunnel was for "business purposes." The winking crew filled in the blanks; they knew how Smiley had made his dough back East; sex never even entered their minds.

Smiley kept the only key and made sure the door on the other side was hidden at the back of a large walk-in closet. Finally, he bribed the county officials to conveniently lose the architectural plans to both homes, which explained why — almost ninety years later —

Factboy didn't uncover a trace of this tunnel during his initial check on the Lowenbruck house.

And why Hardie and Lane were surprised to find themselves in a dank, stone-lined staircase in a corridor that seemed to stretch up into a dark forever.

Thick black smoke had poured in behind them; there really was no time for debate. Charlie used his forearms to push away the semirotted wood and clear the entranceway. There seemed to be nothing behind the wall at first, but Charlie figured nothing was better than dying from smoke inhalation. Maybe there was a crevice between the house and the mountain, and they could squeeze themselves out through it.

"Go," Charlie said, hacking. "Go go go . . ."

Once they were inside the passageway, their eyes began to adjust, and they saw the stone walls, the cement stairs. They crawled up into the darkness. After a few steps Charlie reached out and grabbed Lane's arm. She clutched his hand in return, holding on tight and limping all the way up the cement staircase into what seemed like total darkness.

She wondered if Andrew had any clue this passageway was here. She assumed not. He loved talking about the house, and he wouldn't have been able to resist talking about a secret corridor. For a second, Lane thought he'd be excited by the discovery, but then she remembered his house was burning down, along with everything he owned and created.

174

Mann kept her eyes on the scene of the fire, trying to pull in any kind of detail that would be useful. Every few seconds she would ask O'Neal:

"Anything?"

"Nothing."

Her eyes hurt, though. Their sockets were tender and her face throbbed so much that she couldn't stop tearing up. She couldn't take anything for the pain, because that would just fog her thinking. The more she stared up at the house, the more tears came. Blinking was agonizing, so she did it as little as possible. And with every blink, Mann was convinced the damage to her eyes worsened.

But she couldn't leave. There was no one else to keep watch. What had begun as a team of six eyes had dwindled down to a pitiful two and a half — that's all Mann really had, a kind of pathetic half vision.

If they were dead . . .

And this was where you went after you died . . .

Then they must have stumbled into a part of the afterlife that was still under construction. Hardie looked around at the buckets, the scaffolding, the painting tarps. The room reeked of caulk and cement and dust and paint, and harsh light blazed through uncovered windows. Still, you could tell that you were standing inside what most people would refer to as a castle.

And all at once, Lane figured it out.

"Oh God," Lane said. "I know where we are."

"A new wing of Hell?"

"No. We're in the Smiley Castle. You can't see it from the street, but it's the next house up on the hill. This director I know bought the place a few months ago. He wants to do a movie about the guy who built this place. A real nutcase who turned into a cult leader."

"I'm guessing your friend hasn't moved in yet."

"No. He's having the whole place redone — he's restoring it to the way it looked back in the nineteen thirties, from the flooring to the roof to the fixtures. Half the place is on order from antique dealers around the world, and it won't be finished until early next year. It's kind of his dream home and dream movie project wrapped up in one."

"Groovy," Charlie said.

Lane had read a long piece about it online a few months ago. Eventually, the massive room they were in would be restored to its Depression-era glory. Before that, it was a recording studio. Before that, a storage center for pornographic VHS cassettes. Before that, a playroom. Before that, a crime scene. And before that, not long after its construction, Jimmy Smiley's secret full-service Polynesian-style bar, where the former bootlegger-turned-Hollywood-producer-turned-devil-worshipper would take a few nips of brown lightning before descending the concrete staircase to bow at the feet of his mistress — who, in time, would ascend to the level of Dark Satanic Goddess.

"Come on," Lane said.

They wound their way through a series of halls until they reached the front doors. Outside, the roiling black smoke from the Lowenbruck house was filling the sky, and fire truck sirens were cycling down. Hardie and Lane were up too high on the hill to see the burning house below, so they had the illusion that the faux castle was floating on a polluted cloud. Behind them was the hazy apparition of the Hollywood sign, which only completed the picture. If he hadn't been engaged in a desperate struggle for survival, Hardie might have stopped to appreciate it all, to savor the view. But they had to keep moving in case their tormentors realized they weren't dead.

Hardie told Lane they needed to get the hell off these mountains and back on relatively flat ground — well, flat for California.

Lane shook her head.

"No. We need to go up."

CHAPTER
NINETEEN

It was a grim, desperate struggle for existence, and all of a sudden I was stirred by it, excited by its drama, stirred by its stark, lethal beauty.

— James M. Cain

Up?

Up seemed insane. A dead end at the top of some mountain peak. Enough time to touch the *H* in the Hollywood sign before kissing your ass good-bye.

"Trust me," she said. "I know this area. I used to go running around here all the time."

"What's up there?"

"Come on."

Hardie followed her up a set of concrete stairs that ran away from the castle along the side of one steep slope. Then they were back on Durand Drive and headed up again. None of this made sense. Who the fuck designed Hollywood, anyway — M. C. Escher? Homes were stacked on either side of the road, offering a corridor of sorts. And the road kept climbing up, up, up. The ascent was hard, sweaty work — definitely not something a man who's been skewered and poisoned and choked and nearly burned to death should be doing. Hardie was about to complain, when he saw that

178

Lane was still limping, biting her lip with every step. She was suffering, too.

As they walked past windows, Hardie imagined one of their surprise tormentors popping out of a window, bow and arrow or some other crazy weapon in their hands (*Why didn't they carry guns? What the hell was it about guns?*), ready to take them both out. Halfway up, Charlie realized how hard his heart was pounding, how much his lungs were burning and heaving. Steep fucking steps. Lane, meanwhile, who didn't have nearly as much muscle, bone, and fat to transport, darted up like a dragonfly skimming the surface of a pond.

"Hang on," Hardie said. His chest wound was killing him, his thighs ached, and he was so incredibly light-headed that at any given moment, that hazy feeling in his skull threatened to transmogrify into a giant rock, and then his head would slam into the ground, his body following.

Lane said, "We'll rest at the top."

Up.

Why the hell were they headed up instead of down?

Lane had quickly explained: the killers probably *expected* them to go back down. This was a canyon; all roads funneled back to Franklin, and it was easy to have that covered. But if they continued up into the hills, they could dart around the Lake Hollywood Reservoir and sneak back down on the Burbank side — and then find someplace to hide and sort everything out.

Burbank? Charlie thought. Wasn't that an entirely different city? Not even in Los Angeles?

But he said nothing and followed her up, up, up. This was Lane's town. What the hell did he know, other than that he'd just fucked up royally. Sure, a house he'd watched had burned before. But back then, he had saved boxes of irreplaceable items from the soon-to-be-burned-out shell. (Like the stuff in his missing carry-on.) Hardie hadn't saved jack shit from the Lowenbruck house.

"Why don't we bang on somebody's door and have them call the police?"

"You saw what they're capable of, Charlie. Yeah, we might get a cop sent out here. But they might intercept the call and send a bunch of their own guys in uniform. And then we're done."

Hardie hated to admit she was right — God, it was all so *Invasion of the Body Snatchers*. Trust no one! Warn everyone you see! Look out for trucks full of mysterious-looking pods! But she did have a point. There was only one man he really trusted. And Hardie wanted to make sure they were somewhere safe and quiet before he made that call.

"So, what then?"

"We keep going and go somewhere I can think."

"You mean we keep going up."

"Yeah."

Across the street, O'Neal watched the firefighters continue their work on the house with hoses and water, soaking the living fuck out of everything in sight. They didn't want to be the ones to let this blaze run loose up and down the hills. Mother Nature was bad enough

180

with her cleansing fires. There was no room on the schedule for stupid accidental house fires.

O'Neal stood on the side of the road, pretending to be a landscaper doing a little rubbernecking. Pretty soon he would be shooed away — already he was getting the eye from the captain on site. They needed eyes inside the house, badly. It was possible that Madden and Hardie had found really, really great hiding spots, so good that even the firefighters hadn't been able to find their bodies yet. But that seemed highly unlikely. You're stuck in the middle of a fire, you don't go hiding. You try to get out, at all costs.

Look at the 9/11 jumpers. O'Neal thought that pretty much said it all.

Rather than attract more attention, O'Neal climbed into the driver's seat, adjusted his mirrors, then started the van. He drove up Durand until he reached the point where the road met the downward-sloping hill, then made a hard right, gunning it up the hill until he reached the giant wrought-iron gates that stood in front of the road leading to the Smiley Castle.

O'Neal had been to a party at the castle a bunch of years ago — before he was part of the Industry and still had his mind on movie dreams. He remembered the crazy drive up to the main house and thinking he'd landed on Mars, not in the Hollywood Hills. He'd spent much of the party buzzed by the history of the place.

Pulling a pair of bolt cutters from the back, O'Neal quickly snipped the chains locking the gates, pulled the loose strands free, curled them up into a heavy ball, then tucked them behind a bush. Construction crews toiled on this place nonstop during the week, but it was Saturday. Day off.

Then he gunned the van up the long hill to the castle at the top. At least up here nobody would be able to see him, and maybe he could set up some surveillance from a turret or something. Give this whole operation a little class.

While waiting for word from O'Neal, Mann allowed herself a glass of water from the kitchen tap. Her stomach rumbled, but she didn't dare open a cabinet to scavenge for food. There was already so much to clean up, to reinvent, to explain, to fix. This production should have been over last night. There was no excuse for why it had taken so long, other than dumb, rotten luck. Until today, Mann had always believed that you make your own luck, you create your own fate. Now she wasn't too sure.

She took a final swallow of warm water, decided against having another glass, then used a soft terry-cloth towel to wipe away any finger- and lip prints before she replaced the glass in the cabinet with its mates.

The longer she waited, the longer she just postponed the inevitable — the report to the Industry office, the request for an additional cleanup budget, over and beyond what was already earmarked.

She took out her cell and dialed DG&A.

They'd probably want to take her off tonight's job. But there was one card left to play, and that was the fact that the other production was already moving along, and it would be impossible to pull back now. Doing so would be shortsighted and unproductive. She conceived it; she had to be on the scene to follow it through.

Would that be enough?

She'd soon know.

O'Neal pulled the scanner out of the dash and hooked it to his belt. No sign of any other bodies in the house, which was really starting to bother him. The rescue teams should have found something by now. Even a pair of barbecued bodies.

Then again, he and A.D. weren't able to find the actress when they did a full sweep of the house. They'd been interrupted by Hardie, but still — they *should* have found her. What were they missing? What was wrong with this picture?

A small, paranoid part of O'Neal wondered if the actress had even been inside. He hadn't laid eyes on her since the chase through the canyon. Mann said she'd heard her voice, using the wall-penetrating omnidirectional mics, but that sound could have been something else. Someone else.

Was she inside?

Or had she already escaped them hours ago?

Oh, for this fucking day to be over. The original production should have wrapped in a matter of seconds. Now it had ballooned into this big, sprawling, open-ended thing — the worst kind of production.

He'd been on a few messy jobs before, but nothing like this.

Well, nothing to do but listen. Maybe he could get a few questions answered once he was on top of this castle.

O'Neal was about to step out of the van, when the front door of the castle burst open and two firefighters came stumbling outside. They seemed confused, as if they'd spent the last few minutes in a carnival funhouse, forced their way through a small door, and ended up in Poughkeepsie, New York.

Smoke poured out behind the firefighters; the entire first floor seemed like it was engulfed.

Was the castle on fire, too?

No. That didn't make sense, unless a ribbon of fire had leaped over Alta Brea Drive and crashed down on the roof of the Smiley Castle like a flaming meteor. The wheels in O'Neal's mind spun, and after a few seconds he suddenly understood — both the presence of smoke and why they hadn't found any bodies yet. O'Neal pulled the van door shut and, shifting gears, hauled ass down the front driveway and rocketed back up Durand Drive.

"Mann, I think I know where they are."

Static popped in his ear. "How sure are you?"

O'Neal quickly explained what he'd seen, what he thought.

"How the fuck did we miss this?" Mann asked.

"Don't know, but it's the only thing that makes sense."

"I'll be right up."

"No time. I'm already on my way."

As Hardie chugged up past the intersection of Durand and Heather, he noticed someone had mounted three signs — bright yellow triangles, each with the image of a stick figure falling. He asked Lane to hang on for a minute. They paused in front of the signs to give Hardie a chance to catch his breath. He leaned forward, pressed down on the tops of his thighs, then straightened up again.

"Is that a joke?" Hardie asked. "Do people actually fall off the road enough to warrant a goddamned traffic sign?"

"No, it's real," Lane said. "I read about these. A while back a guy on a bike took a spill. Ended up paralyzed and filed a lawsuit against the homeowners in the area. So they put up these signs."

After a few seconds of frenzied rest, they continued their ascent, up the winding road. Dirt spilled out from the cracked and broken sides of the road, as if the hills were slowly trying to shuck themselves of the asphalt.

Each time Hardie felt like they'd finally reached the peak, there would be another bend in the road, and he'd see more of Durand curving up into the sky. There were no other pedestrians. Just houses, with no signs of life inside them, and cars wedged in every available space.

"We're almost at the reservoir."

Finally, across a valley and through the haze, he could see the ghostly letters of the Hollywood sign. Durand's name changed at some point. Hardie missed

185

the sign, if there even was one. But now he felt like he was at the top of all of creation. Behind him, Mt. Lee and the sign. In front of him, shimmering in the woozy afternoon, was downtown Los Angeles, so faint as to almost seem like a matte painting or a special effect. And in front of it was the promised reservoir — big and blue and looking like the only refreshing thing for miles.

Hardie followed Lane to a strip of honest-to-god sidewalk, which ran along the rim of an overgrown canyon. That said, it barely qualified as a place for pedestrians to walk. The paving was so narrow and so close to the road, Hardie found himself turning his head every ten seconds, to avoid being sideswiped by the cars that would appear out of nowhere. Where the fuck were they coming from? A parking garage behind the *H* in the Hollywood sign?

You had to be careful, too. One good slip and down you would go, all the way to . . . Hardie glanced down and saw a little park where people walked dogs, and little blobs that must be children raced around. So random. Just like the rest of this city.

"All we have to do is make our way down there," Lane said. "There's gotta be someone with a phone. We find a phone, we call my manager, and we'll be okay."

"Right."

"I'm serious. This is almost over."

Yeah, Hardie thought, just like my house-sitting career. This is the second house I've let burn. Got a free pass on the first one. This one — with all the fancy studio equipment inside? He doubted that Andrew Lowenbruck would be all that understanding.

Of course, it was kind of absurd to be worried about a career when you were being hunted by a group of secret killers.

Hardie must have been slowing down, because Lane prodded him:

"Come on, keep moving."

"I'm right behind you."

Hardie threw a glance over his shoulder, then took another step, and then . . .

Wait, what?

There was a white van rushing down the road. Fast. Right at them.

"Fuck?"

"What?"

In that instant there was nothing Hardie could do but push Lane and send her over the edge and then send himself right after her.

O'Neal hit the tiny curb and bounced and cut the wheel hard to the left. He had to fight to keep the van from bouncing right over the edge of the road into the canyon. What had seemed like a flash of brilliance — gunning it and spooking the actress and Hardie right over the edge — now seemed like the stupidest damn thing he'd ever done, because it would do his career no good to end up dead and upside down in the middle of a fucking park.

The van clung to the road, though. O'Neal stomped down on the brakes and brought it to a shuddering halt and immediately, without much thought, jumped into the back to grab a wasp pistol. Same principle as the wasp's nest, only in portable form, with a spray range of about fifteen feet. He pulled a box of vials from a cubby, then loaded the pistol with four shots. Then he stepped out of the van. Time to end this.

And then something slammed into his face.

Which would be Hardie's fist.

Which happened to be studded with cacti spines, and Hardie hoped it hurt like fuck. Because it had hurt like fuck to reach out and grab hold of something, *anything* . . . and realize that it was full of sharp needles. It hurt even more to scramble up through a field of fucking cacti to make it back to the pavement.

So this tall guy had nothing to complain about.

Hardie threw another punch, which made his chest, and fist, throb with agony all over again, but he really didn't care. Something dropped out of Tallboy's hands and shattered on the ground. Hardie grabbed two fistfuls of Tallboy's fake landscaping uniform and slammed him into the side of the van, and again, and again, watching the guy's neck seem to loosen with every blow.

Hardie knew he should put him in some kind of hold now, or cut off his air, something. Slap him around to revive him, then start in with the questions. Who are you. How many of you. Why do you want to kill Lane Madden. Who's in charge. But Hardie's blood was up. It didn't feel right to stop and ask questions. Fuck questions. This guy tried to run them off a road, make them fall to their deaths.

So Hardie adjusted his grip, ran Tallboy over the edge of the canyon, then launched him outward. Tallboy yelled and waved his arms and legs, and that was the last thing Hardie saw before he disappeared.

Hardie took a step back, breathed out, put his palms on his knees. Thought about the events of the day.

Women punched in the face: 2.

Men thrown off something high: 2.

Hardie was nothing if not consistent.

For an instant O'Neal felt his stomach go all giddy. The air blasted across the back of his neck, and it reminded him of a million dreams he used to have about falling to his death. He didn't want to die. Not when there was still work to be done. O'Neal threw out his hands to grab whatever he could to break his fall.

His body made impact and he instantly felt hundreds of spines stab his palms, his arms, his back, crushing the plant that held him before he started sliding backward down the hill. O'Neal pounded his heels into the ground and he clawed at the earth, fingers bent like the teeth of a rake, his brain screaming, stop STOP STOP!!!

For the third — fourth? — time in the past twelve hours, Lane Madden had saved her own life thanks to something she learned appearing in stupid action movies.

She was stunned by how many of these moves had become reflex. For instance: falling.

When you fall, you should go loose and push the air out of your lungs. Basic stunt lesson, straight from Enrico. A tense body is a hurt body.

So, when Hardie shoved her onto her back, she instinctively went loose and pushed the air out of her lungs. She also kept her head up — that is key because, of all the body parts you don't want to damage, your head is at the top of the list. As you go down, you fold yourself like an accordion, collapsing every bendable part of your body one at a time:

ankles
  knees
    hips
      elbows

Finally — if you can remember to do this — Enrico taught her to slap the ground with her palms to help break the fall. Lane ran through these steps countless times while training for *Your Kiss Might Kill Me* — hours of nothing but falls on an exercise mat. Then Enrico took away the mat. If Lane could do anything, it was fall.

There was no mat here. No flat surface either. And her bendable parts were already sore beyond reason. But the technique still worked, and after Lane slapped the ground, she reached out for the fat stubby trunk of a bush. She rolled over onto her back just in time to see Charlie sliding past. Lane reached out and grabbed a

190

handful of his T-shirt. Which ripped six inches and then . . . held, preventing him from sliding the rest of the way down into the canyon.

At the end of her arm, Charlie wriggled like an insect caught until he found some handholds, some footing. One he'd stabilized himself, she heard him hiss:

"I'm going to fuck up that motherfucker."

And then up Charlie went, scrambling through the brush and cacti. He'd just cleared the top when Lane heard a door creaking open.

Lane made it up just in time to see Hardie launching their tormentor over the edge.

The craziest thing was the absolute exhilaration Hardie felt watching Tallboy's body disappear. It was a sensation he thought had been lost to him. Strange that the one thing that made him feel alive for the first time in three years was killing somebody.

CHAPTER
TWENTY

*Listen, Charlie, before we go in, there's something I
have to tell you. It's been on my conscience, and
you can punch me if you want to.*

— Oliver Platt, *The Ice Harvest*

The keys were still in the van, hanging from the
steering column. They climbed inside. Lane eased back
into the passenger seat, not offering to drive, not saying
a word. Hardie was about to give her shit about being
Miss Daisy but then remembered the accident. She'd
probably done enough driving for one day.

He craned his neck around to make sure there were
no hidden surprises in the back of the van.

Now he saw that the back was *loaded*.

Lane heard him move and cracked open an eye.

"Where are you going?"

"Hang on."

The cargo area was packed neatly, efficiently. Row
upon row of plastic containers assembled on metal
racks. Some of the stuff he recognized. Hardie popped
open the top of one container. Syringes, sterile and
sealed in plastic. Hardie checked another. Rubber
tubing, the kind nurses use when they draw blood.
Another container: gauze and tape. Hardie knew he
should grab as much of this crap as possible. He was in

shock and in too much pain to be slapping on bandages at the moment, but they would come in handy later. If there was a later.

Another container was full of small plastic bags of coke, heroin, and other goodies Hardie recognized from his days battling Philly drug gangs with Nate. The street value, based on his best guestimate, was enough to buy a house in the suburbs. And probably a sweet piece of automotive eye candy to park in the front drive.

Other items weren't so familiar. Hardie popped the top of a plastic container that held a bright orange suit that was heavy and reeked of rubber. Another contained little pouches labeled RSDL — "reactive skin decontamination lotion" — and next to it, a box of injectable ampoules of hydroxocobalamin.

Then there was a box in the middle of the floor, half full of little spring-loaded vials. Just like the ones Hardie saw in that box they'd mounted on the front door of the Lowenbruck house. He fished one out, held it up to the light. Inside, clear liquid. Didn't look like anything, really. Hardie slid it into his back pocket. You never know.

There were no guns. With every container top he opened, Hardie kept hoping, wishing, praying. But there was not so much as a slingshot.

"Charlie, come *on*. What are you doing?"

"One minute."

There it was. Tucked into the corner, sealed in thick, opaque plastic.

His luggage.

Hardie reached out and touched it, just to make sure it wasn't a mirage. He pressed his fingertips against it, saw the headless Spider-Man, and *yeah*. Definitely his bag. Hardie wondered what they had planned on doing with it. Burn it? Bury it? Divvy it up with a dice game? Which made Hardie think about the poor courier who'd had the unlucky assignment of delivering this bag. His body wasn't in the van, and his delivery truck was nowhere in sight. Which was further proof that the world was random and mean and didn't really give a shit about anybody. The world would run you down and slam a tire over your exploding skull and not even wonder what it had just hit.

Hardie was about to go back to the front of the van, when he remembered his carry-on. It should be back here somewhere. Maybe tucked away in some secret compartment?

Hardie began opening more tiny doors, kicking others. Had to be here. Where else would they have put it?

"Charlie! Get up here now or *I'm* getting behind the wheel."

"Hang on."

"Seriously? You're really going to do this to me?"

"Coming, coming . . ."

The carry-on bag contained the only thing that couldn't be replaced, the one link to his old life, the one reminder that he used to be a decent person . . .

Had to be here.

Somewhere.

194

While Lane waited, literally on the edge of her seat, trying not to scream at Charlie for taking, like, *fucking forever* back there . . . her eyes fell on the GPS unit mounted in the dashboard. Huh. Maybe this would show where these creepy bastards lived. She tapped the touch screen and cycled backward through the searches until a familiar address popped up.

Her own.

572 Westminster Avenue, Venice, CA.

Goddamn it, did they come to the house last night? How long had they been watching her?

She tapped the screen again and another address appeared. One that made her body turn ice cold.

No . . .

They *couldn't.*

The carry-on wasn't back here. Clearly the fuckers had stashed it somewhere else.

Hardie knew he was wasting time. They had to move. Now.

He gathered up a bunch of first aid-type supplies, unzipped the side of his bag, and shoved everything inside. He climbed back into the front and noticed Lane tapping the screen of a fancy-ass GPS unit on the dashboard. Hardie caught a glimpse of an address in bright white letters — *11804 Bloomfield St.* — before Lane tapped the screen again and it went dark.

"What was that?" Hardie asked.

"No idea," Lane said.

"Hang on. Pull that address back up. Maybe that thing can tell us where these bastards live."

"Already thought of it, already looked. There's nothing. Just a lot of random places. Can we drive already, please?"

Just drive, Charlie.
Please don't ask me to explain.
Thankfully, Charlie let the thing rest . . . for the moment. He slid the van gearshift into drive and tapped the gas and they lurched forward. All at once a horn blasted and a black Audi swerved around them, missing them by inches. As the Audi zoomed forward, a slender feminine hand appeared out of the open passenger window and extended a dainty middle finger. A beat later, a male hand popped out of the driver's side, the thick middle finger lifted high and proud, the driver making sure they could see it over the top of the roof. Both held their salutes until the Audi was a good tenth of a mile away. Just to make sure they didn't miss the message.

Charlie muttered, "Nice fucking town."

"Do you want me to drive?" Lane asked. "Because —"

"No."

After a wide curve, they passed a rocky overlook where a couple of groups of tourists lined up to take photos of one another with the shimmering reservoir and City of Angels in the background. Lane looked at all of their cars parked along the road. The children all bounced around up there, mugging for the camera, some of the older ones flashing fake gang signs.

"Lane."

"Yeah."

"You said you know this area."

"Yeah."

"Well, you mind directing me the nearest highway?"

"I just thought of something."

"What?"

"Do you think they have this thing LoJacked or something? They could be tracking us right now."

Hardie sighed.

"You know what? I don't give a shit. I'm tired of crawling through cactus plants and running up stairs and down mountains. Let's put a few miles between us and them, then ditch the van somewhere."

"So that's your big plan."

"Well, sweetie, to tell you the truth, I'm kind of making it up as I go along here. I should be drunk in somebody else's house, watching *Singing in the Fucking Rain*, okay?"

Lane couldn't stop thinking about that address, what it meant that the address was programmed into *this* GPS unit, in *this* van.

By the time they reached Lake Hollywood Drive, Charlie announced that he did have a plan, as a matter of fact. Charlie wanted to call somebody named Deke, kept repeating, Deke will know how to handle this, Deke this and Deke that, prompting Lane to finally ask who the hell Deke might be. Deke turned out to be Deacon Clark, some FBI agent Charlie knew from his Philadelphia days.

"That's pretty much the dumbest fucking idea in the history of dumb ideas," Lane said.

"Why?" Hardie asked.

"Haven't you been listening to anything I've said? The Accident People are *connected*. Once our names go into the system, any system, anywhere in the world, we're done. That means no police station. No hospitals. Certainly no FBI."

"Then, what's your bright idea?"

"We call my manager," Lane said. "She'll know exactly what to do, who to call."

Charlie frowned. "Right. So don't call my trusted source. Let's call yours?"

Lane said nothing, because she realized that Charlie might be right. Hard to tell who to trust anymore. Every time she thought about who may have sold her out to these bastards, her heart started to ache.

There were very few people who knew what happened.

There were very few people who knew that address . . .

Including Haley, her manager.

How did Lane know that she *wasn't* involved? How else were they able to tap into her alcohol-monitoring anklet, know her every move, and know what was crawling around in her mind over the past week, unless they got to Haley?

She was not prepared — not financially, not physically — to go into hiding. She was too notorious to appeal to the media. Not without them painting her as a drug-addled paranoid nutcase. She couldn't run to Haley. Andrew was in Russia. She had nobody, nobody at all except . . .

Hardie twisted and turned the stolen death van through the streets of — well, he didn't even know where this was. Was it Burbank? The Valley? He just wanted to see a road he recognized. He had L.A. boiled down to a few major routes in his brain: the 101, the 405, the 10. People complained about the gridlock and the psycho drivers, but that didn't matter much to Hardie, since he was usually only passing through on the way to a house. Besides, he understood highways. He was used to Philly's I-95 and the "Sure-Kill" Expressway. After a few minutes he finally saw it: a sign to the 101. He merged into the southbound lanes and headed down into Hollywood.

Lane looked at Hardie. "Okay, so where are we going?"

"Downtown. Or wherever there are a lot of people."

"So you want to get stuck in downtown when we're fleeing a group of unstoppable killers?"

Hardie thought about the one he'd sent flying off the edge of the cliff. *That* sorry son of a bitch didn't seem too unstoppable. The guy's surprised scream echoed in his mind. In fact, Hardie probably should worry about how much he liked replaying it.

Hardie signaled left, then changed lanes.

"What would you prefer to do? Drive out to the middle of nowhere, so they can hunt us down and kill us in total privacy? When you're in trouble, you run toward people, not away from them. If they're going to make a play, they're not going to do it in broad daylight."

"How do you know? I mean, they attacked me on a highway this morning. It was early, but there were plenty of other cars on the road. They didn't seem to give a shit. Charlie, they could be tracking us right now, fixed on a LoJack signal or some crazy shit like that. Any one of these cars could just smash into us . . ."

"They wouldn't do the same thing twice."

"How do you know? Seriously, how the hell do you know *what* they would do? God, I feel like we made it out of that house but we're still trapped, no matter where we go. It's not as if I can hide all that easily. People tend to recognize me. Even when I'm looking like shit."

Hardie glanced over at her. She was still a beautiful woman, despite the dirt and blood and swollen eye. He guessed that's what separated famous people from the rest of humanity. People *would* recognize her.

And then Hardie figured it out. Their next move, until he could call Deke.

"Where's Musso and Frank?"

"The restaurant?"

"Yeah."

Lane shook her head, squinted, held up her hands. "Why the fuck do you want to go to Musso and Frank?"

Hardie told her:

"Lunch."

They blasted past the entrance to the Hollywood Bowl. An electric marquee was mounted in a stately chunk of white stone; a jazz musician Hardie didn't know was performing here tonight, 8p.m. Cars fought their way into the parking lot. Cars full of people who probably had no worries on their minds. After all, they were going out in the cool California afternoon on a Saturday to see somebody play jazz. How tough could life be?

But Hardie had always felt that way — separate from the good times everyone else seemed to be having. Like his own little world somehow sat parallel to the real world, but not actually *in it*.

"Get over to the left," Lane said. "No, really, *right now.*"

"I'm trying."

But other vehicles quickly closed the gap, forcing Hardie to retreat. Somehow he ended up being corralled into the right lane. All down Highland giant billboards advertised movies he hadn't heard of, featuring actors and actresses who were equally unfamiliar. Some of the cars on the road looked bizarre to him, too, now that he was really looking at them. If his life were a DVD, Hardie thought he must have skipped over a couple of chapters.

"Okay, we missed Franklin, so turn right onto Hollywood. We'll have to come around."

"Where . . .?"

"Hollywood Boulevard. The next light. Right. As in turn right . . . *right now!*"

And suddenly Hardie found himself at L.A. Tourist Ground Zero. Some of his homeowners had cautioned him to avoid this area at all costs. The sidewalks were jammed with goofy tourists being preyed upon by people in costumes and photographers and drug dealers and hustlers and punks. Traffic came to standstill a few car lengths away from Grauman's Chinese Theatre. Hardie saw that the marquee read PROXIMITY, which apparently was having its premiere tonight. Another movie he'd never heard of. Outside, along dark velvet ropes, people stood around with vacant stares. Waiting to be entertained, trying to ignore the hustlers and kids hawking CDs.

"So . . . Musso and Frank?"

"Back that way a block or two," Lane said. "You were kidding about lunch, right?"

Right in front of Grauman's, Hardie stopped, put the van in park, pressed down on the emergency brake, flipped on the fourways. The car ahead of him inched forward a few feet. The car behind Hardie noticed, and gave a tap of his horn.

"Okay, this is good. This will work," Hardie said.

"Right, Charlie?"

"Follow me."

And there, right in the middle of Hollywood Boulevard, Hardie turned off the ignition, pulled out the keys, and stepped outside.

Lane stared at him as if he were an astronaut who'd announced he was going for a stroll and just opened the air lock without his helmet on.

"Charlie?"

But what else could she do except follow him? Lane opened the passenger door, unsnapped her belt, slid off the seat, and started limping toward the back of the van. Charlie had already opened up the back doors. He grabbed the suitcase. The guy in the car behind them, just two feet away, moaned *what the fuck* so loudly she could hear it through the glass of his windshield. He blasted them with his horn again. Hardie looked up, smiled, and gave him a tiny Queen of England wave.

Lane touched his shoulder.

"Uh, you know we can't stop here. The cops are going to be up our asses in about two seconds."

"Then I guess it's a good thing we won't be here."

"Please explain that."

Charlie pulled the retractable handle out from the suitcase, then extended his left arm formally.

"Shall we?"

Now other car horns were screaming at them. Charlie didn't seem to care. He looked over at a crowd gathered on the sidewalk — hustlers, moms, dads, punks, homeless guys, toddlers, costumed superheroes, models — and shouted:

"Hey, Hollywood types! Free drugs! Help yourself, right inside the van."

Hardie launched the van keys up in the air toward Grauman's. People jumped out of the way and cursed as the keys made their descent back to earth. Then Hardie linked arms with Lane and pulled his rolling suitcase down the coral-and-charcoal paving block of the Hollywood Walk of Fame.

CHAPTER
TWENTY-ONE

*I found out something I never knew. I found out
my world was not the real world.*

— Robert F. Kennedy

"A Manhattan on the rocks," Hardie said, adding, "lots
of ice." "Yes, sir."

The tuxedoed waiter moved away from the table and
headed toward the oak bar.

Musso & Frank was a Hollywood legend. Even
Hardie was familiar with the place. Countless directors,
actors, screenwriters had sat in these same chairs,
knocking back tumblers of booze and sawing into
chops and making big Hollywood deals. Hardie knew
this because one night — bored out of his mind and
with no new movies to watch — he had watched a
DVD extra that gave a quickie history of the place. As
Hardie understood it, Musso & Frank was where you
came to create dreams, and others could just gawk.

Which was the whole idea.

From the moment they stepped inside, everybody
was staring at them.

Granted, Hardie would have stared at them, too.
Their clothes were dirty and torn and blood-encrusted.
Hardie was pretty sure he had blood caked all around
his head and neck. The gore that had seeped through

204

his gray T-shirt had left it stiff and dark. He was also dragging along his stupid luggage, headless Spider-Man and all, which was probably a faux pas unto itself.

But he was here with World Famous Actress Lane Madden, and that made all the difference.

The maître d', an older gray-haired man in a natty suit, blanched at first but then recognized her face. If Lane Madden wanted a table, then she would receive a table, no matter her physical appearance. He didn't flinch. Maybe he was used to actors showing up in their makeup, looking like they crawled away from a plane crash site.

But everyone else . . .

It was clear no one had ever seen anything like this. Not even this midafternoon crowd of lingering lunch-hour boozers and people hoping to get Saturday night started early.

Oh, the stares.

Hardie looked at her. "Aren't you going to order something?"

"I feel like I need to throw up. Like I'm having bed spins but I haven't been drinking. I should really call my manager."

"Have some bread. Or a drink."

"I don't want any food. And I'm not allowed to have any alcohol. What are we doing here?"

"You're in public, being seen. If everything you've told me is true, then this is the last place They'd want you. Consider this a big ol' thumb in their eyes."

"But Musso's? Why here?"

"Why not? This is a Hollywood power joint, right?"

"Uh . . ."

Hardie was about to tell her about the DVD extra, when someone stood up from the bar and approached their table. Instinctively, Hardie reached for a butter knife, tensed himself. The guy, wearing a designer T-shirt and jeans, held up a phone and snapped a photo, then walked away without a word. So, that's how they do you here in L.A. Quick and dirty. Hardie put the knife back on the table and called after the guy.

"You're welcome, buddy."

They were here to be seen — but not for long. The way Hardie figured it, they'd stay just long enough to have a drink and be photographed and gossiped about. In a world where jacking off in the back of a porno theater makes you notorious, this couldn't help but raise some eyebrows. Hardie saw it as pissing on the burning embers of their failed "accidental death."

They'd get noticed, and Topless's little plans would fall apart, and then they'd get out of here and go ghost for a while and have Deke call in the cavalry.

Lane, meanwhile, looked sick to her stomach.

The guy with the cell phone — a production assistant named Josh Geary — quickly cut through the length of the restaurant and headed out the back to the parking lot. This was insane, what he just saw. Josh checked the photo again, squinting, but yeah. Lane Madden, looking like she'd just crawled out of her own grave. A few key presses later, the photo was on its way to a web editor he knew back in NYC. Geary was leaving for

NYC next month, and hey, it couldn't hurt to send a little gift ahead of time.

The editor, whose name was Zoey Jordan, texted back: I WANT TO HAVE YOUR ABORTION. (Ah, those *Fight Club* jokes never got old.) Jordan worked at a celebrity gossip blog. NYC-based, but they also ran L.A. stuff. Especially L.A. stuff like this.

Within twenty seconds, the photo was online with a snarky headline: LIFE IN THE FAST . . . ER, LANE?

Hardie was confused. Sitting across the table, Lane looked like she'd just been handed a death sentence.

"This is a good thing," Hardie said. "We've just proven you didn't die in a car crash this morning."

"Uh huh."

"They can't do a thing now. They wanted to kill you and make it look like an accident and they failed. You're sitting here in public. That dork in the two-hundred-dollar T-shirt probably just saved your life. He sends it to his friends, they'll send it around."

"But then what comes next?"

Hardie looked around the restaurant. Where was the waiter with his Manhattan? His brain worked better on booze, he was sure of it. Half of the shit that happened to him today wouldn't have happened if he'd had a minor buzz on.

"Look, I know you said that these *Accident People* are connected at the highest levels. Which sounds like a stupid movie line, by the way. Anyway, there's one guy I trust, literally, with my life."

"Now *that* sounds like a stupid movie line."

"Touché. And that's the guy I told you about. Deke. He can't be touched. He's straighter than a grizzly's dick. I can call him, and he'll have an investigation going by the time my drink arrives. He lives for shit like this. He'll investigate. Everything comes out in the open."

Everything comes out in the open.

Charlie's words broadsided her.

That was exactly what she'd been afraid of for three years now, wasn't it? The very thought of it terrified her. Even worse than dying. Because if she had died back on the 101, if she hadn't been lucky with that stupid martial arts move and that fistful of safety glass . . . then at least her worst memory would have died with her.

God, all this time, fighting Them, struggling to survive, escaping, running, begging for a chance to live . . .

Maybe all this time she should have been rooting for them.

Because once everything comes out in the open . . .

This time, Factboy was in the bathroom legitimately — taking a quick leak — when the phone in his cargo pants pocket buzzed. He shook, zipped up, then checked the screen and smiled. A Google alert on Lane Madden. He read it, then read it again, just to make sure his eyes weren't playing tricks on him or somebody hadn't linked to an *Onion* piece or something. Then he autodialed Mann.

"She's at Musso and Frank," Factboy said.

"Right now?"

"Right now."

"Doing what?"

"Having drinks, apparently."

There was a pause on the line; for a moment Factboy worried that Mann would be thinking he was playing a joke, or fucking around with her for some reason (though he'd never dare). Instead she said:

"You know, I could kiss you."

And with that, the call terminated.

Factboy's face melted into a loose grin. It wasn't that he relished a kiss from someone like Mann — even if she was hot, she was still scary as fuck. No, what made Factboy happy was that warm, fuzzy glow of job security, the knowledge that he'd done well, and that he could bask in it for a few minutes. When he rejoined his family at dinner, his wife was pleasantly surprised he'd returned so quickly.

And Factboy told his kids that, yes, they could order ice cream out on the back porch after they finished their meals.

O'Neal eased himself onto a wooden bench in the Lake Hollywood dog park. Hands and legs scraped to hell, bruising all up and down his back, head throbbing, eyes watering. What hurt most, though, was his pride. They have a word for henchmen who fuck up. And that would be . . . *ex-henchmen*. He could imagine Mann berating him. If he hadn't gone after them solo, they wouldn't have a van loaded with gear and sensitive information now, would they?

As if on cue, his cell vibrated.

Mann.

"We've got approval on a budget extension. But we need to wrap this up right now. No excuses, no more mistakes."

"I'm fine, Mann, really, thanks for asking."

Mann ignored him. O'Neal supposed he should know better than to expect concern about his well-being or health. In her mind, O'Neal had fucked up.

"I have two new team members bringing a vehicle," Mann said. "I've got your position. Stay where you are. We'll come get you."

"Do you even know where they are?"

"Yeah. I know."

"And you've got a new narrative in mind?"

"Of course."

At long last the waiter placed the Manhattan on the table in front of Hardie. Sparkling reddish amber, packed with fresh ice, a vision of Heaven if Hardie ever saw one. But he shocked himself by not touching it. Not until he figured out what was up with Lane, who was staring at his drink.

"What is it? What's wrong? I mean, besides the — well, obvious?"

Lane picked up a fork from the table, then pressed her thumbs against it until her knuckles turned white.

"I'm going to tell you something I haven't told anybody."

"Okay."

"You're not going to like it."

"Okay."

Lane told her story.

Three years ago — January.

They'd been goofing around in her new car, speeding down Mulholland Drive in the late afternoon. He said for a real thrill you had to do Mulholland in the dark, in the rain, going like 90 miles per hour. She told him he was ridiculous. He told her that *he* should drive, really show her what the car could do. The car was factory-new. Delivered yesterday. Yesterday she'd been on a shoot, the last day. The car was a present from the director. The car was a thing of high-speed beauty. She loved it, and loved that it made Blond Viking God jealous. She could tell.

The delivery guys woke her up. The shoot had been long, grueling. She was fried to the point of not knowing what day it was, or what a normal routine felt like. This was always the case; it took a few weeks of film detox before she felt normal again. By then she'd be diving back in for her next role. Which was fine. She wanted to keep busy. She liked being busy. She'd heard a term — *journeyman actor* — and liked it. It meant she wouldn't flame out quickly. She preferred to have thirty decent movies on her IMDB page than a handful of spectacular smashes and utter flameouts.

Blond Viking God told her she was lazy; anything less than Total World Domination wasn't worth her time.

Blond Viking God was in a position to say something like that. Even then, three years ago, he was the Blond Viking God.

So she received her new car and quickly showered and dressed and ate a croissant — the first breadlike food she'd had in five weeks — and poured some orange juice down her throat and went off to Blond Viking God's place in Santa Monica. He was hung-over but immediately suggested a drink.

She pouted a little — she'll admit that much. She wanted to go driving around L.A. Something she used to do all the time.

Wait until I show you Decker Canyon Road, she said.

Fuck that, he said. Mulholland or nothing, baby!

He had a few drinks, and then she was coerced into having a beer — again, the first booze she'd had in five weeks, since the start of the shoot. The first sip was a cold, fuzzy blast. Wow. Reluctantly, she accepted another beer, nursing it as he tossed back bourbon. He'd been on a big bourbon kick lately, having come back from shooting a gothic/science-fiction thing down in New Orleans. Bought it by the case. She hoped it was a phase; she didn't like kissing him after a bourbon jag.

She saw the light in his eyes go dimmer and dimmer, and she hated when that happened. He got to a certain point where it was impossible to reach him. So she said, shoes on, we're going for a ride.

He put his shoes on; they went for a ride.

They didn't go as far as Decker Canyon Road — honestly, she was afraid all the twists and turns would make him puke. And sorry, she was not cleaning Blond Viking God vomit out of her factory-new sports car. He egged her on — Mulholland, baby! Mulholland! Until finally she agreed, taking the PCH up to Sunset, then up Beverly Glen.

Finally to Mulholland.

He gleefully told her the story behind the name. Mulholland was a government official who was responsible for the deaths of at least 450 people — including forty-some kids — when a dam burst.

Only in L.A., he said, would they name a road after someone like that.

They stopped at a lookout, at which point Blond Viking God grabbed the keys.

No.

C'mon.

Fuck, no. Don't be an idiot.

I'm fine. I just want to give it a test spin.

And I'm saying no.

He jingled the keys in front of her.

Just a mile or so.

How much bourbon did you drink?

See you at the bottom.

She screamed his name —

But ultimately he won, because he always won, because he was the Blond Viking God and he raced her factory-new sports car down Mulholland Drive, yelling, NOW, THIS IS HOW YOU DO IT.

They didn't die.

They didn't hit anyone.

Frankly, he was actually okay behind the wheel.

And Lane had to admit, maybe she was being silly, because it was a pretty amazing ride, the cool January air making all of L.A. look crystal-clear sharp down to the molecule. And there they were, on top of everything.

They decided to get a bite down in the valley. Somewhere quiet, out of the way. He said he knew the perfect place. They went down Beverly Glen to Ventura. Blond Viking God was confused; he knew it was here somewhere, but maybe he'd passed it. So he hooked a left onto a side street, then another left, onto another side street. I'm hungry, he said, then gunned it. He saw the kid two seconds before — chasing a Wiffle ball into the street. He slammed the brakes. The tires screamed. She screamed. None of it did any good.

The world ended.

Lane saw the white ball spinning, slowly making its way to the opposite curb.

He cursed.

He looked around.

He cursed again.

He put the car in reverse.

Lane screaming, WHAT ARE YOU DOING

He raced around the kid and rocketed the rest of the way up the street, even though doors were opening all around them.

WE CAN'T WE CAN'T

She looked back and saw his little body and she screamed again, but they were cut off by a hairpin turn to the right, and then everything receded into the distance.

Hardie's fingers touched his Manhattan, but he didn't lift the drink from the table. He watched her as she spoke. Low tones, quiet and calm, as if she had been rehearsing this tale ever since it happened. But she wasn't acting — there was a difference. She wasn't becoming someone else. This was the real her, beneath everything else. Letting it all go.

"They never caught you," Hardie said.

"They never caught us," she said, "because of the Accident People."

He called his manager.

His manager gave him shit right away — Lane could tell, even hearing just one side of the conversation. But Blond Viking God put the manager back in his place and made his wishes explicitly clear:

GET ME THE FUCK OUT OF THIS.

See, the Blond Viking God could not be wrapped up in a manslaughter trial. The Blond Viking God had a full slate, and nothing could stop that without the risk of losing a ridiculous amount of money. Even Blond Viking God's death wouldn't stop the production of the next six films — two of them summer tent-poles — because, by God, the money men would find a way to reanimate his fucking corpse to finish them.

And the manager understood that.

So the manager advised his client:

HIDE

And then he called the studio's lawyers, who got word to the top, and it was deemed important enough to bring in the Accident People.

By then Blond Viking God had taken them all the way out beyond the San Bernadinos; they were directed to a garage in Chatsworth. The car would have to be destroyed; the studio was already arranging for a duplicate to be delivered to Lane's Venice address. They were cleaned up, given new clothes. They were told to never, ever speak of this. Because it didn't happen. It would be erased.

The Accident People asked the Blond Viking God for his precise route. A third car was procured — same make, same model, same color. Two actors were hired. They drove around Sherman Oaks recklessly, then disappeared.

By 7p.m. they were having drinks at the Standard, having arrived there in Blond Viking God's own car (which had been delivered from Santa Monica). Cameras flashed; the music was throbbing. Friends were there. They asked how it felt to have a day or two off, wow, what did you do? They told their friends what the Accident People had suggested: just fucking around all day at Lane's place in Venice.

Lane was quiet but compliant. She drank and tried to will her hands to STOP SHAKING.

At the same time, the duplicate car, with stand-ins, was cruising around Studio City. The Accident People listened. The police received calls — reports of

216

someone driving a vehicle like a maniac around their neighborhood. The hit-and-run was huge news. The victim, an eight-year-old boy, had died at the scene. The description of the car had gone out wide. Police vowed to catch these "animals."

The Accident People took care of the loose ends with piles of cash. The car dealer: silenced. The director: silenced — and he didn't even need the incentive. There was no upside to having your movie's star arrested for manslaughter.

Lane's hands didn't stop shaking for days.

Not long after, she and the Blond Viking God split. She stopped calling him, he stopped wondering if she'd call. Still, they were considered a "hot couple" by the various celebrity mags for the next nine months.

Lane went to her manager, told him she didn't know if she could do this. The manager said there wasn't a choice.

The studio threw a ton of work at her. Action movies. Something different for her. Lane thought she'd hate it. Turned out she loved it. Loved the preparation, the intensity, the physicality, the mindless-ness of it all.

She did that for two years.

Then, about a year ago, she caught sight of a billboard for a new reality show:

The Truth Hunters.

It was *America's Most Wanted 2.0* — a fugitive-catching show mashed together with *Unsolved Mysteries* and forensic supercop and cold case dramas. All of it one hundred percent true. Each installment had a single sponsor. The sponsor gave a pile of cash. The producers handpicked cases. The cash was used to reopen the investigation and *get things done.* Stage new forensics tests. New lab reports. New photographs. New simulations.

Famously, the executive producer, Jonathan Hunter, did not take a dime from the show; he claimed to use every available resource to catch "people who thought they could get away with it." He lived in the same, slightly cramped Studio City home that he and his wife, Evelyn, had purchased back in the late 1980s; the family was supported by his wife's income. But what really touched the hearts of viewers was the fact that Jonathan Hunter knew what it was like to have an unsolved case eat away at your soul. His son Kevin had been struck and killed by a hit-and-run driver one afternoon two years before.

Lane told Hardie:

"We're the ones who did it."

And with that billboard on Sunset Boulevard began Lane's final descent.

Now Lane prepared for it — the look of sheer hatred that she'd somehow managed to avoid for the past three years. The judgment, the fury, the disgust. The punishment. Boil it down and Lane realized it was just like being a kid, where the thing you fear the most is *getting in trouble.*

Instead, Hardie said:

"We should go."

CHAPTER
TWENTY-TWO

*The world is divided into three classes of people: a
very small group that makes things happen
a somewhat larger group that watches things happen
and the great multitude which never
knows what happened.*

— Nicholas Murray Butler

The name on the cell phone display screen: DGA.

Code for Doyle, Gedney and Abrams, the law firm that acted as the intermediary between Mann and her Industry employers. She knew the call was coming. That didn't make answering the phone any easier.

"This is Mann."

"Gedney. We see the job from earlier this morning still isn't finished, the second job is looming. We're worried you have too much on your plate."

"I can finish both."

"You can? Are you certain?"

"Absolutely."

"Same time frame?"

"The same."

Never mind that DG&A gave her almost no prep time on this. Zero. Just a call last Saturday giving her the basics: two jobs, and we'd like an operational plan by the end of the day. Sure, no problem, not doing anything else, anyway. A half hour later a courier delivered two thick bio packets. One containing a full rundown on Lane Madden. The other a family of four, with the father involved in television, extremely high-profile, special treatment needed.

Mann spent the next five hours sketching out an operational plan for the family. Their deaths couldn't be something stupid like a gas explosion or a car wreck because of the nature of the father's work. It needed to be logical, compelling, and absolute — no room for conspiracy theories. Mann believed she did her best work under pressure, and by the end of the brainstorming session, she was fairly proud of what she'd concocted. It would mean a lot of work behind the scenes, but it was well worth it.

Planning the Lane Madden job, on the other hand, took about five minutes.

After speeding through the bio materials DG&A had sent, Mann decided on a Sleeping Beauty. Actors were usually easy, and Lane Madden's recent career highlights made it even easier.

Three years ago she'd been involved in a hit-and-run accident. Doyle, Gedney and Abrams had hired a director to wipe it from existence. Madden was sworn to secrecy.

After two years of roles in back-to-back action blockbusters — some that performed okay, the rest abysmal bombs — Madden cracked. An arrest on drug-related charges. A failed stint in a drug-treatment program was followed by another arrest, this time for drunk-and-disorderly behavior. While on bail, Madden was arrested on still another drug charge when her room at the Fairmont Miramar was searched following an anonymous 911 tip. Thanks to California Prop 36, she was given probation instead of jail time. She was also forced to wear an alcohol-and-drug-monitoring bracelet.

(Mann couldn't help but smile at that one. It made her even easier to track.)

After that final indignity, reported pretty much everywhere — and with much gusto — Lane appeared to find Jesus. She cleaned up. The press hounded her, but the new Lane appeared to be the real thing. Rumor had it she was seeing someone, but nobody could pin down a name or a face. For the past three months, no lapses, no arrests. And then, just last week, there was a job offer, her first in a year, and not a stupid action movie. A serious role, portraying a single mother in an adaptation of the bestselling novel *Blood Will Out*. Things looked up for Lane Madden.

And now she had to die.

Because while she may have found Jesus, she'd also discovered a penchant for confession. The past three years had been a living hell for her, she told her new boyfriend, composer Andrew Lowenbruck. She'd thrown herself into work for nearly two years straight, appearing in pretty much everything her manager could dig up for her. As long as she was working, she didn't care what it was. But then she saw that *Truth Hunters* billboard; something in her snapped. The drinking started shortly thereafter in a hotel room, first with two mini-bottles of vodka, followed by two mini-bottles of rum, followed by a small bottle of white wine, followed by a room-service order of a salad with lite Caesar dressing and two bottles of Grey Goose. And then finally a phone call to an old connection, and down she went, right into the scandal sites and entertainment mags.

Was anybody really going to question her overdosing after a party late one California night?

Not even her manager would blink. (That is, if her manager weren't already beholden to Doyle, Gedney — client loyalty was one thing, but agency loyalty was another.)

"Restore some confidence in me," Gedney said now. "Because from where I'm sitting, we have an actress who's gone public, and who right now might be going to the media. We also have a van packed with your toys in the middle of Hollywood Boulevard."

"Taking care of the van already," Mann said. "A friend in the LAPD is keeping it tucked away and off the books."

"And the target?"

"We know where they are, and we will pin them down shortly," Mann said. "Once we have them isolated, I already have a new narrative that will explain today's events."

"You do."

"Yes."

"And this Charles Hardie? What do you know about him?"

Mann didn't want to tell them the truth: that she had Factboy digging up everything on Hardie, hoping to find some kind of L.A. connection aside from his house-sitting gigs, maybe a retired cop he knew and trusted, or a family member somewhere in Southern California. Hardie of all people knew you couldn't just disappear.

"I'm not worried about Hardie. He's wounded and has few friends out here. Or anywhere, for that matter."

Gedney said nothing. Mann hated that worst of all.

"This will work," Mann said, hating the sound of pleading that was creeping into her voice.

"Don't fuck it up. You know what's on the line."

"Of course."

The trip was over; Mrs. Factboy was tired of Factboy's stomach issues and decided to call it quits. Back home in Flagstaff, the kids ran around outside like maniacs while he finally was able to dig deeper into the Charles Hardie mythos. Nice to use a desktop instead of a phone. After hours of that, his finger muscles felt like they were going to permanently seize up.

What Factboy was able to crack open in fifteen minutes was disturbing.

What was even more disturbing: the stuff he couldn't crack open.

"Listen to this," he told Mann. He spoke quickly, but concisely:

"Charlie Hardie was never a cop. Never wore a badge, never did so much as a single push-up at the academy. The "consultant" thing isn't exactly accurate either. According to sealed grand jury testimony, Hardie acted as the Philadelphia PD's secret gunslinger, tacitly approved by high department brass. When a door needed kicking in, they called for Hardie. When a witness needed to be kept safe until trial, they asked Hardie to step in. And sometimes, when the law considered itself impotent in the face of some greater threat, and a force of evil needed to be eliminated, they handed the gun to Hardie."

This was not explicitly stated in the grand jury testimony, Factboy said, but you could easily read between the lines.

"Hardie's handler and "rabbi" — the man who brought him in — was a legendary detective named Nathaniel Parish. The two had grown up together in a rough neighborhood on the fringes of North Philadelphia. Each had taken his separate career path until they met up one night nine years ago when Hardie came back to the old neighborhood and found himself at war with a drug gang on a witness-intimidation kick. By the time Parish arrived at the scene, Hardie was in a rowhome, surrounded by bodies, drenched in blood that was not his own, having tea with the owner of that rowhome — an eighty-four-year-old witness to an arson/torture/murder. They were talking about the old days, Hardie even chuckling, despite the carnage around him. Parish arrested him, but all records of the arrest were destroyed. In exchange, Hardie agreed to work with Parish. And in Philadelphia, there was much work to be done.

"I've got most of their secret case files," Factboy said. "You could write a series of novels based on these damned things."

This highly illegal strange partnership, born of a massacre in the heart of the city, came to an end in another massacre — almost three years ago to the day. "I told you all about that thing," Factboy said. "His origin story, if you will."

"Uh-huh."

"In the aftermath, it was left to a fed named Deacon Clark to pick up the pieces. He helped Hardie's family go ghost and acted as a conduit between husband and wife. Whatever money Hardie made as a house sitter, he sent the bulk of it to his family."

"We can get to the family," Mann said. "We have their address."

"Uh," Factboy said, "that address turned out to be Clark's home. I haven't been able to dig up the real address yet."

"You will. And if not you, somebody else."

Factboy didn't like the sound of that. Not one bit. He decided to change the subject slightly.

"There's something else."

"Right," Mann said. "The thing I won't believe."

"Well, before he hooked up with Parish and became this unofficial gunslinger guy for the cops? Charles Hardie didn't exist. Not for, oh, ten years. We have birth records, vaccinations, grade school, high school . . . and then nothing. No military, no taxes, nothing. They've made it look like these records were destroyed in a flood, but it's impossible to have nothing for a ten-year period."

"You're right. It is impossible."

"Not for lack of trying, I'm telling you."

"Forget that for now. I don't care about what he did ten years ago. I want to know what he's going to do now. Who he'll call when he's in trouble. This Deacon Clark sounds like the man."

"Agreed," said Factboy. "Which is why I'm already tapping his phones, e-mail, both at home and at the office."

Outside, one of his kids — Factboy really couldn't tell which one when they were being this loud — shrieked and slammed something heavy into the side of the house.

CHAPTER
TWENTY-THREE

The tougher they are, the more fun they are, tra la.
                              — Rudy Bond, Nightfall

They sat there for a few more minutes, Hardie staring down into his drink, Lane chewing on a roll, unable to bring herself to swallow it. The bread tasted synthetic. She spit the small chunk out into a napkin and sipped some water instead.

More people were staring now. Cell phones coming out, total strangers snapping more pics. Coming here to Musso & Frank was simultaneously going to save her life and ruin her career. But there was such a thing as going too far.

"You're right," Lane said. "We should go."

Hardie nodded.

Lane reached out, touched his hand.

"Please say something."

"Are you up for a little acting?"

"What do you mean?"

"Can you pretend you're trying to score?"

"What — why?"

"Just follow my lead when we reach the parking lot."

Hardie stood up. Lane stood up, shaky, ankle really hurting now that she'd had a little while to rest it. Hardie moved toward the front entrance, but Lane quickly hooked his arm and pulled him in the other direction. "It's back that way." She allowed Hardie to take the lead, and he wound his way through the dining area and past another bar until he reached the back of the restaurant, which opened up into a valet-parking area.

While the two attendants were busy trying hard not to notice Lane but totally noticing her, anyway, Lane saw Hardie inch closer to the cabinet of keys. Then she leaned forward toward the attendants, smiled, and asked if either of them was holding. While both guys shook their heads and smiled, Hardie helped himself to a set of keys, slid them into his jeans pocket, then pretended to notice what was going on with Lane.

"Hey?" he barked. "What the fuck do you think you're doing? C'mon."

Hardie took her by the wrist and yanked her forward. She fell, limping toward him, then hooked her arm through his and leaned in close, the two of them walking past the rows of parked cars.

"Nice," she whispered.

"Not nice until we get a car."

He pressed the security button. *Thhhweep-weep.* The headlights of a Saab a few cars up blinked. Quickly they scrambled inside. By the time the attendants realized what was happening — wait! They didn't let customers park their own cars back here — Hardie was already backing up and then rocketing out of the lot and onto North Cherokee.

The full story hit the gossip sites — including Zoey Jordan's — within ten minutes of their daring grand theft auto. The story was supported by photos and eyewitness accounts and plenty of conjecture and groan-worthy blog-post titles: RELAPSE DANCE. CAREER-END. MUSSO & TANK(ED). Actress Lane Madden, thought to have been involved in a crash on the 101 early this morning and to have fled the scene, reappeared at Musso & Frank in the late afternoon, ordered a meal, then quickly fled with some unknown male (dealer? bodyguard? dealer, bodyguard, and enabler all rolled into one?) into the parking lot . . . where they promptly stole a car and raced off. "She tried to cop from me." "The big guy took the keys." "She looked like hell — and she was definitely not wearing that ankle bracelet." "Looked like she was in the mood to celebrate." "Yeah, the end of her career."

Mann speed-read the posts with her tired, damaged eyes and rewrote the narrative in her head. She forced pieces together, tore them apart again. Tried it from another angle; it fell apart. Laid out the pieces in her mind fresh and told herself to forget what came before. Work with what you have now. She rewrote and rewrote and rewrote.

"Aren't you going to say anything?" Lane asked.
  "About what?"
  "About *what?* Come on, Charlie. I just told you I was responsible for killing a little boy. You're probably a

dad or something. You probably hate me right now. You've gotta hate me right now."

Hardie said nothing as he made another random turn onto an uphill street. He gave it more gas. Halfway up, he finally said:

"I killed my best friend and his family."

Lane blinked.

"What?"

Hardie continued in a low voice, speaking slowly and carefully, keeping his eyes on the road. Just narrating.

"I told you I used to be a kind of cop. Well, I wasn't. Not really. I just helped a cop buddy of mine out from time to time. We worked Philadelphia. One of our last cases, we were up against a drug gang. Bunch of Albanians, trying to carve up the Northeast into territories. They also had ties to terrorist groups, which really pissed us off. So we started fucking with them. *Hard.* Maybe a little too hard. But I'm thinking, we're fine. The bad guys don't know where I live, the bad guys don't know where Nate lives. See, when we really got into it, we put our families somewhere else. Nate even got permission to break the charter rule that said cops had to live within city limits — and I followed him out to the burbs. We used trains, buses, cabs. We never drove our own cars. We were superclever about getting in and getting out. So we thought. But these Albanians, they were ruthless motherfuckers. Somehow they found out where I lived. And one night they showed up at my front door. One of them beeped his car horn, the other shouted out my name. I recognized the accent — I knew who was outside. Har-DEE, Har-DEE, they yelled. It was audacious as fuck. In a weird way I admired it."

"Your family . . . ," Lane said.

"My family was with my in-laws, thank God. I'd been working too hard, and when you work too hard at your job, you start to take your loved ones for granted because, after all, you're working for them, right? And you think they'll just suck it up and understand? Well, that's not the case."

"Yeah," Lane said. "I can understand that."

"So anyway, I'm there alone, and these fuckheads have the nerve to come to my home, shout my name, like they're bullies picking a fight. I pull out two of my guns, and in my head I'm already putting up a For Sale sign, thinking that I'll just take a few of these bastards out and start the process of moving. The place was nice while it lasted. I sneak up to the second floor, crack open a window fast, and start firing. They fire back. *Hard.* They've got Remington eight-seventies, they've got gas-operated, air-cooled M-fourteen carbines, and they start chopping apart the top floor of my house, the bottom floor, the whole damned thing, wood chunks flying, glass spraying. I'm hit once, I dive behind this huge dresser my wife inherited. Thick wood, should be able to block anything. They keep firing for a few more seconds, and then . . . that's it. It's over. I hear a few words in Albanian, the screech of tires, and they're peeling down my street."

"God."

"No, God wasn't exactly paying attention to me, because if he had been, maybe he would have stopped me from making the worst mistake of my life."

"What happened?"

"I went to save my friend Nate."

The logic in Hardie's lizard brain went something like this:

If they'd found his home address, then no doubt they'd uncovered Nate Parish's home address, too. After all, he and Nate bought their houses around the same time, they were partners, and it was understood that whatever happened to the one happened to the other. Yeah, Nate was the one with the official job, and the big brain, but they were in this together. They were two soldiers in a war.

And if the enemy was going to show up and fire some shots over the bow of the Hardie residence . . .

Then clearly the Parish residence was next.

"I bolted out my backdoor, kicked down the door of my own garage — because you see, I didn't want to even bother unlocking it — then got in my car and took off. Peeled right down the street, praying to God I wasn't too late. Praying I wouldn't be rolling up to Nate's house to see windows smashed and the door swinging open. I think I did seventy in a thirty-five zone, and I didn't care.

"But when I arrived, everything was fine. Quiet. Normal. Nate and his wife and his two kids were huddled on the couch, doing their usual thing, which

232

was reading or playing little computer games or drawing pictures. They weren't the kind of family who got together to play board games or sing "Kumbaya," but whatever they did, they did together. I always admired that about Nate. Somehow, he'd found a way to keep it all together. The family, the job, that big brain of his, everything.

"Right away, Nate sees me in the doorway, sees I'm bleeding and trembling. He pulls me inside, asks me what's going on, and I tell him about the Albanians. Nate's wife, Jean, is already taking the kids upstairs, saying she'll bring down the first-aid kit, knowing this night is probably going to turn into a work night and that she won't see her husband until the next afternoon or night at the earliest. But you know what? She's never going to see her husband again, because the moment Nate sits me down at the kitchen table, they all burst in. The real hit team."

Lane lowered her eyes, breathed softly.

"As it turned out, they *didn't* have Nate's address. Nate was too clever for that. He'd never leave a single clue as to his primary residence — he wouldn't, for example, carelessly chuck a magazine away in a downtown recycling bin. Certainly not a copy of a magazine he subscribed to at his primary address. Not with Albanian hatchet men and spotters bird-dogging his every move, all around the city. He just wouldn't be that stupid."

"No . . . ," Lane said.

"But his good friend Charlie, the one with the lizard brain? Well . . . you know, Charlie's Charlie. He's brash,

233

he doesn't play well with others, and he does stupid shit like that. Heart's in the right place, though. Which is why he drove like a maniac all the way to his buddy Nate's secret address, with the Albanians following him the whole way."

"I'm so sorry, Charlie."

"The thing with me was just a ploy. They weren't supposed to hit me at all, in fact — the one who winged me got lucky, I guess. They were supposed to rattle me and send me scurrying to Nate's. The real target. The man who could have shut down their entire operation — and was about to do just that.

"Nate. His wife, Jean. His daughters, Adeline and Minnie. I killed them all. Might as well have been me holding the weapons, pressing the muzzles to their foreheads, pulling the triggers. They made us watch. Then they finished us off. Yet somehow here I am, driving around with you in this car. I don't understand it. Life stopped feeling real to me three years ago. Sometimes I think I actually died back there, in Nate's house, only I'm too stupid to realize it."

This was the first time Hardie had spoken the truth, out loud or otherwise.

Hardie had plenty of experience making random moves. Back in Philly, Nate and he used to do it on a daily basis. It was essential to the job. And for the sake of their families. Your enemies can get a lock on you only if you become predictable. So you start becoming unpredictable.

After winding around the streets of greater Hollywood, Hardie drove to Hollywood and Vine. Before abandoning their stolen Saab, he checked the trunk. God was smiling upon him. Inside were two wire hangers, both with paper spanning the gap proclaiming I ♥ MY DRY CLEANER. He handed one of them to Lane.

"What's this for?"

"You'll see. Shove it in the suitcase. C'mon. We've got to move."

"You going to break into a car with a wire hanger?"

"No, not a car. Let's go."

Lane didn't move.

Hardie looked at her.

"I'm really sorry, Charlie," she said.

"About what?"

"About everything that happened to you. That happened to us. I mean before. It's kind of fucked up and unfair, isn't it? Not as if we woke up one morning and decided to become bad people."

"Come on."

They took the Metro to Hollywood and Western, then a cab to the fringes of downtown, and then another cab back up to Los Feliz until Hardie saw what he wanted.

The Hollywood Terrace didn't have a terrace, nor was it really in Hollywood. It had originally been built as a set for a Poverty Row studio that cranked out a series of 1940s film noirs set in New York City apartments and San Francisco dives and Chicago slums. One building held them all. After the studio died, the building sat vacant for a few years before somebody decided to make it a hotel for real. Of course, it needed real plumbing, something that the set version had lacked. It enjoyed some popularity among up-and-coming musicians in the 1960s, then faded back into obscurity from the 1970s on. The place was a pit. Not really meant to last longer than a few films, let alone seven decades. Still, it held on, out of the developers' eyes for the time being. Soon enough somebody would "discover" it and make it a landmark and put it on bus tours and hawk DVD copies of the film noirs that had been set there. Someday, but not now.

Hardie picked it at random. Lane looked up at the exterior.

"You really want to hole up in a hotel room?"

"If they're after you, they've probably been watching you. They know your friends, your family, everybody. But they don't know me. I don't have friends or family here, and I only go to the houses I sit. I have no pattern. I'm nobody. So this nobody is taking you somewhere random. Just until I can call for help."

"No, you're missing my point. They can trace credit cards. They ask for ID. This isn't the nineteen fifties, where you can scribble I. P. Freely in the dusty ledger on the desk."

"Who said anything about checking in?"

After getting out of the hospital, Hardie spent over half a year living in hotels. When you boiled it down, there were two kinds of hotels: ones with ice machines and ones where you had to call room service. Hardie stayed in the hotels with ice machines. After a while they began to blur together. Same plastic ice bucket, same flimsy plastic liner that took you a while to pry apart. Same thin bars of soap, same sample-size bottles of allegedly luxury shampoo that refused to rinse out of your hair. Same rug. Same phone. Same flat-screen TV. Same shows on the TV. Same A/C. Same smell. Same theft-proof hangers. Same No Smoking signs. Same key-card door locks.

Absolutely the same in almost every hotel.

Hardie had mastered those key-card door locks late one night after walking back from an Applebee's across the street and realizing that, at some point, he'd lost his plastic key card. The sensible thing would have been to approach the front desk, produce identification, and ask for a replacement card. Hardie had not been in a sensible frame of mind. He'd been downright contrary, in fact. That night, he'd downed three double bourbons, seven (maybe eight) pints of Yuengling, and then somebody down at the other end of the bar started buying shots of Jäger for somebody's promotion at some firm somewhere, and Hardie joined in, then realized that he should probably hold that all down with another double bourbon, or two, just to settle his stomach. So by the end, Hardie reasoned, he couldn't form the words to ask for a replacement key card. His tongue had begun refusing commands from his own brain.

But his hands still worked.

And he could fish a wire hanger out of the trash, run it under his own door, and open the handle with a quick jerk.

Hardie didn't want to burglarize an occupied room; they needed an empty room. The easiest way to do that would be to check the maid's pencil charts. There was usually some kind of floor diagram, printed each morning, to tell the maids which rooms to bother cleaning and which had gone unsold for the night. It was late afternoon, but the cleaning staff was still out working the floors. After only a few minutes of roaming the halls, he found a cart, helped himself to the floor list. A lot of empty rooms on the floor, which was great. Room 426 was open, and near a staircase. Even better.

Once inside, Lane announced:

"I'm going to take a shower."

"Okay. I'm going to make that call. And hey, help yourself to whatever's in my bag. There's nothing fancy in there, but at least they won't have blood and smoke all over them."

She gave him a deadpan look.

"You think you have something in my size? Maybe a bra, too?"

Hardie looked at her and smiled.

"Now we're *really* delving into personal territory."

Finally Lane cracked a smile. A big, unabashed, toothy smile. And God, did it make her look stunning.

When Lane rooted through Charlie's luggage, she saw a tiny leather bag. She unzipped it. There was a plastic deodorant stick — Momentum. A metal razor with replaceable blades. Worn toothbrush. A small hard-plastic prescription bottle made out to Charles D. Hardie. Vicodin. Lane glanced over at Hardie. He wasn't paying attention. She grabbed a T-shirt and tucked the bottle inside, then stepped into the bathroom.

She was tired of being hunted, of having the guilt gnaw away at her heart. If it came down to it, Lane would go out on her own terms. She wasn't going to hurt any more people.

And she wasn't going to let Them win.

Hardie sat on the edge of the king-size bed, listening to the springs groan under his weight, trying hard not to think about Lane undressing on the other side of the flimsy door.

He wanted a beer — just a little bracer — before calling Deke. Maybe he should go out and get one. There had to be a tavern or bodega somewhere nearby that would sell him a single or a six. He'd earned it. God, how he'd earned it. Maybe there was even a liquor store that would sell him a bottle of Jack.

But he stayed put. A sliver of sun blasted through the dirty gold blinds. Dust motes floated in the air, suspended by some unseen forces. On the other side of the door, she turned on the shower.

Time to call.

Hardie really wanted a beer.

Usually he didn't mess around with beer. He went right for the bourbon. Beer sloshed around in your gut and only numbed the brain in the faintest of ways. Good old American bourbon knew how the brain worked, knew which wires to pull, which to leave on. But Hardie didn't want his wires pulled. Not yet. He wanted a beer.

Yet he couldn't leave the edge of the bed.

If he stood up and walked out the door, maybe all of this would disappear and he'd wake up on a leather couch with a bottle resting in his crotch and he'd realize this was all a dream. And as awful as things had been, he wasn't ready to accept all of this as a dream. Not yet. Not until he figured it out.

Behind the door, a door slid open, then slid shut. She was inside the shower now.

It was as if he were a corpse slowly coming back to life. Blood surging through veins that he'd long thought withered away. Brain cells in the animal part of his mind suddenly shocking themselves back to life. Charlie Hardie Frankenstein. *It's alive!*

Hardie stood up suddenly and walked to the bathroom door. Listened to the water hiss from the shower fixture. He should have gone for that beer. Instead, he picked up the room phone and dialed a number collect.

It was three hours later in Philadelphia — Eastern Time Zone. Deacon "Deke?" Clark was turning over some carne asada on his backyard grill, nursing his second Dogfish Head Pale Ale, when his cell phone buzzed. Never failed. He didn't recognize the area code either.

"Deke, it's me. Charlie."

240

"Hey. How ya doing, Hardie."

Deke knew how terse he sounded. He just wasn't a phone person.

"I'm kind of fucked, Deke, to tell you the truth. You don't think you could get out here sometime tonight, do you?"

"Where's here?"

"Los Angeles."

Deke paused, tongs in hand, smoke rising, coals burning deep hot. "What's going on, Hardie?"

Hardie started speaking quickly, about a house-sitting gig and finding a squatter inside — then realizing there were people outside the house trying to kill the squatter, and how they barely escaped with their lives. We shouldn't have escaped, Hardie said. It was a ridiculous miracle that we did. And somehow, it seemed to be related to a three-year-old hit-and-run case in Studio City. A kid named Kevin Hunter was the victim.

"You're not putting me on, are you?"

"Would I really make this up?"

"You seriously telling me this is about *The Truth Hunters* people?"

"What's that?"

"Oh, right. You've unplugged yourself from the modern world. So you have no idea that there's this true-crime reality show called *The Truth Hunters*, created and produced by the father of Kevin Hunter, who was killed in a hit-and-run three years ago."

Sure, he'd heard about it. Just this afternoon, from Lane herself.

"She told me about it."

"And you're saying this is part of it? The actress was involved?"

"Yeah."

"Got any evidence?"

"Not a shred. But then, that's what these Accident People do. Cover up all traces."

Deke knew how much Hardie drank. What he did with his life. How he'd removed himself from everybody and everything. This was all a lot to swallow in one phone conversation.

"So, let's make sure I have this right: these shadowy agents or whatever want the actress gone before she tells the truth, right? Hell, if they're already going through all this trouble, why not just bump off the Hunters, too? They're the ones pushing for the answers. They could even do it on live TV."

"I know how this sounds, Deke. About ten hours ago, I wouldn't have believed me either. But this is real."

There was a painfully long pause as Deke looked at his sizzling meat and tried to figure out the best move.

"Look, Hardie, how about I send somebody? A good man I know lives in West Hollywood, works at Wilshire. He can help you sort this out. And if the actress is in some kind of real trouble, and not drugged out of her mind, he'll give her protection and get an investigation started. His name's Steve —"

"No. Only you, Deke. You're the only person in this world I trust, and right now that means everything.

242

They're smart, they're connected, and it's only a matter of time before they find us again."

"You sound a little paranoid, Hardie."

"You can call me whatever you want. And I'm guilty of a lot of things. But have you ever known me to exaggerate?"

Not while sober, no. Deke had to admit that. Not even while drunk, come to think of it.

"And one more thing."

"You means besides dropping everything and traveling to Los Angeles?" Deke asked.

"This is serious. Triple the protection around Kendra and Charlie. They know your address. If they can find you, they can find them. Do you understand?"

"What do you mean they know my address?"

"Swear to God, Deke, I'd only been around these fuckers for maybe a half hour, and it was like they had a complete dossier on me. They know I have a family. They know where I send checks. They've either got sponsors who are connected or have enough money to buy connections."

"Hardie, what have you gotten me into?"

By the time Deke thumbed the Off button on his phone, he'd agreed to drop everything and fly to Los Angeles. He had a go-bag in the closet; he could probably book a flight on the way to the airport — they tended to cut FBI agents slack when it came to last-minute travel. But what the hell was he going to tell his wife? Here, enjoy this plate of carne asada all by your lonesome while I go off and help a guy I've bitched about nonstop for three years now?

Hardie placed the receiver back on the base and stared at it for a few moments. There was no man he trusted more than Deke Clark. The agent was essential to his family's survival. But he knew that Deke didn't like him much. And never had. Some things, though, transcended the personal.

After a while Lane came limping out in nothing but a towel and started picking through Hardie's suitcase. She asked if he minded. Hardie said no, of course not, and tried hard not to look. None of his jeans would fit her, of course, but one of the T-shirts worked. Black, advertising a Northeast Philly bar called the Grey Lodge, coming down to midthigh.

Hardie said, "You look a lot better."

"Ugh. I'm banged up and cut and scraped to hell. I'm finding bruises I didn't even realize I had this morning. Guess I won't be on any magazine covers for a while."

"But you're alive."

"I am alive."

Hardie saw her differently now. Not just because the grime was gone, or because she was wearing his T-shirt. All day he'd more or less dismissed her as a snotty bitch who'd gotten herself into trouble. But for the past three years, their lives had been more similar than Hardie ever would have guessed.

"It's going to be okay," Hardie said.

"I know."

There was an awkward moment of silence before Hardie excused himself and walked into the bathroom and closed the door behind him. The off-white tile walls were still damp with condensation from her shower. Hardie put his palms on the enamel sink and looked at himself in the mirror. Hey, tough guy. How handsome are you?

He stripped off his dirty, bloody clothes — ripping the rest of his T-shirt, actually, because that seemed easier than pulling it over his head. He stepped into the shower, cranked up the water. The pressure sucked. The water spat out in a weird pattern that hurt his skin but didn't actually get him very wet. But it didn't matter. As long as he could wash off most of this day. The crusted blood, the smoke, the dirt, the film of sweat. His wounds still bled but at least he could replace the old blood with some new.

After tucking the bottle of Vicodin under the pillow, Lane lay back on the bed and allowed herself the luxury of closing her eyes for a moment. She couldn't remember the last time she'd done that without worrying about something — her choices, her career, the incident. Usually when she closed her eyes, the demons would pounce. The middle of the night was the worst. That's when she'd pop awake and think about all the things that could go wrong in the world. Everything from never working again to drinking too much to a global pandemic to catastrophic financial meltdown to an asteroid smashing into the ocean and obliterating every living thing. She hated the night. The morning sucked, too, because most days the pounding behind her eyes was relentless. But at least it wasn't night.

Now, though, she felt a little more at ease.

Because after three years, God had finally called her on it.

Her worst sin.

And she was still breathing.

He hadn't reached down from Heaven to smite her in a flash of blinding white. Maybe he'd tried with the Accident People, but if so, it wasn't a full-on, full-court-press try, because she was still alive.

Still breathing.

Until she chose not to.

The air conditioner hummed in the corner, and the water beat against the shower tile steadily, incessantly. She wondered if she could fall asleep. Just for a few minutes. Her protector was in the next room. They were hidden away, at random in the middle of nowhere L.A. Maybe she could indulge herself, just a little.

The total blackness and icy numbness came faster than she thought.

But it wasn't the kind she'd been hoping for.

CHAPTER
TWENTY-FOUR

This time it's personal.

— Tagline from Jaws: The Revenge

Hardie turned the cheap metal handle to the Off position. He used mostly cold water so the steam wouldn't make him sweat, and the cold was nice and bracing and had the curious effect of calming him down a little. After patting himself dry, he took a stab at taping up his chest wound again. As soon as Deke made it here, he'd go have it checked out. He promised. But in the meantime, one little Vike couldn't hurt. Hardie rooted through his toiletries bag, trying to feel for the familiar round shape of the bottle. Nothing. He looked. Everything else seemed to be here. Toothbrush, razor. No painkillers, though. Great. He probably left them behind at the last gig.

So instead, Hardie busied himself with brushing his teeth, halfway through when he realized that all his clean clothes were in the suitcase out in the other room. He wasn't about to wrap a towel around his midsection and go parading around out there. The towels were ideal for preteen girls, not for a guy the size of Hardie. The actress might get the wrong idea. So Hardie put on his smoky, torn, blood-splattered jeans again and looked at himself in the mirror. He was a big mess. But at least it was better than the towel. His mouth still felt metallic, stale, so he squeezed out more toothpaste and started to brush again and had just opened the door when something pinched his neck and he found himself, inexplicably, on his knees.

Someone whispered:

"Shhhh, now."

Hardie's arms felt like rubber. The toothbrush started to slip out of his fingers. Tightening his grip didn't work. His fingers didn't want to do what they were told. The toothbrush slipped completely out of his fingers.

A gloved hand caught it before it hit the carpet.

More gloved hands picked him up.

The lights were off.

But he could see what they had done to Lane over on the bed.

Factboy had put a standard trace on all calls and e-mails coming to Special Agent Deacon Clark, Philadelphia office, Federal Bureau of Investigation. Home, office, and cell. Again, not hard to do with the magic of the Patriot Act, even when the subject was a federal agent. Hell, Clark's being a fed made it easier. Still, Factboy couldn't believe it when a hit popped up almost immediately — a call from a hotel room in Los Feliz, near Hollywood.

Not only was Mann's new team already assembled, but they were rolling up and down the streets of old Hollywood already. The hotel was two minutes away. They were pulling up within forty-five seconds.

Mann actually thanked Factboy and told him he did good work. Factboy was too stunned to reply and stammered something about the trace being a good one (like what the fuck did that even mean?). The line disconnected and Factboy wondered if he was actually done for the day, if he could go upstairs and rejoin his family. That's what he really should do. Try to smooth things over with the wife, look at his kids and tickle their bellies and tell them that he loved them. That he did all these awful things because he loved them.

Isn't that what all fathers did?

Lane was there, on the bed, waiting for him. She'd been stripped naked. Only her panicked eyes seemed able to move, along with a slight up-and-down motion of her chest. They'd let her continue breathing. For the moment. Hardie tried to look away but a gloved hand pushed on his jaw, facing him forward.

"Uh-uh-uhhhh," a soft voice said. "Look at her. You've wanted her from the minute you saw her. Haven't you, Charlie? Your little celebrity."

Hardie recognized the voice. Topless. Why was it that whenever he heard her voice, he happened to be staring at naked breasts? And why was it that, at the same time, her voice chilled his blood and made him think of death?

The gloved hands guided him over to the bed, holding his midsection, working his legs. The sensation was horrible. He was completely helpless, a pile of rubber meat hanging on plastic bones, ready to be posed and moved and positioned any way they wanted.

As Hardie was moved closer to the bed, he saw that Lane's eyes were open — glassy, but open. They'd given her something, too.

"Isn't she beautiful, Charlie? We found all her movies and photos and torn-out magazine pages in that duffel bag you carry around with you all the time. Admit it. You love to look at her, and, wow, you finally have her here now, in the flesh, right in front of you. To do with as you please."

The bag. Oh God, they still had his bag, not the one with the stupid T-shirt and jeans, but the real one, *the important one*, the one he swore to keep with him at all times. The one he'd lost anyway.

"Go ahead, Charlie. Get closer. You know she wants it. She's practically begging for it. Look at her."

They arranged his body so that he straddled hers. His body was at once tingly and partially numb, but he could still feel her naked form beneath him. Her skinny, tired, bandaged, cut body.

"Only maybe she doesn't want you. Maybe you've read the signs wrong. You totally want to fuck her, but she's repulsed by you. Wouldn't want you even if you paid her. Even if you threatened to kill her."

They forced his arms up, then placed his thick, scarred hands around her throat. Carefully, they arranged his fingers around her pretty throat. He could see a vein throbbing there, and her throat working hard to swallow. There was a fleeting terror in her eyes, like she'd realized what they were going to do before Hardie did.

"Anyway, it doesn't matter. You're the kind of guy who can't get it up, no matter how badly you want it. You try to get yourself all worked up, but in the end it's an exercise in futility, you're just too out of shape to make it happen."

The men in the gloves paused for a moment to change positions; Hardie could feel them adjusting around him, like puppeteers struggling behind a black felt curtain. Pay no attention. Keep your eye on the maniac on top of the beautiful naked actress.

"She got you so mad, you thought to yourself — well, then, yeah. Fuck it. I *will* kill her. Squeeze the life out of her stuck-up obnoxious face."

Gloved fingers pressed down on Hardie's numb, useless fingers. Gloved thumbs guided his naked thumbs to the middle of her soft throat and then pressed down hard, joined by the rest of his fingers, tightening around her neck like a vise. Hardie tried to push back, but there was nothing for his mind to seize control of; his hands weren't talking to him right now. They were busy acting. Choking Lane Madden to death in this crazy psychotic fucked-up fantasy version of real life.

"Feels good, doesn't it, Charlie? Choke that bitch out. Go on. Break her little scrawny neck."

As they pushed Hardie's hands down, something shot out from under the pillow and ping-ponged across the carpet.

"Ooh, what was that, Charlie? A secret weapon, maybe?"

Hardie felt one of his puppet masters leave to retrieve the mystery object. He must have handed it to his boss, because she said:

"Now, this is interesting . . . Vicodin, prescribed to . . . oh, to you, Charlie. I suppose it's painful being a hero. But what was this doing under the pillow? Did you put it there, or did the actress? I think it was her, wasn't it, Charlie?"

Hardie looked down at Lane. Her eyes were filled with still tears. After a moment, his puppet master rejoined the group on the bed and pressed Hardie's hands down again, squeezing Lane's throat. She blinked. Tried to look away. She couldn't do anything.

"Wait, I get it now. Your girl took your pills and hid them under the pillow. Now, why would she do that? Maybe because she'd rather swallow a fistful of pills than spend another second with you?"

Lane's legs twitched. Her stomach heaved, and her head started to move slightly, from the left to the right, from the left to the right, just a few millimeters. Hardie felt her hips jolt beneath him. She was trying, God, she was trying.

"But we can't have that. No no no. We don't want a suicidal actress. We want an actress who was cut down in her prime. Choked to death by a man who lusted after her. Murdered by *you*, Charlie."

Hardie wanted to open his useless mouth and tell Lane he was trying, too, that everything was going to be okay, he wasn't going to let them do this. But he was. Strangling her. Murdering her. And there was nothing

252

he could do about it, because his body was no longer his own.

Percentage of murder victims killed by someone they know: fifty-eight.

Only now, in these desperate moments as the capillaries burst in her face and in her eyes, did Lane Madden realize that punishment had come for her after all. Over the past three years she'd ping-ponged between despair and hope, damnation and redemption, wondering where she'd land.

She wanted to tell Charlie: *It's not your fault. You couldn't help this. This was my war. You just wandered into it. It's not your fault.*

She wanted to tell the Hunters: *I'm sorry I didn't tell the truth. I prolonged your suffering because of my own self-interest and greed and narcissism.*

She wanted to tell the world: *I'm not this person you thought I became. I'm really not, it's not me, it's not me . . .*

And then, at the last possible moment, it came to her.

This wasn't about her.

This was about the family at that address.

She had to let Charlie know, she had to tell him, because there was no one else who could do anything about it but Charlie . . .

Save them, she tried to will her mouth to say, struggling to make her jaw move and her lips form the words, one last line to run, her final performance, God, please let Charlie understand what I'm trying to tell him . . .

Save them.

They continued pressing down on his hands until her body was still. One of the gloved hands freed itself to feel her wrist for a pulse, then slid over her eyelids, forcing them shut. They guided Hardie back to a corner of the room, then eased him down into a sitting position. Something sharp poked at one of his ass cheeks, but he figured that was the least of his worries. The taller of the two men slid a syringe out of a zippered case. Hardie recognized him now. He was the second intruder, the one who had Tasered him, then crawled backward out of the Lowenbruck house. The tall, vicious one, he thought he'd sent flying off the top of a mountain. Now he caught Hardie eyeing the syringe.

"Oh, don't worry, big guy. We're not going to kill you."

"Oh, no," Topless said. "After all, you're Unkillable Chuck. I guess we finally learned our lesson about you. No, we've got something else in mind."

Hardie struggled to make his mouth work. He thought he managed to sputter out a couple of syllables —

"I . . . I'll . . ."

— but he wasn't sure until Topless responded.

"You'll what? You'll talk — is that it? About what? What proof do you have? You have nothing, Charlie. Absolutely nothing."

She gave a curt nod. The tall one slid the needle into his arm, but Hardie didn't feel it. He could hardly feel anything, except maybe the burning ingot of rage in his brain.

"This is just to keep you comfortable," Tallboy said.

"And before you do open your mouth," Topless continued, "I'd keep Kendra and Charlie Jr. in mind."

As he passed into total paralysis, Hardie couldn't stop staring at Lane's lifeless body. Her eyes, still slightly open. One eye staring at him. The one he'd punched. Accusing him, blankly. Why couldn't you save me? What have you been doing for the past three years except taking up space, breathing other people's air, consuming natural resources? You not only failed to save your partner's family — you got them all killed. It was even worse with me. You actually killed me. With your own hands.

You happy, Charlie?

You happy you let all of this happen?

O'Neal made one last visual sweep of the hotel room. No fibers had been left behind, no trace of them whatsoever. This was familiar turf — he'd worked dozens of hotel jobs before. He felt like he knew how to hit the Reset button on a hotel room better than career maids did. No trace of them was left. The only evidence left behind told the sad tale of . . .

Charles D. Hardie, a police consultant turned house sitter turned raging alcoholic, finally breaks with reality once he crosses paths with his favorite movie star, Lane Madden.

Hardie has been to Hollywood before and spies on Madden whenever possible. He takes another house-sitting assignment because he knows she'll be in town — he's been reading about her in the entertainment rags. Friday night Hardie follows her back to her Venice apartment after a party in Brentwood, then all the way through the mountains, past Mulholland Drive, and down the 101.

But he's too eager. He brakes his rental vehicle too fast, causing an accident. Panicked, he loads Madden into his car, then flees the scene. His unbalanced mind creates a "hero" fantasy where he's saving her from unknown attackers — just like in the action movies featuring Ms. Madden.

Hardie brings her to the house he's been hired to watch, up in the Hollywood Hills. Madden tries to escape, at one point even stabbing Hardie. Enraged, Hardie beats her savagely and sets the house ablaze and then forces Madden into a landscaping-company van just up the hill, then drives down to Hollywood proper to continue his psychotic fantasy.

Believing this a date, Hardie forces Madden into the famous Musso & Frank, much to the shock of the staff — but no one summons the police, because Madden is well known for exhibiting strange behavior in public. Madden, to her credit, tries to play along, hoping to defuse the ticking time bomb that is Charles Daniel Hardie.

But the ruse breaks down. Hardie brings her back to a hotel in Los Feliz, breaking into a room, where he proceeds to beat and eventually strangle Madden to death. The police find him on the floor of the hotel room, paralyzed with shock, still rambling about these "Accident People" who were trying to kill her.

Mann wasn't exactly proud of the narrative. It was far from her best work, and there were holes galore to plug (the flight times, accident reports, rental-car damages to duplicate). But there were no easy narratives once Hardie had injected himself into the narrative so audaciously and publicly. So the narrative was rewritten to give him a supporting role. Hell, Mann was giving Hardie immortality. From now on, Charles Daniel Hardie would be mentioned in the same breath as Mark David Chapman and Robert John Bardo and Anthony Gary Silvestri. Names that would be uttered in celebrity circles for years to come; Hardie would become a spook story, a cautionary tale.

And considering the dirty laundry Hardie had left behind in Philadelphia, it was doubtful people would fall over themselves to clear his name. Trying to prove otherwise would dredge up a lot of shit that the city would prefer stay buried.

Now it was time to summon the police and make their way to the real job — the one that, until this morning, she'd thought would be the tricky one. Not the case. Compared with the miracles her small team had had to perform during the past fifteen hours, this would be relatively simple. They didn't even have to do anything. Just sit in the van with O'Neal and let things happen.

"We good?"

"All clear," O'Neal said.

Mann knew she couldn't touch Hardie, even though she longed to smash his eyes back into his skull with her fists. Instead she contented herself with stooping down, lifting his chin with gloved fingers, and saying:

"See ya in Hell, tough guy."

CHAPTER
TWENTY-FIVE

Acting is all about honesty. If you can fake that,
you've got it made.

— George Burns

The drive into L.A. from Barstow was pretty boring.

Dusk started creeping across the land, the sun receding and fading away into a smoky gray. They didn't say much — "Jane" staying in character, of course, and "Phili?" wanting to save his energy.

He drove because Philip Kindred always drove and they wanted to make sure it was clear that it was Philip Kindred behind the wheel all the way from Barstow to L.A. But the actor behind the Philip Kindred identity was tired of driving, wanted a little rest. This was a demanding role, both mentally and physically. And the forced torture session at the gas station this morning had taken a lot out of him.

Plus, he had to admit — he was more than a little jealous of the actress playing the role of his sister/lover Jane, who basically was able to sit around just watching everything happen. What a gig.

Not that she didn't cram as hard as he did. The job came up midday Wednesday; by that evening he was shaking hands with "Jane" and holing up in an anonymous hotel room in Flagstaff, AZ, reading through the piles of reference material and photographs and recordings about the infamous Kindreds. Plenty creepy stuff, but kind of a thrill, too — even the man playing Philip had to admit that.

Part of the cram session was getting to know the actress playing Jane and becoming comfortable with each other — familiar. The real Philip Kindred had a habit of touching Jane whenever possible, as if to claim her by physical touch or to reassure her. They kissed until it felt natural, familiar. They listened to the Kindreds' favorite music (1960s orchestra pop and psych rock LPs that their dead parents kept around — "Crimson and Clover" especially — over and over and over), watched clips of their favorite movies (1980s slashers, 1990s teen sex comedies, 2000s torture porn), stared at the crime scene photos, and touched each other some more. Not that anyone would be quizzing either of them. But the more immersion the better.

The truly surreal thing was watching the *Truth Hunters Special: The Kindreds* as it was broadcast live Thursday night. As usual, ultimate family man Jonathan Hunter introduced the show, but he seemed even more somber than usual — almost like he knew what was coming Saturday night.

"Kind of creepy," the man playing Philip muttered.

The woman playing Jane, staying in character, said nothing.

(See! She didn't even have to learn any lines!)

Most of the show featured reenactments from previous installments, focusing on two sad sacks who didn't look much like the real Philip and Jane Kindred

260

at all. Which was really fucking insane, considering that Philip and Jane Kindred were notorious for abducting innocent victims, then forcing them to play out — reenact, if you will — scenes from their favorite horror movies. At gunpoint. So, as the man who was playing Philip watched the screen, he recognized the occult link between them all: he was watching a reenactment of another reenactment, and he himself was preparing to perpetrate still another reenactment — only one that everyone would think was real. All of it made his head hurt. He wished he could twist the cap off a cold beer.

But no booze of any kind: the Kindreds were teetotalers.

(Which just went to show you how seriously nuts these people *were*, he thought.)

And the man playing Philip would have loved to point out this strangeness to the woman playing Jane, but what could she do — nod? Shrug?

The show ended with Jonathan Hunter's usual plea for the truth, that if you have any information that will shed some light on this case, please don't hesitate to contact a Truth Hunter either by phone or e-mail or Facebook, and be sure to follow all *Truth Hunters* updates on Twitter . . .

Blah blah blah.

Jonathan Hunter supposedly disliked episodes on serial killers and their ilk; he preferred smarter, less gruesome quarry, like corporate criminals and con men. But the cable network — for all its generosity in pouring hundreds of thousands of advertising dollars into research — practically *insisted* on serials because the numbers spiked whenever the show featured a lunatic with a knife. Especially a lunatic who made out with his own deaf-mute sister and liked to reenact slasher flicks.

The man playing Philip had to admit, this one was probably the most exciting job he'd ever done working for Mann.

In fact, he still had a hard time believing he was actually *in* this line of work.

He'd come out to L.A. in his early twenties with a set of head shots, just like everybody else. Scored a part in an indie film, just like everybody else. Had visions of being discovered, landing the big role, just like everybody else. Waited for his cell to ring, just like everybody else. Worked another, totally unrelated job in the meantime, just like everybody else. Saw his early twenties slip into his midtwenties, just like everybody else.

But unlike everybody else, his cell rang one day. He was called in, given a number 2 pencil and a battery of psychological exams, then a series of interviews, then a bizarre play-acting screen test. More time went by, and then all of a sudden he was signing an inch-thick nondisclosure agreement and told to memorize a script, and then instructed to burn it and then drive to a certain street corner downtown near the Bradbury Building, where he watched someone get murdered. He followed the script when he talked to the police, and then he went home and wondered if it was all a practical joke. That is, until he went online and looked at his checking account balance.

262

The actor soon learned that other hopefuls had fallen into this line of work; there was a loose network of them spread throughout the world. You didn't audition; you were simply chosen. In a way, it made him feel like a secret superstar.

And this was his biggest role yet.

Still — all of that preparation Wednesday night, Thursday night, Friday night (because the real Philip and Jane liked to sleep most of the day away, curled up with each other while movies and music played nonstop in the background), left him exhausted. He was eager just to get this job done — impress them, then move on. The gas station part was fun, but it was a long slog to L.A. Lots of highway and hills and sun and then chain stores and houses and more hills.

As he drove, the man playing Philip wondered what the real Philip Kindred was doing right now. The official story was that the Kindreds were still on the loose; the FBI had kept them on their Ten Most Wanted list for the past year. Unofficially, they were told not to worry about the real Kindreds, because they had been apprehended a year ago and were being confined in secret and wouldn't be talking to anybody.

Probably safe to say that nobody told Jonathan Hunter this little bit of news.

CHAPTER
TWENTY-SIX

I wanted a symphony of powerful men . . . ..
of lonely women . . .
of thick-necked losers . . .
of human ships that crash in the night.
— Sylvester Stallone

The arrest was straightforward. They eased the handcuffs on him, pulled him to his feet, shuffled him down the hallway, digital cameras capturing the scene, the cops shooing them away. He had feeling back in his legs now, and in his arms. Middle of his chest still felt dead, though. They read him Miranda. They put a hand on top of his head as they eased him into the back of the car. Slammed the door shut, ready to bring him in.

They figured out who he was, and his connection with the Philly PD, fairly quickly. They called in more uniforms when they realized they had a celebrity death. Their goal was to get Hardie away from the scene and let the tech guys start working it over.

Hardie wanted to save them the trouble and shout: *I did it.*

You won't find a shred of evidence that'll say otherwise.

His hands around her throat.

His fist that smashed into her badly bruised eye.

264

His skin cells all over her body.

They'd even helpfully left his duffel bag behind, the one that used to contain the one irreplaceable thing in his life.

Now it contained Lane Madden DVDs, photos, magazine articles, and other stalkerish paraphernalia.

Used to work with the Philly police or not . . . Hardie did it, and he was going down for it.

Hardie wondered how soon they'd let Deke know, if they'd try to contact him on the plane. Cell phones didn't (allegedly) work up there, but many airlines had Internet. Hardie's name was in the system, and he couldn't imagine Deke wouldn't have alerts in place in case anything went wrong with Charlie or his family in hiding. Deke would probably head right to the station house, ask for time alone with Hardie. Would Deke believe him? No idea. Even if Deke did, who would he go looking for? Where would he start?

And what did it matter, anyway? Their mission was accomplished. Delayed maybe. But Lane Madden still ended up dead, and the truth along with her. The truth about what had really happened to poor little Kevin Hunter.

In her last moments, she'd begged him, wordlessly pleading with him:

Save me.

Hardie couldn't get rid of the image of her racked with pain, struggling to speak:

Save me.

The more he thought about it, *me* wasn't right. Her lips hadn't come together to form an *m*. Her tongue had darted out first, and a moment later, she ended the word with an *m*.

She wasn't saying

Save me.

Lane was saying

Save them.

All it once it came to Hardie, his lizard brain finally snapping the last piece into place. Why hadn't he realized it earlier, after Lane had confessed her sins?

As Deke had put it:

These shadowy agents or whatever want the actress gone before she tells the truth, right? Hell, if they're already going through all this trouble, why not just bump off the Hunters, too? They're the ones pushing for the answers. They could even do it on live TV.

The address in the GPS. 11804 Bloomfield. The one that Lane quickly dismissed from the screen.

11804 Bloomfield, Studio City, CA.

Oh fuck.

They weren't done yet.

O'Neal didn't say it out loud, but he couldn't keep the thought from rattling around in his fuzzy, sleep-deprived mind.

They shouldn't be doing this.

Seriously, it should be some other unit. He knew what Mann was thinking: turning this assignment over to another production team midstream was a sign of weakness. And you never showed weakness to your employers, because suddenly they'd lose your number and you'd never receive another assignment.

There were other directors out there — some legends, others rising stars. They were all known only by their monosyllabic code names, inspired by Hollywood directors. O'Neal had worked for "Fritz" (after Lang) as well as "Ray" (after Nicholas). He'd heard rumors of a "Hitch" as well as a "Brian" (after De Palma). Some Guild wags joked that Brian was actually the *real* Brian De Palma, moonlighting between thrillers. Meanwhile, some directors specialized. There was a "Howard" who was an expert on faking plane crashes, from Cessnas to 747s; an "Oliver" who worked on assassinations.

Deputy directors like O'Neal typically took on the names of famous actors, dead or alive. O'Neal took his name from Ryan; in the past he'd worked with an Eli (Wallach), a Van (Hefflin), a Sam (uel L. Jackson), a Myrna (Loy), a Bob (Culp).

The code names made it easy to keep Guild members straight. The code names also provided a nice protective layer of absurdity. Even if you were to stumble upon their plans, what were you going to say? Some dudes named "Oliver" and "Kevin" were plotting to assassinate a Rwandan president?

Mann's code name, however, was both clever and a big fuck-you to the boys' club that was the Guild. She chose it in honor of Anthony Mann, western and film-noir director extraordinaire, and claimed to be a huge fan of his work. But O'Neal knew it was just her way of saying:

Oh, I'll show you who's the fucking Mann.

No doubt about it, Mann was extremely talented. She worked with efficiency and innovation and with small, agile units. Not only did she smash through the glass ceiling of their peculiar little business, but she did it without leaving a fingerprint.

Fact remained, though: they were all injured and tired and punchy and twitchy and in no condition to be conducting an operation like this. But Mann didn't give a shit. She didn't care how tired you were or what your plans might be or what day it was. When Mann had a production and tapped you, you dropped everything and hung in there with her until it was complete.

So here they were.

Securing the perimeter in the lovely San Fernando Valley in a brand-new white van, new communications gear. And boy, it must have galled Mann to break the new gear out of storage.

Awaiting the arrival of a new A.D. — henceforth to be known as A.D.2. (Underlings never received cool code names, just job descriptions.)

Trying to stay awake.

Waiting for 8p.m.

Which apparently . . . was when everything was going to happen.

Mann was keeping the details of this mission extremely close to her chest. All O'Neal knew was that there were two other teams out there; one offensive, one defensive, and O'Neal's job was to observe and block communications as needed. Police squawks, cell-phone calls, people with digital cameras, whatever.

Complete blackout, on demand. Now he was in the van, awaiting her command.

Hardie needed to get out of this police car immediately.

But he had nothing.

No shirt, no shoelaces, no socks, no underwear, no weapons of any kind. Nothing on his body but a pair of bloody, ripped, dirty jeans on his legs, and a pair of his own shoes — minus the laces — on his feet.

He was handcuffed and sitting inside a suspect-transport enclosure, which was locked and moving through the streets of L.A. on the way to the North Hollywood station.

Let's face it: there was nothing he could do.

He eased back into the seat and closed his eyes when he felt it dig into his ass cheek. Took him a minute, but he remembered.

The tiny spring-loaded plastic vial.

The one he'd plucked from the white death van. Hardie had figured if they were forced into a corner again, he'd spray that shit all around and play the game of See Who Wakes Up First. Use their own poison against them. He'd forgotten about it, though — not that it would have done any good back in the hotel room, as they pretty much pounced the moment he stepped out of the bathroom.

Now, though. In an enclosed space . . .

The barrier between the backseat and the front was a hard layer of bulletproof plastic, with a group of air holes the size of quarters in the middle.

Hardie remembered what Topless had said about the stuff in the vial. The dose was designed to kill a man in two stages — first knock him out, then convince his heart to stop beating for a short while. If he sprayed this stuff in the car, all three of them would die. Hardie first. That wouldn't do any good.

And if he waited until he was in an interrogation room, same deal. And even if he lived, there was no way he could fight his way out of a station house. Nor would he want to, because then he'd be hurting cops.

So it was now or never. While they were still on the street, where he maybe had a chance at controlling things.

Otherwise, it was like letting the Hunters just die.

God knows if he thought there was even a chance they'd believe him, Hardie'd tell them everything. Much better to have a SWAT team descend on the house and deal with the situation. But Hardie knew he was in the worst position possible — the guy absolutely nobody would believe.

He used his fingers to slide the vial out of his back pocket.

The way it worked seemed clear enough. A simple pump on one end would send the poison mist shooting out on the opposite end. But how was he supposed to lift it to the holes in the plastic barrier?

Ungracefully, he supposed.

Hardie started turning around in the back and the cop in the passenger seat immediately noticed and warned him to sit the fuck down now. Hardie ignored him and focused on the strange task of kneeling on the seat, then raising his cuffed hands — along with his ass — to the barrier. Again the passenger cop screamed, asking what the fuck he thought he was doing, and the driver joined in and began braking the vehicle — which was good news, all things considered. Hardie felt the edges of one of the air holes with the tips of his fingers and quickly put the vial through, took a deep breath, and closed his mouth and eyes and pushed it.

PSSSSSSSST

The effect was immediate. The car, with an unconscious driver slumped over its wheel, lurched to the right and came to a bone-rattling stop on the side of a parked car. Hardie's cuffed hands were crushed by his own ass against the barrier. The vial slid out of his hands. He continued to hold his breath.

Come on come on come on . . .

Falling forward, Hardie led with his right shoulder and landed on his side. He flipped around and smashed against the window with both feet. First time nothing. Second time nothing. Third time was a charm.

KRESSSSHHHHH

The rest Hardie accomplished by rote, walking himself through his improvised plan step by step. It was the only way to do it. Skip to the end and realize how impossible this all seemed, and you might just lose hope.

So go ahead, Charlie.

Kick away the jagged glass from the frame. Sit up. Lunge yourself through the opening. Land on your shoulders. Breathe. You're outside. You can open your mouth now. Suck in that air. Stand up. Come on, stand up. Get to that driver's-side door. Turn around. Grab the handle with your fingers. Open it. Really yank it open. Cops never lock their doors because they have to get out quickly at any given moment, and the perps are always locked up in the back, so what does it matter? Open the door and let the driver come tumbling out, because many cops don't wear their seat belts, either.

He's down on the ground now. Good. Take the keys from his belt and uncuff yourself. You're not going to do anybody any good with hands behind your back. Unsnap. Jam the key in. Twist. You're doing fine, doing fine . . . and look, you're free.

Now throw away the cuffs and give this poor bastard his life back. Don't worry about 911. They'll come soon enough, with all these bystanders with cell phones. Focus on the CPR. Chest compressions . . .

Survival rates for people experiencing cardiac arrest outside of in a hospital: eight percent.

Hardie knew that the mouth-to-mouth part wasn't key. An EMT had told him so over a beer once, many moons ago: it was the chest compressions, stupid. When somebody's heart stops, they still have oxygen in their blood. If you can get their pumper a-pumping again, the oxygenated blood will begin to circulate. Simple as that. In fact, blowing into someone's mouth can be a bad thing, the EMT explained. You see a person drop, you tend to freak out. Freaking out increases your level of carbon dioxide. So you end up

272

blowing carbon dioxide down their throat — when what they really need is oxygen.

The EMT shared a personal tip with Hardie: when compressing someone's chest, play the Bee Gees' "You Should Be Dancin?" in your head. That keeps you pumping at one hundred beats per minute.

At the time, Hardie, being a wiseass, had asked: Wouldn't "Stayin' Alive" be more appropriate?

The EMT responded: "So fucking cliche, man."

You should be dancing.

Yeah . . .

The cop started coughing and sputtering and waving his arms around, wondering what the fuck was going on. Hardie scrambled up, his body screaming at him, and made his way to the other cop. Yanked him out of the passenger seat, started in with the compressions. *Come on, come on,* Hardie thought, all the while noticing that they were about the same age, about the same build.

CHAPTER
TWENTY-SEVEN

Ouch. When you get those feelings, insurance companies start to go bankrupt.

— Reginald VelJohnson, *Die Hard 2: Die Harder*

Yes, the whole *hurting somebody* thing sucked.

But he told himself this was just a role he was inhabiting. Other professions did it. Soldiers inhabited a role when they were sent to foreign countries and told to drop bombs on people and they tried to avoid running over bombs set by other people. It was never "Dave White of Clifton, New Jersey" sent over to kill people; it was "Sergeant White," stripped of his full identity and given a new one by his superiors, with orders to terminate with extreme prejudice. Same thing here.

(The man pretending to be Philip Kindred played these ethics games in his head right before a job, just to keep his sanity.)

He pulled the car to the side of the street. Parking was carefully orchestrated on a San Fernando Valley block such as this one. While there were no signs, everyone knew which spaces belonged to which abode. He had been told to park directly in front of 11802 Bloomfield, which was next door to 11804 Bloomfield.

Okay.

274

Immerse yourself in the role.

Your name is Philip Kindred, and you're here for revenge.

You and your sister were watching TV Thursday night and you saw all the awful things Jonathan Hunter said about you.

Worst of all, your sister Jane saw them, too.

Saw them refer to you both as "monsters" and "evil adults with childlike desires."

That was not a nice thing to say, Mr. Jonathan Hunter.

So we're going to show you what we do.

"Philip Kindred" opened his eyes, opened the driver's-side door, strode up the street, reaching his gloved hand inside the pocket of his Windbreaker for the heavy automatic that hung inside. Hoodie up, moving forward.

You are Philip Kindred.

You're just about to the door, and the guy behind the wheel notices you. Now's the time. You pull the gun out of your pocket, you squeeze the trigger and shoot him in the face. The guy next to him, the other half of the Hunters' usual security detail, reaches inside his jacket, but you're too fast for him and you shoot him in the face, too, followed by another shot to his chest and then another shot to the driver's seat.

You are Philip Kindred. You don't wait to make sure you've killed them both because you know you have, and you jog around the car and then up the Hunters' driveway and you immediately cut to the left, along the eight-foot hedge that blocks the front yard from the street.

You are Philip Kindred. You move along the hedge, following it into the very corner of the yard, where you crouch down in the darkness and wait. You are Philip Kindred . . .

As the minutes ticked by, it became clear that nobody had reported the shots, or the brief cries. Not even the Hunters, who were busy preparing for Family Movie Night, waiting for their takeout pizza to arrive.

All clear.

Mann thumbed a text message. Down the street, the woman playing Jane Kindred stepped out of the stolen car, gently pushed the door shut, then went to the trunk, from where she removed an insulated bag. Holding it in her arms, she quietly darted up the street.

In the back of the house, under a cover of bamboo trees, A.D.2 killed the security system, as well as the floodlights along the side of the house and in the backyard.

As the two cops slowly choked themselves back to life and started scrambling around, trying to figure out what the fuck had happened to them, Hardie peeled away, finally beginning to understand why he'd been kept alive all this time.

276

God, you wily bastard. You don't work in mysterious ways. No, your ways are pretty fucking clear right here at the end.

And it was the end; Hardie didn't doubt that. He had been kept alive on this planet for one job, and one job only: to atone for the sins of letting an innocent family die. And how was he going to do that? By saving the lives of another innocent family.

Thanks for the clarity of mind here at the end, God. Glad to know you don't leave us guessing forever.

Further proof that God wanted him to do something: all of the gifts.

A few minutes ago, Hardie had nothing. Now he had two Glock 23s, four loaded .40 S&W magazines. He had no idea what kind of fancy shit his old friend Topless was planning. Didn't matter. He'd fucked up her shit this morning, so let's fuck up her shit in the evening. Let her bring on all her syringes and magic blow darts and gases and poisons and the rest of her Agatha Christie crap. Hardie planned on squeezing the triggers of these Glocks and not stopping until Topless and her Tall Boyfriend and anyone else who *wasn't* the Hunter family were dead.

He also had a button-down black polyester police shirt, taken from the second of the arresting officers. Hardie didn't want to go traipsing around town bare-chested in a stolen police car. People tend to notice shit like that.

Finally, Hardie had a police car, and he'd disabled the two-way, the MDT, the vehicle tracking systems, the CCTV, as well as the supposedly secret LoJack device mounted in every department vehicle. Turned out to be the same gear as in Philly. Nate had shown him how to turn off all this shit years ago. *Sometimes, Nate had said, you want to go ghost.*

CHAPTER
TWENTY-EIGHT

An act of God; a natural and unavoidable
catastrophe that interrupts the expected
course of events.

— Definition of *force majeure*

A hand-scribbled sign was taped to the wooden door leading to the path along the side of the Hunter home: PLEASE KEEP THIS DOOR CLOSED WE DON'T WANT TO LOSE OUR DOG. The man playing Philip Kindred knew this was a simple anti-burglary ruse; the Hunters didn't own a dog.

He quietly scaled the wooden fence and dropped down loosely, sneakers slapping on concrete. Inside the house the TV was already on, the THX sound from the start of the DVD blaring superloud.

He quickly made his way down the cement path, past tidy trash cans and recycling bins, a perfectly coiled hose, a well-manicured berry tree, and then finally to the backyard. Right about now the actress playing Jane should be approaching the front door, ringing the bell . . .

Jonathan Hunter answered the door; he always answered the door. He had the exact total plus tip ($38) ready in his pocket, because each week they

279

ordered the same items (one large Sicilian red, one round medium white, boneless wings with mild Cajun spices) from the same pizza parlor over on Ventura Boulevard. They always played the DVD past the FBI warning and the THX sound and the previews and paused it right on the company credits so they'd be ready to watch once the food arrived.

This was Family Movie Night; this night was sacred. Nothing could trump it. No business meetings, no travel plans, no matter how allegedly "important." The network knew that, his staff knew it, and no one would dare suggest otherwise to Jonathan. His precious boy, Kevin Hunter, had been killed by some coward on a Saturday afternoon. Saturdays the family gathered to be with one another.

And while this ritual didn't make the night terrors go away, it was a steady reminder of what mattered most.

Now the food was here, and Jonathan opened the door, already reaching into his jeans pocket for the cash. He never worried about who might be on the other side. Harry and Marvin vetted everyone who approached the Hunter home. Sometimes they even placed their own orders with the same pizza parlor.

Which was why Jonathan was stunned to see a girl, a plain-looking girl with a tiny face and stark eyes who pulled a .38 out of the insulated bag and shoved it into his throat, then pushed him back, stumbling, into his own vestibule.

The surprise was fleeting, however. Jonathan processed what was happening within a second and knew he was able to respond accordingly.

He pretended to flail a bit, his right hand brushing against the wall — where a big fat rubber button marked CLEAR would summon the police instantly. There would be no alarm, no sounds, no warning of any kind. But the LAPD would know.

The girl pushed the gun into his throat just as he tapped the button, then allowed himself to be guided back into the living room, backward, the girl's creepy eyes never leaving his. It was a matter of waiting for the cops to arrive.

There was no recognition in these early moments; Jonathan's mind was honestly on Harry and Marvin outside, because if this girl made it to the front door without an ID check (and Harry and Marvin knew every deliveryman who worked at Perelli's Italian Kitchen), that meant they were incapacitated or dead.

But she did look familiar. Something about the eyes. Her small, angry little face . . .

When Jonathan was finally allowed to turn around in his own living room, and he saw his wife, along with little Peter and Kate, arranged on the living room floor, and a sneering punk with a gun standing over them . . . everything clicked.

"Hey, Mr. Hunter," Philip Kindred said. "Are you ready for some fun and games?"

Hardie didn't know the Valley. He'd never sat a house there, never had occasion to drive through it, unless he was forced to fly into Burbank.

As he sped through the streets now, though, he was relieved that the landscape was strangely familiar.

Except for the mountains in the background — which you really couldn't see in the dark, anyway — it was one big fat sprawl, kind of like the suburbs of Philadelphia. No multimillion-dollar dollhouses clinging to the side of a mountain. Hardie felt like he'd come back down to earth.

Plan? There was no plan, other than forcing his way into the Hunter household and demanding to speak with Jonathan, even if he had to use his guns to convince him. Hardie had seen too many movies where the would-be hero tries to communicate some vital piece of information only to have it be too late — the dagger's already sticking out of a back, or the bullet's already taken off the top of a head. No, Hardie would stick a gun in Hunter's face if he had to, force him to call Deke, and start the process of untangling this mess and, incidentally, saving all of their lives. Deke was beholden to no one. Deke was the real hero. Deke would figure this out.

Hardie was snapped out of his reverie when the street sign started to whizz by in a black-and-white blur — Bloomfield Street. He braked hard, screeching a little, then made a sharp right and cruised up the block.

When he reached 11804, there was a car parked out front. Even in the early evening, Hardie could see the tiny splatter of dark fluid on the windshield.

They were already here.

It was already happening.

Mann freaked the moment the LAPD cruiser made it halfway up Bloomfield.

282

"Who the fuck is that? How did that slip through?"

O'Neal pecked furiously at his netbook. "No idea. I'm tracking all of them, and this guy isn't showing up. He's not real."

"Somebody with a broken transponder?"

"No. All others are accounted for."

But when the rogue vehicle stopped directly in front of the target's home, Mann went absolutely ballistic.

"We have to intercept NOW! There hasn't been enough time."

One look in the rearview and Hardie spotted the white van parked in a driveway a few doors down and across the street. Topless and her gang must have seen him by this point. Right now, they were probably preparing some quick way to kill him. Loading darts or needles or pain rays or some other crazy shit.

So . . .

Fuck it.

Most police cars were equipped with a push bumper — aka, nudge bars — welded to the chassis so that you could ram up somebody's ass to ensure they'd pull over or never move again. He hoped this was one of those cars.

Hardie shifted gears and slammed his foot down on the accelerator. The squad car jumped over the curb and smashed through a thick shrub and raced across the lawn. Hardie cut the wheel — hard — to the right. The car spun and skidded to a halt a few feet from the front door. He didn't think. He just opened the door and grabbed a gun and went to the front door, which was unlocked. Cocky bastards.

CHAPTER
TWENTY-NINE

Guns, guns, guns.

— Kurtwood Smith, RoboCop

Things had just gotten interesting. The father, Jonathan, was shirtless and kneeling in front of his wife, who had two steak knives in her trembling hands and the muzzle of a .38 pressed up against the nape of her neck. Both were crying. As were the children, who huddled together on a small blanket in the middle of the floor, with Jane, arms wrapped around them, squeezing them reassuringly, her .38 dangling from one hand.

The wife was going on, *please please please,* and the man playing Philip Kindred went through the usual lines, direct from transcripts of interviews with survivors: *You're a good mommy. A good mommy would do this for her children. Shut up, Daddy. You're a bad daddy. You have to be punished, Daddy!*

All of it meant to be some nutball wish-fulfillment do-over fantasy concocted by Philip Kindred to amuse his younger sister, to change reality so that Daddy didn't break Mommy's neck, and somehow Mommy was able to overpower Daddy and stab him forty-seven times with a high-end steak knife.

So Evelyn Hunter had to be compelled to stab her husband, Jonathan, in his bare chest repeatedly.

The man playing Philip Kindred delivered his lines with gusto. But it was hard to believe in the lines, to truly *inhabit them*, because he knew exactly how this would play out. After all, he'd read the rest of the script.

There was no way Evelyn Hunter here would stab her husband, Jonathan, in the chest. No way. Even with her kids' lives on the line. Mann had put the statistical probability at 0.5 percent. No. All psychological profiling pointed to the likelihood that the Hunters would prefer to die together rather than live on with the death of yet another family member staining their souls.

So, when all the lines were run, and all the tears were shed, the man playing Philip Kindred was supposed to pull the trigger and put a bullet into the back of Evelyn Hunter's head. Immediately to be followed by two in the chest for Mr. Hunter, right in the pumper.

Then it would be time to make their getaway through the back, the path already cleared for them, the keys in the black van, ready to go.

And the kids?

Again, the woman playing Jane had it easy. The kids *had* to live, because the Kindreds never killed kids — supposedly they identified with them way too much. Which seemed to be even more cruel than the alternative, forcing them to watch their parents die horribly and begging for their lives . . . but hey, he wasn't the one writing the script.

Still, "Jane" didn't even have to kill anybody, while "Philip" would rack up a quadruple murder.

And no lines! "Jane" had no fucking lines!

So now it was winding up, and the fake Philip was already thinking ahead to the shot, trying to steel himself for it, because no matter how many ethical games you play with yourself, you're still squeezing the trigger and putting a bullet into the back of a *living, breathing person's head*. No matter how much of a badass you think you are, that still gets to you. Deep inside.

And then the front door blasted open and this crazy-looking guy in an LAPD shirt and bloody jeans raced in, guns in each hand, charging right for them, and the man playing Philip thought to himself — did he miss a page or two of script or what?

This was not what Hardie expected.

He expected Topless or Tallboy or one of the other faceless minions skulking around, flicking their fingernails against a syringe, trying to get the air bubbles out, unzipping body bags and working over every surface with a rag and a can of Pledge.

He didn't expect to see two punks with guns holding a family hostage in the middle of a modest, tastefully appointed living room.

Frankly, he didn't expect that they'd still be alive. Hardie thought he'd burst into this room on a mission of pure vengeance, a biblical reckoning.

Hardie lifted his right Glock and fired. The bullet struck the male punk in the shoulder and spun him like a top, sending him crashing into a small table littered with framed photographs.

Then Hardie turned and pointed the gun at the punk girl, who was already on her feet and climbing backward over the living room couch. Hardie gave her one in the arm. She shrieked as the bullet propelled her off the top of the couch and sent her crashing to the floor. She shrieked again, in one hot, angry burst, then started moaning.

Hardie closed the distance between himself and the fallen male.

"Stop stop stop," he was murmuring, actually cowering as Hardie approached. "Please don't shoot me again, this is not what you think, oh God, please."

A voice behind Hardie croaked to life.

"That's Philip Kindred. He's a serial killer, along with his sister over there behind the couch. Don't listen to anything he says, because it'll be a lie."

Hardie turned to the shirtless man who'd spoken — Jonathan Hunter — and instantly felt twin pangs of kinship and guilt. Kinship because they were two fathers who wanted nothing more than to keep their families safe. Guilt because Hardie knew the secret history of the Hunters' worst nightmare. In another life, they could have had a beer together. The sort-of cop from working-class Philadelphia and the television producer from Los Angeles. But not today. Not after what Hardie would be forced to ram down their throats.

The truth.

"You know him?" Hardie asked.

"We ran a special about him, and his sister, a few days ago. I guess he figured he'd come here to tell me what he thought of the show. Isn't that right, you son of a bitch?"

The lizard part of Hardie's brain raced to keep up, but he thought he had it. Topless's big plan. She'd set this in motion days ago. She couldn't do it alone either. Lane had been right. The Accident People were indeed connected at the highest levels. Hardie wished more than ever that Deke were here right now.

"By the way, who are you?" Jonathan Hunter asked.

"I'm Charlie Hardie."

"Yeah, but *who* are you? Why are you here? How did you know these people would be coming for us?"

"You've got a guardian angel somewhere."

HARDIE.

The name lit up in Mann's brain like pure neon rage.

HARDIE.

She knew they should have killed him in that hotel room, she advocated for it, pressed it, almost begged for it. You don't leave a man like that alive. Not after what he's seen. But Gedney insisted: his bosses wanted

HARDIE

kept alive, to be dealt with later, in a manner of their choosing. The narrative would be stronger for it, more airtight, they argued. One living psycho was always better than one dead one found at the scene. Even Lee Harvey was allowed to live for a period of time after the big job at Dealey Plaza. Mann again disagreed, saying that

HARDIE

was a god who needed to be put down, no fucking around, no fancy shit, because a man who's too stubborn to die will be too stubborn to stay put, and god-fucking-damnit she should have listened to her gut on this one because now

HARDIE

was going to fuck everything up unless she was quick and smart and decisive and ended this now.

Now Hardie had this sputtering psycho — "Philip Kindred" — to deal with. He was still inching away, eyes rolling around in his head, as if waiting for someone to tell him what to do. Hardie crouched down next to him, poked him with the muzzle.

"How are they talking to you? Do you have an earpiece? Are they telling you what to do?"

"W-What are you talking about, man?"

"I know all about her, your boss with the big tits, so don't pretend, nutboy. Just tell me how you were supposed to get out of here after killing the Hunters."

There was another shriek on the other side of the living room. Hardie could only see the top half of the action, but clearly Evelyn Hunter was kicking the living shit out of the shot and bleeding psycho sister. "Honey, honey, honey," Jonathan Hunter said, rushing across the room to his wife. Hardie turned his attention back to Philip. Stuck the gun in his face.

"I really don't care if you live or die. I want to know the plan."

290

"Okay, I'm not Philip Kindred. I'm only pretending to be him, oh please, God, don't kill me."

"Well, duh."

"How were you getting out?"

"Th-Through the backyard."

A.D.2 and Grip were supposed to have been the first ones in, anyway.

When enough time had elapsed, and the kill shots had rung out, A.D.2 and Grip were to play the roles of innocent bystanders — or in this case, gay Studio City joggers — just two lovers out after work, blowing off some steam, when suddenly they hear gunshots coming from a house, and they rush in because they swear they hear kids screaming (and how are they supposed to ignore that?) and they get to the living room just in time to see two grubby-looking people making their way out the sliding doors that lead to the backyard, and oh God, the mom and the dad on the floor, shot in the head and in the chest respectively, and then would come a frenzied call to 911 and the job would finally be over. A.D.2 and Grip had clean backgrounds that would check out. They'd be paid over the next few months to live their lives and serve as witnesses to this awful, senseless tragedy, make a court appearance or two, talk to the media when directed.

But now Mann sent them in early because there was really no other option.

And she sent them in with guns.

She hated guns on jobs, but now the narrative absolutely demanded it, accepted no substitutes.

The instructions were simple: kill Hardie —
especially HARDIE

— and wipe out the entire family, kids, too,
everybody, and then get the actors the fuck out of there
to the black van and get out of Studio City as quickly as
possible. O'Neal would provide some backup from the
Moorpark side of the block. Mann would then place an
anonymous 911 call — though when the gunshots rang
out, it was very possible one of the neighbors would
save her the trouble.

And then she would have to come up with a new
narrative, but things were evolving too quickly to worry
about that now. Action first; explanations later.

She repeated the instructions as A.D.2 and Grip ran
toward the house, pistols tucked in their waistbands,
looking like two rookies from the academy.

"Kill everyone. Especially Hardie. If Hardie does not
die, I will find you both and kill you myself."

CHAPTER
THIRTY

Did I ask you to be his psychiatrist? No. I asked you to fucking kill him.

— Ralph Fiennes, *In Bruges*

Psycho Phil handed over the keys with a trembling hand. He said they would open a black van parked out back, over a fence and between houses, right on Moorpark. Tank full of gas. Please God don't kill me. The two of them were supposed to leave the Hunters dead and go out there and fade into the Los Angeles night and please God don't kill me.

"I'm not gonna kill you," Hardie said. "I want you alive so you can talk to a friend of mine."

Deke, right this very moment (hopefully) was flying across the whole country just to be here. Deke was still their only chance, their light at the end of the tunnel.

"I can't, you don't understand . . . they'll . . ."

"Yeah, yeah, they'll kill you and make it look like an accident. Really horrible. I feel for you, brother. I really do."

Hardie dragged Psycho Phil into the middle of the room and told Jonathan to do the same with Psycho Sis. Dark blood smeared across the buff-colored carpet. The last thing he wanted to do was find himself trapped in yet another house, with faceless killers

293

swarming about everywhere. They needed to get out of here. Like right fucking now. Hardie kept Psycho Phil's gun and handed the Glocks to Jonathan, told him to give his wife one of them.

"They're still loaded with plenty of bullets. You or your wife see somebody you don't know, squeeze until they drop."

Jonathan nodded quickly and handed his wife a Glock. She looked down at it with not so much fear as grim determination, as if steeling herself. *You know what*, her face seemed to say, *if it comes down to it, I could point this fucking thing at somebody and shoot.*

Still holding the .38 in his right hand, Hardie fished the stolen handcuffs from the back waistband of his jeans with his left. His plan was to run the handcuffs through a support pole in the middle of the Hunters' entertainment center and then click them around the right wrist of Psycho Bro and the left wrist of Sis. What a sight he must be. Dirty pants and stolen shirt and no shoes, pretending to do real actual police work. Hey kids, meet Hobo Cop. *He rides the rails! He carries a bindle! He solves crimes!*

Jonathan Hunter, meanwhile, was holding his smartphone up in the air like he was offering a sacrifice to God. "My cell," he said. "I can't get a signal."

"They can jam the signal. And don't bother trying the landline. They've probably cut it."

"They?"

Hardie almost smiled. Just this morning he'd been thinking the same thing. *They? Who the fuck is They?* But there was no time to convert Jonathan Hunter to the Church of the All-Powerful and Immortal THEY. He needed the Hunter family to survive, and to know the truth.

Hardie slid open one of the glass doors leading to the backyard. This being California, of course there was a pool. Modest, but still. Plastic Adirondack chairs were scattered on the grass, along with an assortment of inflatable pool toys. He had to make it across the yard, to the fence, and out to the other side of the block. But did *They* have anything out there in the way of backup? Were they watching to make sure the Psycho Twins got out safe and sound?

The moment was so fucking familiar — the realization, the horror, the feeling that everything was happening right in this very second and there was no time to think, to react, to act —

C'mon Nate, let's move let's move let's move, out the front, my car's out there, we've got time . . .

Evelyn Hunter, meanwhile, had her two kids under her arms and was looking at her husband with wild desperation. "We can't call anybody?"

Hardie had to tell Hunter the truth. Before it was too late. He took Hunter's arm and leaned in close.

"Lane Madden wanted me to tell you how sorry she was about what happened to Kevin."

Jonathan's face — totally ashen. Just at the mention of his boy's name. "What . . . what did you say?"

"She was a passenger in the car that hit your son."

"Who was driving?"

And then Hardie said the name of the man behind the wheel — the Blond Viking God. Hunter ran

through a rapid-fire series of emotions within seconds
— disbelief, confusion, anger, grief.

"I saw it on the Web, Lane Madden is the one
who —"

"— who died this afternoon. I was with her, and she
told me everything. This is why she was killed. The
same people are trying to kill you, to cover it up. To
make sure no one ever finds out."

Invisible wheels turned behind Jonathan Hunter's
eyes, and then he moaned out loud. "The show," he
said.

"Huh?"

And then his eyes lit up.

"The show. They forced me to run that show about
those two. Oh, those bastards. They told me it was
because of ratings, but that's bullshit, I should have
known it was bullshit. They forced me to do that show
on those animals —"

and with that, he gestured at the shot and bleeding
people on the living room carpet

"— to give them an excuse to come after my family."

"They're actors. This is all a performance. They
planned this to the last detail."

"Except for you."

"Yeah. I guess —"

There was a loud noise. A bullet smacked into
Hardie's left arm, and then another hit the side of
Hardie's skull, which propelled his body through the
plateglass sliding doors and down the stone steps
leading to the backyard.

296

A.D.2 and Grip burst in through the door, with Grip going right, into the dining room, and A.D.2 charging full speed ahead down the hall. He saw Hardie, the stubborn old bastard, right away, so he aimed and fired. "Hardie's down," he muttered, then immediately moved to the left.

"Thank fuck," Mann said through their earpieces.

There was much screaming and confusion — people running into the backyard, diving behind furniture. A.D.2 looked at Grip from across the hallway. Gesturing with their hands, they split the living room into two. Simple enough. A.D.2 would take the left, and Grip the right. Adults first, obviously. With the kids, they'd try to make it as clean as possible.

A.D.2 nodded.

Grip stepped into the living room, eager for a target.

As he fell, Hardie closed his eyes.

This was it, at long last:

Death,

He felt the burning hot/cool sensation throughout his brain, which he knew was strange, because the brain doesn't have any nerve endings. Maybe what he was feeling was his soul departing, his life force ripping free from its physical prison.

Maybe it would all be over soon, and he'd be numb.

Maybe Lane would be there when he woke up, and she'd be patting his hand, telling him everything was over, he could rest now.

Right?

At least he told the truth.

297

The Hunters still had a chance . . .

No.

Of course he wasn't dead yet. Sure, there was a bullet swimming around in his brain — he'd felt the impact, which was like a baseball bat to the side of his skull — and blood pouring out of his head, wet and hot, but he was still conscious, still alive. Because this was purgatory, and he still wasn't finished atoning for his sins.

You were on the right track there, Chuck. You stopped those two fake crazies and set the record straight with the father about the hit-and-run. Really great stuff, Chuck. Much better than you sitting around drunk in your boxer briefs watching Jimmy Stewart movies. You've come a long way in a day.
But it's not over yet.
Oh, no.
The family is still in trouble, so we're not letting you off the hook that easily. You're part of the bigger plan here. So open your eyes.

Hardie, against his better judgment, opened his eyes. He could still see. He could still breathe.

Now sit up.
You've got a gun in your hand, sit up and raise your arm.

No, God. I can't sit up. I can't move either arm. One is numb and the other feels like a bag of granola. The gun's still in my hand but it might as well be my dick, because I can't lift my arms to save my life.

This isn't about your life. So sit the fuck up. I could make Lazarus rise from the dead, you think I can't make you perform one measly situp?

God, please, that's enough. Really. Send someone else down there. I'm through.

Sit up.

I can't —

Sit up.

I —

Sit up.

So Hardie sat up.

A.D.2 was trying to decide if it was worth shooting through the couch, or if he should try to flush them out first. Because the father was obviously cowering behind the couch, no question about it. But the insides of the furniture might stop the bullet or, more likely, cause some weird ricochet effect, and it could get messy.

This was why A.D.2 didn't see Hardie sit up, gun in hand. What clued him in was the tinkling of shattered glass falling from Hardie's chest.

A.D.2 turned to see Hardie's eyes glaring back up at him, and a blood-splattered face that now twisted into a wicked grin, and then there were three miniature explosions ripping through A.D.2's body and he was floating in the air and the house tumbled around him and then, all too late, he remembered his gun, in his hand, which would have been really useful about two seconds ago.

Hardie heard the next one approaching long before he appeared in his field of vision. To Hardie, it seemed like he had a weird out-of-body thing going on, because it was all happening like slow motion. The second gunman was taking what seemed like forever to get to him, to his line of fire. And when he finally did, seemingly *hours* later, it wasn't difficult at all to turn his wrist a few degrees and line up the shot. Two in the center of gravity. The first one exploded a lung, sent the gunman spinning, and the second shot really put the English on it, striking breastbone and knocking him backward through the air. But Hardie didn't bother to see where he landed, because he was already collapsing backward himself, back onto the stairs.

There, God. Am I done yet? Can I come home now?

CHAPTER
THIRTY-ONE

You know what the trouble with you is?
You're too violent.

— Sylvester Stallone, *Cobra*

Jonathan Hunter counted the shots — three, followed by some frenzied footsteps, then two more. He didn't dare move. He was covering his daughter's body with his own, praying incoherently yet fervently. Waiting for the right moment.

All of his night terrors, those 3a.m. torture sessions where his eyes popped open and he was again reminded of what happened to Kevin, how he hadn't been here, how he was never here because of his stupid job . . .

Nothing compared with this nightmare.

He had a gun in his hand but he was frozen, unable to sit up and use it. Because he'd watched too many stupid cop shows in his time where somebody thinks it's safe and looks around a corner and ends up with his brains splattered all over a brick wall.

Just like that poor bastard — Charlie? Is that what he said his name was?

The image of the man's blood leaping out of his arm, his head jerking to the side, was horrible, almost pornographic.

But now there was no sound at all.

Except —

"Mr. H-Hunter?"

Jonathan hesitated. Could be a trap. One of the gunmen, trying to get a fix on his location. He'd seen that a billion times on TV, too. He'd produced countless shows featuring those kinds of tricks.

"Mr. Hunter, it's me. Ch-Charlie Hardie. Out here on the steps. You might want to get over here quick. I have a way out for you g-guys, but it's not going to last forever."

Only then did Jonathan Hunter release his grip on his daughter's tiny curled-up body and take a careful glance over the top of the couch. There were two more bleeding people in his living room, both in T-shirts and jogging shorts. This made a grand total of four shot and bleeding people, all struggling to stay alive. And there, on the steps leading to their backyard, was their savior, Charlie Hardie, blood pooled around his head.

Jonathan Hunter rushed to Hardie's side and made all kinds of ridiculous promises about calling 911 and getting him help, he'd be okay, the worst was over, blah blah blah. But Hardie knew better. He also knew there wouldn't be much time, so he had better spit it out now.

"Take your family out the back. There's a key in one of my hands. It belongs to a black van one block away on Moorpark. Do you know where that is?"

"Of course, yes."

302

"Get your family into the van and just drive. Go somewhere random, wherever there's a large crowd of people. Your cell phones should work. I don't think they can jam the whole city. Call FBI special agent Deacon Clark, and tell him that Charlie Hardie sent you."

"Charlie Hardie," he repeated.

"Yes, but the most important name here is Deacon Clark. Deke for short. Got it?"

"Deke for short, Deacon Clark."

"I've told him some of this, but it's important you tell him the rest. Use whatever power you've got and look into the hit-and-run. Lane Madden's alibi will unravel if you push it hard enough. Tell him to check the car-dealer angle. There's going to be paperwork somewhere. But trust no one except Deacon Clark."

Hunter nodded, not really understanding the words, but trying to commit them to memory, anyway. Everything had happened so fast. Life was blurring by him again, just like it did three years ago. He needed to slow down. To think clearly. Except this man, their savior, was telling him to take the guns and run, run for their lives.

"Good, now go."

"What are you going to do?"

Hardie smiled. "Hold them off."

Hunter took his family through the backyard, past the pool, past the bamboo trees they'd planted in honor of Kevin — they'd been his favorite. Jonathan leaped the fence first, then had Evelyn pass Kate over, then Peter, but as she handed Peter over, her eyes went cold and she damn near dropped the boy, and Jonathan wanted to scream, What the hell are you doing? and then —

O'Neal could hear the shots, all the way over on Moorpark. He counted them. *Bang bang.* Pause. *Bang bang bang.* Still another pause — a little longer this time, and then finally *bang bang.* Seven shots in all. Plenty for Hardie, a father, a mother, and two children. Two to spare, even. O'Neal hoped they'd used them on that stubborn son of a bitch.

Then O'Neal waited.

Soon this would be over.

He promised himself that he would sprawl out on his king-size bed and just sleep for days after this one. Days on end, with pauses only to eat, shower, and drink, and then crawl back into his big, soft bed.

And then out of nowhere Mann came screaming over the line — Get in there, A.D.2 and Grip are down! Kill them all! — and O'Neal realized that his night was far from over. He took his gun and jogged down a path between the two houses leading to a lush, overgrown backyard. Something in his pocket vibrated.

It was his other boss.

Gedney.

A text message:

WALK AWAY

Every director was required to work with someone who would report directly to the employer. A built-in fail-safe to prevent directors from going rogue or pursuing their own agendas. Every director knew about this fail-safe position; however, the identity was kept

304

secret. When the director submitted the script along with the requested crew members, the employer would discreetly contact a particular crew member and say: "You're up." A secure connection was established, along with a panic button in case of emergencies.

O'Neal was the fail-safe for the Lane Madden jobs; he'd hit the panic button four times since this morning. Each time, the employer — in this case represented by Gedney — had responded: STEADY ON

Now it was finally over:

WALK AWAY

was meant to be taken literally. O'Neal was to simply leave the scene, taking along any compromising materials. He was to go to any one of a number of safe houses and dispose of the materials, then disappear for a while and await further instructions.

O'Neal slid the gun back into his pocket and stepped backward into the trees. He plucked the earpiece out and snapped it with his fingers, then slid that into his pocket, too. He waited.

"Thought I saw something."

"Come on, hurry up," Jonathan said, easing his son down onto the grass. After helping his wife over the fence — though she didn't need much help — they walked through their neighbors' yard and straight out onto Moorpark. The van was there, just like Charlie had promised. The key opened the door. Jonathan loaded his family inside, made sure everyone was buckled up. He turned on the ignition, shifted it to drive, pulled out of the space, and drove down the street, trying to tune out the cries and questions and the general bedlam in the car.

Deacon Clark, he muttered to himself. *Deke for short. Charlie Hardie. Look into the car dealer. Lane Madden. Deke for short. Charlie Hardie.*

Jonathan didn't know if he was escaping the nightmare or simply driving into another.

O'Neal stepped out of the shadows and followed the same path toward Moorpark. Once the van was away and clear, he stepped out onto the sidewalk, looked both ways, then hurriedly crossed the street. He headed north.

Mann knew why O'Neal refused to answer.
Why no one answered.
HARDIE
HARDIE
HARDIE

CHAPTER
THIRTY-TWO

Michelle Monaghan: *Oh cool!*
This stopped the bullet, Harry.
Robert Downey, Jr.: *No, not really.*

— *Kiss Kiss Bang Bang*

Okay, God, really, you can take me home now.

Hardie's battered and broken and shot and burned and lacerated and cut and dizzy and sweating and bruised body lay in a glittering field of broken glass. There were no lights back here, but the moon was up, and the stars were out, and they provided a little bit of illumination. Hardie heard sirens off in the distance. Always coming. Never here. He supposed some of the Hunters' Studio City neighbors had finally decided that all those popping noises weren't firecrackers, and the screams weren't screams of delight but rather terror, and they'd called 911.

He closed his eyes. Might as well try this again.

God, I've done it.

I managed to screw up one set of lives, but I've replaced it with another. You were nudging me in this direction the whole time, only I was too stubborn to see it. I get it, now, Lord. We're done, you and I. Even-Steven. You can send me wherever

307

you see fit. While it would be nice to see Nate Parish again, I realize that's probably not in the cards. Not sure Nate would want to see me, anyway; considering everything that happened.

So I guess that leaves the Other Place, which . . . you know, I can't say I don't deserve. But even Hell would be a change-up from this purgatory of a life, so go ahead. Do your stuff. Banish me, embrace me, whatever. I'm done. This body is finally broken, forever and ever Amen.

Please tell me I'm done.

Anything.

Any kind of sign at all.

"Hello, Charlie," a voice said.

Hardie forced his eyes open. His girl was there, his Topless killer beauty, his demon from the patio, standing on the top step, looking down at him, hideous smile on her face, and a coldness in her cut, bruised, and ruined eyes.

"Despite what you think, you're not a hero," she said. "All you've done is waste a lot of time and effort."

Hardie coughed up blood.

"You're not invincible," she continued. "You're just a man. You can be killed."

"Yeah, I kn-know," Hardie said. "Pull up a lawn chair and you can watch it happen, any minute now."

The smile stayed frozen on her face, but Hardie could tell she didn't quite understand the joke. Hardie didn't either, to tell you the truth. It just seemed like something badass to say.

Behind her, back in the living room, there were assorted moans and cries. He heard someone call out *man* insistently, urgently. Someone else — or maybe the same dying man — pushed aside a table and knocked over a lamp, followed by a sharp hollow pop. The sound echoed out into the backyard. "Man," someone cried again, "get us out of here."

Hardie didn't make the connection for another few seconds. Why would a guy dying of gunshot wounds sound so informal — *Man, help me, I'm dying ova hee-uh. Yo, got a gunshot wound, bro.* Then it clicked.

"Wait . . . your name is Mann?" Hardie asked. "Seriously?"

Mann didn't reply. Instead she kicked the .38 out of his hand, then grabbed Hardie by the fabric of his stolen police shirt and started to drag his body across the broken glass and pavement, away from the broken sliding doors. The world moved sideways and started to shake. Mostly because he couldn't contain the crazy, wheezing giggles that were escaping his chest.

"All this time I've been fighting the Mann?"

He broke into full-on laughter. He'd never heard anything funnier in his life, honest-to-fucking Christ. Wordlessly, she continued dragging his body, across the dry grass now, the smell of it mixing with the blood and the gunpowder in Hardie's nostrils.

"You're the M-Mann?" Hardie cried out, tears welling up in his eyes.

And then when he was at the edge of the pool, Mann nudged him over into the water. More concrete steps, meant to help someone adjust to the chilly water gradually. Hardie didn't need to worry about that. He was mostly numb, anyway, except for the burning sensation in the places where the chlorine touched his open wounds.

Mann waded in next to him, put a foot on his chest, and pushed him under the water. His laughter was cut off in a messy gulp. Water swirled into his partially open mouth, his back slammed into the bottom of the pool.

"You can be killed," she said, though she had no idea if Hardie could hear her. "You're not immortal."

Mann honestly couldn't pinpoint her first mistake, where it had all started to unravel. She'd made split-second decisions like always. Had written her narratives like always. But this one had spiraled out of control early this morning, on the 101, when a spoiled bitch had shoved broken glass into her eye. She couldn't even blame Hardie solely for this horrible abortion of a day.

But it would feel good to kill him, anyway.

Give her one last bit of accomplishment before . . .

. . . the next part of her career.

A director has one major fuckup, that director is finished. That did not mean death. Oh no. Mann had heard stories about another director — code name Stanley — who'd botched a production in London once, and rumor had it that they kept Stanley locked away somewhere in a secret prison, toiling away in the darkness, concocting narratives, gaming out possible futures endlessly, relentlessly. Good directors were assets, too valuable to be squandered. They'd keep you working. Working until your body and mind finally gave out.

Still, it was better than the alternative.

It was *some* kind of life.

Maybe she'd even impress them by killing Hardie. Prove to them that she was still valuable, that, yes, this assignment spiraled out of control but she was still one of the best death directors around. The very thought gave her a strange exhilaration. Some hope was better than no hope. She pushed down on Hardie's chest with renewed strength.

Die, you stubborn bastard.

Aren't you going to fight back?

What's the point? Drowning's not a bad way to die, so I've heard. After you stop fighting it, that is, and let it all happen. Once the air runs out, you faint. You start seeing crystal formations and hearing high-pitched tones and the crystal formations turn into a tunnel and then everybody starts telling you it's okay, you're going to be okay.

You are wrong. Drowning is an incredibly painful way to die. Your head is soon going to feel like it's going to explode. Your body will go into violent convulsions. So, fight back. There's still more to do.

No, there isn't. It's over. I'm done.

You're being drowned by the woman who threatened to kill your family. What do you think she's going to do the moment you're dead? She knows the address. She'll track them down. She'll hurt them, just to hurt you after your death.

No.

She knows you know this, too. She's hoping it makes drowning all the more painful.

NO

So, fight back. Fight back with everything you've got.

I've got nothing.

Fight!

I told you, I've got nothing.

Then what's that in your hand?

Mann felt him wriggling down there, but she thought it was the start of death spasms. Earlier in her career she'd assisted on a job on the beaches of the Black Sea, a "drowning by misadventure" job, and she'd had to help hold the subject under. She knew the stages; she knew when someone was truly gone.

So she was surprised when an arm shot up out of the water and slapped her on the wrist. Like she was a schoolgirl being chided.

Mann was about to say —

You're going to have to work a lot harder than that, Charles Hardie

— when she looked down and saw that he'd cuffed her.

The other cuff around his own wrist.

Then he jerked his arm, and she tumbled forward, splashing into the pool. She coughed up water. Tried to regain her footing. Slipped on the bottom. Tried to steady herself, maintain balance, but her arm was rudely jerked forward again. And again. Suddenly she realized what Hardie was doing. He was pulling himself along the bottom of the pool, one-handed, fingertips digging into the rough cement at the bottom . . .

Dragging her to the deep end of the pool.

If the stubborn bastard made it out that far and was able to drag her body out there — and then he passed out and drowned — she was done. Game over. He was too heavy. Dead weight, cuffed to her wrist, and she'd have no way of breaking through to the surface.

"No!" she screamed and finally maintained her footing. This tug-of-water had to be won here, where the water was only four feet deep, where she could still draw air into her lungs. She was stronger. She knew that. But he had sheer mass on his side. And stubbornness, the likes of which she'd never encountered before.

Mann pulled and dug her feet into the cement and pulled and wondered why he hadn't drowned yet and pulled and, seriously, what was keeping this stubborn son of a bitch alive, jerking at her, even when he had to know this was completely and utterly hopeless?

As she finally won and reached the edge of the pool, pulling herself out and steadying herself on the metal railing, Hardie's head broke the surface. He gasped and sucked in air, choked, coughed, and sucked in more air. His eyes rolled around in his head. He choked again.

Hardie concentrated on forcing water out of his lungs as she dragged him back onto the grass. He could hear sirens closer now. Something cold and hard pressed against his temple. A gun. The .38. Held by Mann, who was dripping wet and shaking with rage. He looked up as she fired and —

CLICK

Nothing. A dry fire. He'd emptied the gun. Used the last few bullets on her employees, apparently, who were still moaning and writhing in the Hunters' living room. Hardie wasn't Dirty Harry. He hadn't been counting shots and didn't have a line prepared where he would ask his girl here if she thought he'd fired five or six shots, that it was difficult to tell in all the confusion. Though it would have been funny if he had.

Mann dropped the gun, let out a sad shriek, and then did something that startled Hardie. She began to laugh. She lay down next to him on the ground and laughed her ass off.

As they lay there, handcuffed to each other, the police burst in.

CHAPTER
THIRTY-THREE

Who is Dirty Harry?
— Arnold Schwarzenegger, *Red Heat*

Four hundred miles away in San Francisco, in a hotel suite overlooking Union Square, Mr Gedney sat and talked to Mr Doyle about the events of the past nineteen hours. A bottle of Johnnie Walker Blue sat unopened on the marble desk between them, as well as a fine array of artisanal cheeses and hand-carved meats. The management always sent it up. Neither Gedney nor Doyle ever touched the stuff. Somewhere, a very lucky member of the cleaning staff probably had a kitchen cabinet full of the Blue.

Down on the square, a lone and mournful trumpet sent jazz notes ricocheting off the buildings. Late commuters scrambled for streetcars or squeezed past tourists trying to do a little shopping before the stores closed for the night.

"How are we feeling about containment?" asked Doyle. "Do we have a prayer?"

Gedney shook his head. "Jonathan placed three calls to reporters before he got smart and threw away his phone. I understand they're already calling car dealerships. I don't think they quite know what they're looking for, but that won't last. This thing is going to

315

blow up. Getting rid of Jonathan now would be pointless, and actually work against us."

"And the merger?"

"I think the merger as we know it is finished. We can rework it without McCoy, but that's going to take many more months of negotiations and . . . well, I don't have to tell you."

Until today, the Blond Viking God — actor Allan McCoy — was the lynchpin of an agency deal that could move a lot of assets in the right direction.

A few weeks ago, they'd launched a quiet exposure assessment. Someone brought up the hit-and-run; it was included on a bullet-point rundown. The likelihood: low. Then came the tip from their source, Andrew Lowenbruck. The actress had told Lowenbruck: it's tearing me up inside. Destroyed her confidence, her career, her soul. Lowenbruck reported this. The risk suddenly went way up. Especially with Jonathan Hunter's TV show — which they owned, interestingly enough — pressure was mounting. It wasn't a question of whether Lane Madden would snap, it was when.

And how long would it take her to call the Hunters?

Taking a cold look at the numbers, and gaming out the scenarios, they'd figured the elimination of Lane Madden and the Hunter family would remove the risk entirely and actually tweak potential profit even higher.

Now all that was lost.

Doyle was good at looking into the future; he saw that Allan McCoy really had no future.

"There is an upside," Gedney said.

"And that is?"

"I think we have a new asset to consider. One who'd be ideal for another project."

Doyle thought it over.

"You think so?"

"Based on what Mann says, he sounds perfect."

"Okay. Send a team over to fetch him."

CHAPTER
THIRTY-FOUR

My dream role would be some kind of tour de force where the character goes through hell and still comes out on the other side alive.

— Bruce Campbell in *Cashiers du Cinemart*

Hardie lay in the dry grass, bleeding, handcuffed to his demon girl. She'd stopped laughing, thankfully. It had started to creep him out.

"Now, if I can just wait until the cavalry arrives . . . ," he said, wondering if Mann would get the reference. If she did, she gave no indication.

The police arrived, along with a flotilla of EMTs. Somebody used a key on the cuffs and separated the two. Somebody else checked his neck, his vitals, shined a light in his eyes, and then he was loaded onto a gurney and carried through the Hunter home. Psycho Phil and his sister were still groaning — they would probably live. Same deal with the gunmen, which meant that Hardie was losing his touch. Either that, or nobody died in purgatory.

Of course, all of this was kinda sorta deja vu-like in a bizarro universe kind of way. Being shot and beaten to the brink of death and then carried through some innocent family's home. Just like when he was carried

318

through Nate's home, after all the shooting had stopped three years ago.

Maybe this was it, finally, at long last — the end credits that had been waiting three long years to crawl across the screen.

Please, God, let me just fade out and realize that the past three years have been an elaborate imagined fantasy sequence as my dying brain fired off its last few synapses. Please tell me I actually died at Nate's house, and all of this has been some kind of fire I had to pass through before making it to the next life. Please tell me this was meant to purify my soul, and now I can rest in peace.

God — if listening — declined to respond.

Some time passed. Hardie wasn't sure how long, exactly. A minute maybe. He felt his eyes go out of focus. His mind wandered, like he was on the edge of sleep. His life didn't flash before his eyes. There were no last-minute revelations or epiphanies. Everything was just gray and soft and numb.

An EMT appeared next to him. He ripped open some plastic. Pulled out a syringe. Pried off the plastic top. Slid the needle into a glass bottle. Flicked the syringe with a finger. Drew back the plunger.

"Oh, they're going to have fun with you," the EMT said, then slid the needle into Hardie's arm.

Thanks & Praise

This book has many fathers, as well as a mother or two. Three of those fathers are named David, strangely enough.

A little over two years ago, David J. Schow invited me to his birthday party in the Hollywood Hills, and the moment I almost died backing out onto the edge of Durand Drive, I knew I had to set a novel there. The germ of *Fun and Games* (at least the germ of the *setting*) was planted then; it would reach full bloom this past summer when Schow took me on a crazy driving/walking tour of Beachwood Canyon, from the Hollywood Reservoir to the Bronson Caves — the setting for countless genre films over the years. Hardie and Lane didn't make it over to the caves, but they hit pretty much everything else Schow showed me. I owe him a huge debt. If there were such a title as "locations manager" for a novel, that would be Mr. Schow. Read his short stories (my personal favorite collection: *Lost Angels*), read his novels (faves: *The Kill Riff*, *Internecine*), pray your kids grow up half as cool and kind as him.

My longtime novel-baby daddy (aka literary agent), **David Hale Smith**, who was right there at conception, as well as on the day I heard the happy news *and*

320

delivery day. He's not the kind of agent who paces and smokes out in the lobby; he's right in the room with you, holding your hand, telling you to breathe.

I'll save my third baby daddy, also named David, for the end; you'll understand when you get there.

This book's fourth baby daddy — the one who force-fed me prenatal vitamins and made pickle-and-ice-cream runs at 4a.m. — is a non-David. His name is John Schoenfelder, and he's the editor of Mulholland Books. We kicked this baby around in a *Scarface*-style restaurant not far from Grand Central Station, then kicked it around a little more in a bustling Irish joint. And thanks to John, this little runt of an idea I had grew up into this big, crazy trilogy you'll (hopefully) be reading. His creativity knows no bounds; his enthusiasm is like Ebola — one lunch with John and you'll be bleeding *awesome* from every orifice.

Also in the delivery room were Miriam Parker, Wes Miller, Luisa Frontino, Michael Pietsch, and the rest of the stellar Little, Brown/Mulholland Books team. Pamela Marshall's spot-on copyedits made sure nobody would make fun of this child in school someday. And let me thank two members of LB's extended family, in the "kindly uncle" category: Michael Connelly and George Pelecanos. Their novels set the standard; their kindness and support are legendary.

If I could hand out cigars, I'd be giving some fancy Cubans to Danny and Heather Baror, Lou Boxer, Ed Brubaker, Angela Cheng Caplan, Jon Cavalier, Joshua Hale Fialkov, James Frey, Sara Gran, McKenna Jordan,

Anne Kimbol, Joe Lansdale, Paul Leyden, Ed and Kate Pettit, Eric Red, Brett Simon, Shauyi Tai, and Jessica Tcha, as well as everyone else I somehow forgot to mention. But please forgive me; I'm a new father and kind of frazzled.

Last but nowhere near least is my real-life family: I could not have written this novel without the patience and support and love of my wife, Meredith, my son, Parker, or my daughter, Sarah. They watched me write this book as we traveled across the United States and back again, and they don't mind that I have all these baby daddies. Which would freak some people out, to be honest.

I mentioned a third baby daddy named David; that would be my friend **David Thompson**. Sadly, I am not able to thank him in person; David passed away unexpectedly at the insanely young age of thirty-eight.

As I type these words a few short months later . . . well, *fuck*. I still can't believe I'm typing those words. I thought David and I would grow old together, and that someday — if we were lucky — we'd be the cranky old men of the genre, commenting on all of the young whippersnappers coming up, and trading our favorites back and forth via e-book readers or direct mental implants or whatever. David was literally the second person (after my own agent) to congratulate me on my Mulholland deal, which was appropriate, because David's been there from the beginning. *Literally*. Whenever I meet someone who's read my stuff, more often than not — and I am *not* exaggerating here — it's because David Thompson put one of my books in their hands and said, "I think you'll really like this." I can hear him speaking those words now, in that wonderful Texas accent of his. He spoke those words often; he was a tireless promoter and supporter of crime fiction, and had this uncanny ability to match reader with novel. I don't say this lightly: I owe my career to him.

So of course I couldn't wait to send David an early peek of *Fun and Games*. I was still writing the first draft when he died; I finished it in a Houston hotel room the weekend of his memorial service (which was packed with family, friends, and a veritable who's who of mystery and crime fiction). This novel is dedicated to David not because he's gone; it's because he was my ideal reader, and forever will be. There's no replacing him. There will never be anyone else like him.

Someday I hope to tell the whippersnappers all about him.

ISIS publish a wide range of books in large print, from fiction to biography. Any suggestions for books you would like to see in large print or audio are always welcome. Please send to the Editorial Department at:

ISIS Publishing Limited
7 Centremead
Osney Mead
Oxford OX2 0ES

A full list of titles is available free of charge from:

Ulverscroft Large Print Books Limited

(UK)
The Green
Bradgate Road, Anstey
Leicester LE7 7FU
Tel: (0116) 236 4325

(Australia)
P.O. Box 314
St Leonards
NSW 1590
Tel: (02) 9436 2622

(USA)
P.O. Box 1230
West Seneca
N.Y. 14224-1230
Tel: (716) 674 4270

(Canada)
P.O. Box 80038
Burlington
Ontario L7L 6B1
Tel: (905) 637 8734

(New Zealand)
P.O. Box 456
Feilding
Tel: (06) 323 6828

Details of **ISIS** complete and unabridged audio books are also available from these offices. Alternatively, contact your local library for details of their collection of **ISIS** large print and unabridged audio books.